Devil's Prize

Devil's Prize

JANE JACKSON

With best wishes,

Jane Jackson

ROBERT HALE · LONDON

ISBN 978-0-7090-8480-8

Robert Hale Limited
Clerkenwell House
Clerkenwell Green
London EC1R 0HT

www.halebooks.com

2 4 6 8 10 9 7 5 3 1

For Mike, with love.

Typeset in 10/13pt New Century Schoolbook
by Derek Doyle & Associates, Shaw Heath
Printed and bound in Great Britain
by Biddles Limited, King's Lynn

CHAPTER ONE

'For God's sake, it's not worth the risk.'

Devlin Varcoe glanced at his brother across the long slender form of the galley in its wooden cradle. He saw narrow sloping shoulders that the greatcoat's four shoulder capes could not disguise, and guessed that the beaver hat's narrow brim was the height of fashion. Irony twisted his mouth.

'Concerned for my safety?' Devlin hauled a filthy oilskin over his salt-stained blue jacket and thrust the ends of a knotted red neckerchief into the throat of his woollen shirt.

Thomas's gaze flicked towards a hulking figure waiting beside the wide doorway of the vaulted cellar, water dripping off his oilskin to pool around his booted feet. 'Wait outside,' he ordered.

'Round up the others, Jared,' Devlin interrupted. 'Fast as you can. I don't want that crowd from Brague getting in first.'

With a nod the big man disappeared into the driving rain.

'I don't give a damn about your safety,' Thomas snapped. 'But you have a run to make tomorrow night—'

'The schooner's here now. Once I get a line aboard, she's mine.'

'Father would never have permitted—'

'Father's dead.'

'Better if it had been you.'

Hardened to his brother's hatred, Devlin ignored him and began lifting long oars from wooden pegs, laying them in the galley.

'I've always thought it strange,' Thomas said, 'that no one else was killed.'

Devlin laid another oar in the galley. 'Nothing strange about it. None of my crew had time to stand still. The sea was rough and we were carrying every stitch of canvas. I warned Father that the privateer would probably have a sniper in the foretop. But he refused to go below.'

Thomas bristled. 'Naturally. Father was no coward.'

'He was stubborn as a jackass.'

'You're glad he's dead.'

'I'm not sorry.'

'I wouldn't put it past you to have killed him yourself.'

Devlin straightened up. After a moment one corner of his mouth quirked in a half-smile that left his eyes cold. 'You'll never know, will you, Thomas?' He saw his brother swallow.

'No wonder they call you *Devil.*'

Devlin hefted another oar into the galley. 'Ah, but without me you'd be right in the shit. You won't take the money across to Uncle Hedley, and who else can you trust?'

'I'm needed here.' Thomas said quickly, his voice climbing. 'The business doesn't run itself.'

Devlin eyed him briefly. 'You get seasick.'

'Bastard,' Thomas hissed. His chin jutted as he gathered his shredded dignity. 'I'm calling on Colonel Trevanion tomorrow. It's to be hoped—'

'He's sober?'

'That he has the money for next month's cargo.'

'Bled him dry, have you?'

'It's a cut-throat business. You have no idea how complex—'

Devlin bared his teeth. 'Seems plain enough to me. Uncle Hedley buys the goods in Roscoff to your order. Colonel Trevanion provides the finance. I pay our uncle, collect the cargo, land and store it until it's distributed. I don't have your book learning, Thomas. But I'm no fool. You'd do well to remember that.'

Thomas couldn't hide his loathing. 'We didn't need you. Father could have hired another boat.'

Devlin eyed his brother in the wintry grey light that spilled through the open doorway. The rain had stopped but the wind howled and waves thundered against the sea wall, splintering into great plumes and fountains of spray.

'He'd never have done that. Whatever he felt about me he'd never go outside the family. Besides, I'm the best skipper on this coast.' He reached for his sou'wester.

'You!' Thomas's face contorted. 'If it hadn't been for you she'd still be alive. Everything was wonderful with just the three of us. Then you came. No wonder he hated you. It wasn't just his life you wrecked. I was only seven—'

'Jesus Christ!' Devlin exploded. 'Listen to yourself. Your life was wrecked? You went to a decent school. He wouldn't pay for me. While you were studying accountancy and attending assemblies up in Truro I was out in the North Sea fishing for herring on Arf Sweet's boat. Father needed me in the business, but he made you a partner. When he put money into the lugger so I could make the runs faster, he charged me interest until I'd paid him back.' His laugh was brief and harsh. 'And you want sympathy?'

Thomas smirked. Having provoked a reaction he was relishing the illusion of power.

The anger that balled Devlin's fists was directed at himself. He should know better. He let it go and uncurled his fingers. 'Go home, Thomas. You're in my way.'

'You're mad to go out in this weather.'

Devlin's wolfish grin held amusement and brief satisfaction. 'Worried, Brother? You should be. Now father's gone you're on your own. Just remember, you need me more than I need you.'

Jenefer Trevanion laid her pen beside the account book and pulled her paisley shawl closer as a flurry of hail splattered against the window. A wood fire crackled in the grate but the warmth hadn't reached as far as her writing desk.

Once again the columns showed a drop in profit. She had checked her totals twice. Something was wrong, and it wasn't her addition. But convincing her father that Thomas Varcoe was cheating him would be impossible without some sort of proof. How and where was she to find that?

'People are gathering at the top of the beach,' Betsy said as she swung the long glass on a tripod that spared her the effort of holding it steady. 'It won't be long— Oh!'

The shock in her sister's voice made Jenefer look round. 'What?'

'There's a galley pulling out of the harbour. It's Devil Varcoe.'

Jenefer bolted from her chair to Betsy's side and peered through the window down the sloping garden to the cliff edge and the sea beyond.

The house was situated on a narrow headland separating the village, harbour and beach on one side from a series of rocky coves and inlets on the other. But while Betsy always had something of interest to look at, the position of the house meant they were visited with annoying regularity by the Riding Officer.

Jenefer found his barely concealed scepticism in the face of her denials infuriating. Particularly as in this instance she was speaking the truth. Did Lieutenant Crocker really think her father stupid enough to allow contraband to be hidden in the house?

She gazed down at the galley, the turmoil in her mind echoed in her stomach. Her fingers strayed to the fine gold chain about her neck. But the instant she touched the tiny painted miniature of Martin suspended from it she jumped as if it had burned her.

If only she hadn't accepted his proposal. But there had been so many pressures: grief, anxiety, guilt and a relief that made her ashamed. If she hadn't gone for a walk instead of accompanying her mother and Betsy, she would have been in the carriage as well. She might now be dead like her mother, or crippled like her sister.

After the accident her father had been obsessed with arranging a match for her, and this one promised a solution to so many problems, not least where she and Betsy would live after his death, for the house was entailed to a male cousin. Martin's promise that Betsy would be welcome to share their home was very generous and Jenefer had felt the net tightening around her.

She knew she should be grateful. In so many ways Martin was ideal. He was 27, came from a good family, was well educated, enjoyed a private income from his French grandmother, and his diplomatic career was flourishing.

Nor could she offer the excuse that her heart was engaged elsewhere. For though she had enjoyed several flirtations none had been serious. So, hoping that where liking existed love would follow, she had accepted.

But since their Easter betrothal, the war had kept Martin busy and away from Cornwall, she had met Devlin Varcoe, and now every waking moment was an exhausting battle between her duty to her family and to Martin, and foolish yearning. At least Devlin didn't know. Doubtless she had already slipped from his memory. Yet the thought that she might have made no impression on him pricked like a thorn.

'He's mad,' Betsy whispered. 'The water is seething down there. They'll never get out past the point, let alone close enough to throw a line.'

Jenefer wrapped her shawl tighter as she gazed through small windowpanes misted with salt. The gale had whipped the sea into heaping waves. Dirty grey clouds with ragged edges raced low over broken crests and spindrift. But even from this distance she recognized him. He had lost his sou'wester and his dark curly hair lay flat against his scalp. Seated in the stern he wrestled the tiller with both hands as he steered the galley through wild water that bounced off jutting outcrops and surged back to meet the incoming rollers.

Facing him, their backs to the rearing waves, eight men strained at the long oars and another crouched in the bow, ducking his head against drenching spray. Forcing her gaze from the galley she glanced towards its target, a helplessly wallowing schooner.

Broken spars and tangled rigging were snarled around a jagged stump that had once been the foremast. Somehow the schooner's crew had managed to drop the huge gaff mainsail. But the main topmast had gone and shredded canvas flapped uselessly on the mizzen. The heaving deck was crowded with people clinging to the lashed boom and any other handhold they could find. They were flung first one way then another by the wild gyrations of the stricken vessel as the howling wind hurled it shoreward.

'There's a woman by the companionway hatch,' Betsy said. 'Why doesn't she use both hands? She'll be swept overboard if she's not careful. That bundle can't be worth her life.'

Unable to see details without the aid of the long-glass, Jenefer glanced instead at the beach where, on either side of glistening sand and grey shingle, the ebbing tide revealed fingers of black rock that jutted out of the cold foaming water like broken teeth.

Switching her gaze to the galley once more her breath caught as the long slender craft climbed the vertical face of a giant roller and disappeared over the top. Seconds later the comber crashed on to the beach with a thunderous roar that rattled the windows and made the house vibrate. The galley was already climbing the face of the next wave whose crest was breaking and curling. *It would swallow them.*

'They'll never survive.' It was only when she heard her own voice sharp with fear that she realized she'd spoken. She dreaded seeing the galley flipped over to be smashed to splinters, the men pulped by the avalanche of water. Yet she could not look away.

'Of course they will.' Betsy was fierce, using both hands to hold the long-glass steady as she leaned forward in her wheeled chair.

'Devil Varcoe has the best crew in West Cornwall. They've faced worse than this. They've done it,' she breathed. 'They're out past the point. Pull, Jared. Pull,' she whispered.

'Pull, you bastards!' Devlin bellowed above the roar of a wind that slashed his exposed skin like a gutting knife. Braced in the stern he fought to keep the galley heading into the waves. Kicking like a wild horse, the tiller demanded every ounce of his strength to hold it steady. The crew's oilskins were shiny with spray, their weather-beaten faces contorted with effort as they bent and hauled in unison born of familiarity and practice. Despite the roar of wind and waves Devlin heard their grunts as they dragged the long sweeps through wild foaming water and the rasp of in-drawn breath as they reached for the next stroke.

He looked ahead. As the gap between the galley and the crippled schooner narrowed he could hear terrified yells begging them to hurry. Back on the beach the crowd was swelling as more people arrived. The spume and spray made it impossible to see clearly. But he knew most would be carrying a hatchet, crowbar, ropes and every container they could grab. They stood and watched in silence, waiting.

Careful to keep the galley upwind of the schooner, Devlin signalled to Charlie Grose who reached for the coils of rope. Rising to his feet, instinctively adjusting to the pitch and roll, Charlie flung them high toward the figures waving desperately from the schooner's side. His aim was true but a gust caused the vessel to lurch wildly, forcing those waiting to grab a handhold or risk being hurled into the raging sea. The arcing rope fell into the water.

Quickly Charlie retrieved it. But his numbed hands were clumsy and the sodden coils awkward to handle. The schooner was now only yards from the rocks.

Devlin knew this would be the last chance for all of them. He clamped his teeth together, fighting the urge to shout instructions. Charlie knew what to do.

Balancing the heavy rope, Charlie judged his moment and threw. The bow of the galley reared on a breaking wave forcing him to his knees as he grabbed the gunwales.

The rope arced over the broken foremast and men rushed to haul it in and make it fast.

Devlin raised a clenched fist. 'Right on, Charlie! We've got her, lads,' he roared. Quickly checking that the towrope was securely lashed to the reinforced seat in front of him he pushed the tiller over and the men redoubled their efforts. As the slack was taken up the rope sprang tight and the dead weight of the schooner dragged at the galley and her labouring crew.

Devlin knew he couldn't prevent the stricken ship from beaching. But if they could tow her away from the rocks so that she grounded on sand, she'd be easier to salvage *if* the waiting crowd could be persuaded to respect salvor's rights. The pistol's cold steel was hard against his side. It would help. But it wasn't enough. He hoped some of his landsmen were among the watching crowd. He sensed the villagers' anger. They were willing him to fail.

For a few moments the crew's valiant efforts seemed to be paying off. Then, hit by a breaking wave, the schooner tossed her head violently. The sharp crack of wood fracturing near Devlin's feet was as loud and potentially lethal as a musket shot. His heart clenched and the crew froze momentarily on a collective intake of breath. They watched him. *Cut or continue?*

Cursing in fury and frustration Devlin reached for the small razor-sharp axe stowed beneath the sternsheets. With two swift strokes he severed the taut towrope.

Free from the burden that would have dragged them to their deaths, the galley leapt forward. Screams of renewed terror erupted aboard the helpless schooner. Devlin ignored them. He'd done his best. Braving the storm had been a calculated risk. Trying to maintain the tow would be foolhardy. Losing the salvage was bad enough. He had no intention of sacrificing the galley or his crew.

He pushed the tiller, turning the galley towards the beach. Though they had lost the vessel as salvage, the men had a right to pick up whatever they could.

They headed shoreward, surfing the curling breakers and using the long sweeps for balance. But the urgency had gone and their disappointment was palpable.

Devlin heard the grating splintering crash as the schooner was dashed on to the rocks. It was followed a heartbeat later by an animal roar. Presented with this gift by the storm the villagers had become a ravening mob. Desperate to seize anything they could use or sell, men, women and children surged down the beach.

As the galley reached the shallows the crew shipped their oars, jumped over the side and carried the boat to a spot beneath the cliff well away from the wreck. It would be safe there. No villager was stupid enough to touch anything belonging to Devil Varcoe.

'Jared, stay with me. The rest of you look to the crew and any passengers.'

'You want 'em brung up 'ere, skipper?' Charlie Grose shouted above the noise.

'Then can we go?' Danny asked, clearly anxious for a share of the spoils.

'What time tomorrow night, skip?'

'Eight. With a fair wind we'll reach Roscoff by dawn.' He turned away. Anyone missing or turning up drunk would be off the crew for good. Not a man among them would take that chance.

With Jared Sweet lumbering along at his side, Devlin started running down the beach. Already some men from the village were braving the frothing surf and wet slippery rocks, determined to be first to reach the tilted schooner, drawn like flies to carrion. Starving and desperate since the copper mines started closing, the tinners were always first to reach any wreck, and the most dangerous.

Looking past the yelling crowd already squabbling amongst themselves as they scrambled across the rocks and floundered through the bone-chilling water, Devlin could see a bare-headed man in a dark blue coat standing defiant on the schooner's slanting deck, his hands raised to repel the raiders.

'Daft bugger,' Jared growled.

Behind the captain, able-bodied crew helped their injured and bloodstained mates over the side while two well-dressed men Devlin guessed were passengers, demanded assistance.

A few feet from the captain another younger man, also in a blue coat, was trying to control a violently struggling woman.

As Devlin and Jared fought their way through the mêlée, villagers whirled, snarling as they raised axe or crowbar to smash aside anyone trying to stop them, but, as they recognized Devlin and Jared, murderous glares dropped and they resumed their race to reach the hatches and holds.

'Captain,' Devlin bellowed through cupped hands. 'Get off the ship.'

'I can't. The cargo is government stores—'

'What are you carrying?' As the words left his lips, Devlin caught a waft of heavy burnt-sugar sweetness and heard the frenzied roar.

Devlin and Jared exchanged a glance. Spirits inevitably meant some of the howling mob would not live to see daybreak. How many would be found broken on the rocks or trapped and drowned in the wreckage? How many children would be left without one or both parents?

'Rum,' the captain confirmed. His weathered face was grey and etched with strain. Exhaustion had sunk red-rimmed eyes deep into their sockets. How long had he been fighting the storm, nursing the schooner towards home and safety? He looked as if he hadn't slept for days. 'And thirty casks of flour.'

'Stay aboard and you'll be killed,' Devlin was brusque. 'Is it worth your life?'

'Surely they wouldn't—'

'They would. They will,' Devlin said grimly.

'Can't you help?'

'What the hell do you think I'm doing?' Devlin retorted. The captain began to sway. With agility surprising in a man of his height and bulk, Jared leapt for the gunwale, swung himself up and immediately leaned down to haul Devlin on board. 'Take him up the beach,' Devlin murmured, as he reached the deck.

Releasing Devlin's hand, Jared grabbed the captain and, before the exhausted man could utter a word of protest, swung him overboard and immediately followed.

Frantic now, uncaring of the damage to their elegant coats, pale pantaloons and polished boots, the two passengers had scrambled down and were stumbling across rocks through waves that one moment were thigh-deep, and the next retreated, gurgling and hissing, into dark fissures.

That left only the man Devlin guessed was the mate and the woman whose struggles had grown weaker and more erratic.

'What are you waiting for?' he snapped.

'She won't – I can't—'

'Oh, for Christ's sake,' Devlin muttered, and strode up the slanting deck. 'Come on, Miss—'

'Mrs,' the mate rasped. 'She's my wife.'

Meeting the man's eyes, Devlin's angry response died on his tongue. He'd never seen such devastation. His gaze flicked to the bedraggled woman clasped in her husband's arms, trembling as if racked with fever.

13

'Is she ill?'

The mate's head moved once, a brief negative. 'Our baby—'

'Where is it?'

'He.' The mate's chin lifted in painful dignity. 'My son. James Henry Vanson. He—' A spasm crossed his face and he swallowed audibly. 'My wife was holding him while I helped with your line. Then the wave – Mary fell. The deck was awash and' – he swallowed again, his mouth quivering – 'he's only three months old.'

Jesus.

'Why?' Vanson's voice was as raw as a wound. 'In God's name, why did you cut the tow?'

Devlin didn't reply. To give reasons would be pointless and to offer sympathy an insult. He looked towards the beach. Two of his men, Sam Clemmow and Ben Tozer, both teetotallers and armed with heavy staves, fended off would-be thieves as they shepherded the survivors up the beach. Without protection the schooner's people, injured and able-bodied alike, would be set-upon, stripped, and left naked and helpless. Any alive after that would not last a night of bitter wind and squalls of icy rain.

Already the afternoon light was fading to dusk. Here and there a flickering light glimmered. Using a lantern, even a shaded one, was a calculated risk. It might reduce the chances of falling into a rocky gully and breaking a limb, but it also betrayed the holder's presence.

By now news of the stricken schooner would surely have reached Lieutenant Crocker. As one of his duties was to prevent the looting of wrecks he would call out the dragoons. But it would take them at least an hour to get here. Given the speed at which night was approaching it would be dark by the time they arrived.

As he was due to bring back a cargo in the next few days, the Riding Officer was the last person Devlin wanted to see. He turned back to the mate. 'Leave the ship now or you'll die.'

The mate shook his head. 'The baby's things – I have to—'

'Forget it,' Devlin snapped. 'Can't you hear? They've broached the casks.'

'But it's all we have left.'

'Do you want to see your wife used like some dockyard whore? Fought over by men mad with drink? Do you know what she'll look like when they've finished?' He did. He and Jared, eighteen years old, had been part of a salvage team. The brig was carrying cognac and they arrived too late. They found the crew spread in bloody pieces over the beach and the captain, out of his senses, crooning to what was left of his wife.

Seared into his memory, the image had haunted him for weeks. Now, nine years later, he saw it only in the occasional nightmare.

Vanson recoiled, eyes wide, his mouth working as if he were about to vomit. '*No*—'

'Then get over the side. I'll pass her down to you.' Putting his arm around the young woman's shaking shoulders, Devlin felt the wet chill of her saturated clothes. She stiffened and let out a shriek of such despair that the hair on the back of Devlin's neck rose.

'Go *on*,' he shouted roughly as the mate hesitated.

Vanson hoisted himself over the gunwale.

'No, no! My baby! I can't—! Jamie, where are you?' Peering round wildly, Mary Vanson lashed out with feet and fists, struggling to free herself.

It was like trying to hold on to an eel. Grimly aware he was bruising her but not daring to loosen his grip, Devlin half-dragged half carried her to the ship's side. Sweeping her off her feet, jerking his head back to try and avoid some of the blows, he dropped her into her husband's arms then jumped down. 'Here, give her to me. Mind where you put your feet. The rocks are slippery.'

Vanson seemed dazed. 'Where should we—?'

'Over towards the harbour, as fast as you can.'

Jared and the captain were halfway across. Ahead of them the rest of the schooner's crew limped and stumbled.

Hearing screams and shouting, Devlin glanced over his shoulder. Two men lurched across the deck, arms swinging wildly as they fought. Others pushed past, their arms full of blankets, casks of flour, lengths of wood. Still more were dragging the wooden chests that held the crew's belongings. Women and children formed chains passing buckets, pans, jars, and even pewter chamber pots filled with rum down to others waiting on the rocks.

Turning his back on the destruction he saw a figure running down the cliff path. The wind had whipped back the hood of her dark wool cloak. Above the pale blur of her face, her hair was barley gold. In one hand she carried a lantern, the other kept her long skirts clear of her feet. *Jenefer Trevanion.*

Jumping down on to the beach she hurried over the sand towards him.

'Mr Varcoe, we saw – my father has asked me to offer food and shelter—' She was breathless and in the fading light there was an unmistakable flush on her cheeks. *The wind, fool. And her headlong dash down the path*. Though her words were directed at him, her gaze darted from the wreck to the crew sitting hunched on the sand, their heads turned away from the mate who held his inconsolable wife, to the captain, dwarfed by Jared, watching his ship ravaged. Not once did she meet his eyes.

'Your father?' Devlin enquired with heavy irony. He would not play her game. Not until she had looked at him, acknowledged his presence. It worked. Her eyes flew to his. But the dim light made reading her expression impossible.

Jenefer flinched at his tone. Since securing her betrothal her father had showed little interest in anything but his brandy and whatever schemes he and Thomas Varcoe discussed closeted in his study. Devlin Varcoe was probably well aware of this.

'He's not a well man, Mr Varcoe.' Cool and steady, her voice gave no clue to the heartbeat thundering in her ears, or the surge of heat beneath her shift. 'But I know he would want to help these unfortunate people.'

He leaned towards her and she steeled herself to remain absolutely still.

'The mate's wife,' he spoke quietly, indicating the couple with a brief nod. 'Her baby went overboard.'

'Oh no.' A hand flew to her mouth. 'The bundle – Betsy was watching through the long-glass. She couldn't understand why – Oh God. The poor woman. There's no chance?'

Devlin shook his head. 'None.'

Jen swallowed the stiffness in her throat. She couldn't begin to imagine – *and now wasn't the time to try*. 'Their name – did you—?'

'Vanson,' Devlin replied.

As she started towards the couple, Devlin crossed to Jared. 'Miss Trevanion has offered everyone shelter for the night. Will you show them where to go? Captain and mate to the house, the rest to the stables.'

'You coming?'

Devlin shook his head. 'I'm going back to the cellars.' He hesitated as a girl came running across the sand.

Wild black curls tumbled over the shoulders of her poppy-red greatcoat. After a searching look at the group of survivors now shuffling towards the path she turned to Devlin and smiled, her teeth a white flash in the gloom.

'Tamara.'

'Devlin. Father would be grateful for masts, spars, sails, ropes and any brass.'

He gestured towards the ragged line of villagers staggering up the beach bent double under the weight of plunder ripped from the wreck. 'Too late. Still, in a couple of days he'll be able to buy anything he wants at Helston Market.'

She shrugged. 'Oh well. In that case you can walk me home.'

He shook his head. 'I've got things to do.'

She caught her lower lip between her teeth as her gaze swept over him from sand-caked boots to wet tousled hair.

'You don't look busy. You look' – she tilted her head to one side – 'lonely.'

'Go home, Tamara.'

'By myself? With all these drunks around?'

He leaned towards her. 'Walk fast. They'll never catch you.'

'Oh, you.' She stamped her foot, making her curls dance. Then with the mercurial change of mood that made her so appealing and so unpredictable, she laughed. 'I'll have you, Devlin Varcoe.'

His groin tightened and he folded his arms, clenching his hands into fists as he resisted the desire to ravish that laughing mouth, bury his hands in those black curls, crush her soft supple body against his. 'Threats, Tamara?' His tone was dry.

She shook her head and her curls flew. 'Oh no.' Her teeth gleamed. 'A promise.'

CHAPTER TWO

Slumped in a high-backed armchair beside the fire in his study, Colonel John Trevanion gulped more brandy. His sagging cheeks were the purplish hue of a ripe plum, and he glared at his elder daughter through bloodshot eyes. 'You had no right bringing them here.'

'I couldn't leave them on the beach, Father. They've lost everything but the clothes they are wearing. Even those would have been taken had I not brought them away. Poor Mrs Vanson is in a desperate state—'

'Who's Mrs Vanson? No.' He flung up a hand before she could reply. 'Don't tell me.' He waved her away. 'Do what you must. But I want them all off my property by tomorrow. Now, find Treeve and tell him to fetch Dr Avers.'

'Oh, Father, that is kind of you.'

'Kind?' He frowned blankly. 'What's kind about it?'

Each day Jenefer found it more difficult to make allowances for her father's violent lurches between foul temper and maudlin self-pity. She fought for patience. 'I meant that it's very generous of you to offer those poor people the services of—'

'Not for them, you stupid girl. If they want a doctor they must find their own. It's not my responsibility. I want Avers here for me.'

Suppressing the all-too-familiar surge of anxiety and exasperation she tried to summon sympathy. 'Is it your stomach again?'

'None of your damn business!' her father retorted. But his speech was slurred and his tone more peevish than angry.

'Father, Dr Avers has already warned you about the brandy.'

He swivelled his head against the worn and faded fabric. 'That's enough, miss!' Spittle gathered at the corners of his mouth and his colour darkened ominously. 'Who d'you think you are, lecturing me? You're getting above yourself. And I won't have it, d'you hear? I'm master in this house. You mind your own affairs and leave mine to me.'

Smarting, Jenefer bit her lip. Whether he liked it or not, his drinking was her affair. He might resent what he termed her interference, but she couldn't remain silent and simply watch him destroy himself.

Her father never allowed her to remain in the room during the doctor's visits. But last time Dr Avers had told her bluntly that the amount of brandy her father was consuming would see him dead within a year.

What then? What would happen to her and Betsy, to Maggie and Treeve? The house was entailed to a distant cousin, and she hadn't heard from Martin in months.

What was she supposed to do? Her father wasn't bedridden. She couldn't physically stop him drinking. Nor, even if there was the remotest chance of him listening, could she plead cost. Not when he funded the cargoes of contraband that Devlin Varcoe collected from Roscoff every few weeks.

One of the benefits of being a venturer was unlimited access to tubs of the finest cognac. Considering the recent bewildering decline in profits from his investment, brandy was rapidly becoming his only reward. Yet how could she think of it as such when it was killing him?

'I'm sorry, Father. It's only because I worry about you.'

He snorted. 'You'd be better off doing something useful. Worry doesn't change anything. I should know. You'd think an officer injured fighting for his king and country would receive some recognition. That musket ball finished my career and I don't even get a decent pension. The pittance I'm paid is an insult, a mockery. But nobody listens. Nobody cares. Out of sight, out of mind.'

His hand shook as he lifted the glass and gulped the spirit down like water. 'Then losing your mother – and my poor little Betsy crippled for life.' His chin sank to his chest. 'All because some damned fool couldn't handle his horses.'

Jenefer slipped out, closing the door quietly behind her. Bitter and befuddled, he would pick over all his grievances and not even notice she'd gone.

Trying to shake off the sense of helplessness and accompanying frustration, she entered the kitchen. Large and warm, it was fragrant with the scent of recent baking.

Her gaze swept over a rack of scones and another containing two large round cakes. An inch thick and stuffed full of currants and lemon peel, their tops had been scored in a lattice pattern and sprinkled with sugar, now pale gold and crunchy. Her mouth watered.

'White flour, Maggie?' Jenefer considered this more of a luxury than the usual brandy and tobacco, lace and silks. Two seasons of difficult weather and poor harvest had led to desperate shortages. In past years grain had been imported from France, which usually produced a surplus. But now the war and resulting naval blockade meant Britain was dependent on supplies from America. These were erratic and even when some did reach Cornwall, it was expensive and far beyond the pockets of ordinary folk.

Behind the huge scrubbed table, the cook-housekeeper was loading a tray with plates of sliced barley bread topped with jam, buttered scones and squares of heavy cake. She looked up, beaming.

'The boys brung back a few casks with the last cargo. Jared Sweet carried one up when he come to see Miss Betsy. Dear of'n.'

'That was kind of him.' It seemed so wrong to envy Betsy, who had loved dancing and walking the cliff paths, and now depended on a wheeled chair to get her from one room to another. But Jenefer envied her sister for Jared's silent devotion, demonstrated in such practical ways.

Jared had constructed the chair and ignoring Betsy's protests, lifted her into it. On warm summer days when he wasn't fishing, Jared had come up and carried her into the garden then sat on the grass at a respectful distance while she painted or worked at her needlepoint.

Jenefer mentioned that he didn't appear to talk much. Betsy's wan face had softened in a smile Jenefer had never seen before.

'You're right, he doesn't. He speaks when he has something to say. But he doesn't chatter, which is very restful. And he's a wonderful listener.'

It was Betsy's expression as much as her words that had made Jenefer think briefly of Martin, then for far longer of Devlin Varcoe, until she realized what she was doing and, hot with shame, quickly redirected her attention to household tasks.

That Betsy and Jared loved each other Jenefer had no doubt. But there was as much chance of her father giving his blessing to such an unequal match as there was of him giving up brandy.

'I've jest took a great pot of tea into the drawing-room, miss,' Maggie broke into Jenenfer's thoughts. 'Miss Betsy's in there keeping an eye to the captain and the others.'

'What about the crew? Have you had time—?'

'Treeve just this minute took a tray out to the stables, miss. I made coffee for they. I daresay Treeve'll put a drop of brandy in it, to help them over the shock, like. How's master?' At Jenefer's brief head-shake Maggie sighed. 'Off again, is he? Oh well, you done your best. You can't make him heed you.'

'I shouldn't let him have it.'

'There idn no way you can stop him.' Maggie was pragmatic. 'Even if you was to hide it away he'd find it. And if you wouldn't give it to him, others would.' She lifted one plump shoulder in a helpless shrug.

'And we both know who.' She sighed. 'I'm sorry, miss. I've warned 'n if he don't do his work proper we'll both be out on the street—'

'I wouldn't do that, Maggie. I'd never find anyone who'd work as hard as you.'

'Nor you would, miss. But 'tis better if Treeve don't know he's safe. You throwing 'n out is the only threat I got.'

'Father's asking for the doctor.'

'You want me to send Treeve for 'n?'

Jenefer shook her head. 'Treeve's got enough to do. Besides, by the time Dr Avers arrived, father would have forgotten asking for him. Then he'd be rude. I'll see how he is in the morning.'

Maggie nodded. 'I fetched a blanket down for that Mrs Vanson. Poor dear soul.' Her eyes glistened with tears. 'Don't bear thinking about, her babby snatched from her arms like that.' She shook her head. 'Break your heart, it do.'

Jenefer swallowed the tightness in her own throat. 'She shouldn't stay in those wet clothes. Take in the tray, Maggie, then boil up some water. I'll go and find a dress for her to change into.'

'Tamara, what were you thinking of?' Morwenna Gillis closed her eyes as she wafted the vinaigrette beneath her nose, flinching as the pungency bit the back of her throat. 'Riding out alone at this time of night. And in such weather.'

'It's not much after six, Mama. It got dark early because of the low cloud. And it wasn't raining when I left. Well, only a little,' Tamara's incorrigible honesty forced the admission.

Beneath a long-sleeved gown of peach-coloured silk Morwenna's spine, normally ramrod straight, wilted in distress as she pressed a handkerchief sprinkled with lavender water to her forehead.

It must be very difficult, Tamara mused, being her mother. To work so hard at being someone she wasn't, to live in constant dread of her family letting her down. Which they invariably did, though not through malice. It was just that both she and her father had more important things to think about. Matters far more vital than the stifling rules and nuances of social behaviour that occupied her mother's every waking moment. Of course, pretty manners were useful if you were attending balls and assemblies. Tamara knew well enough how to impress the stuffy matrons in Helston and Truro. But here in the village her father's main concern was his

21

boatyard. Hers was Devlin Varcoe.

'I despair,' Morwenna wailed, fluttering the handkerchief in her daughter's direction. 'Just look at you.'

'What?' Tamara glanced down at her gown of primrose sprigged muslin. 'I thought you liked this. You said the style—'

'Your hair, Tamara.' Her mother closed her eyes as if looking at the glossy curls that tumbled wildly down her daughter's back was too painful to be borne.

'Oh.' Tamara shook her head. 'Maggie wanted to put it up or thread it with ribbons but I didn't want the bother. Anyway it wasn't dry.'

'Didn't want the bother?' Morwenna's voice climbed, reflecting her shock. She shuddered. 'I've done my best to bring you up properly, to be a *lady* And what do you do? You throw it all back in my face.' She bowed her head and dabbed her eyes.

Gazing at her mother's elaborate turban of gold and peach chiffon threaded with ribbon and decorated with a jewelled pin, Tamara sighed.

'Oh, Mama, don't make such a fuss. I was wearing a coat, and a little rain never hurt anyone. Papa was hoping for some salvage.'

Morwenna's head flew up. Her eyes wide, she gave a little shriek. 'Tell me you didn't go down to the beach! You did, didn't you?'

'Well, that's where the wreck is,' Tamara said, with what she felt was perfect reasonableness. She was growing bored with her mother's histrionics. Surely dinner must be ready? The ride, the fresh air, and her conversation with Devlin – though that had been all too brief – had sharpened her appetite.

'Oh!' Morwenna pressed the lavender-scented handkerchief to her bosom as she lifted the vinaigrette. Inhaling deeply she gasped and coughed. Opening her eyes she turned a long-suffering gaze on her daughter. 'Your father and I have devoted our lives—'

'Papa's life,' Tamara said, over her shoulder as she moved aimlessly about the over-furnished room, picking up ornaments and miniatures from cabinets and side tables then replacing them, 'is devoted to the yard.'

'As it should be,' Morwenna agreed, oblivious to her contradiction. 'Naturally, I know little of such matters. Business is a gentleman's province and not something with which ladies need concern themselves. But it is thanks to your father's boatyard that you were able to enjoy a proper education, with dancing lessons, painting classes and—'

'Yes, Mama. I know. You keep telling me.' Tamara was heartily sick of the constant reminders. Sighing, she flung herself on to a gilt sofa upholstered in ivory brocade and stretched out her legs so she could admire her primrose kid slippers. The little rosettes were pretty and made her feet look remarkably elegant.

'Don't sprawl, Tamara. Sit up properly. Why must you be so contrary? If Miss Mitchell could see you now she would have a spasm. And then there are your clothes.'

'What about them?'

'You have two wardrobes full—'

'I do indeed, Mama. Isn't it fortunate I have one talent you can be proud of?' Tamara jumped up again, unable to sit still. She wished she were still down on the beach, or out on the cliffs. She had no fear of the dark. 'Designing new gowns is such a useful accomplishment.' Experience had taught her that if her mother even noticed the irony she would ignore it.

'My dear, we only want what's best for you.'

'Mama, your opinion of what is best—'

'Is what any loving and responsible parent would want for their daughter: marriage to a man of substance who will—'

'Bore me to sobs.'

'Tamara!'

The door opened.

'Mr Gillis, thank goodness you are come,' Morwenna cried, her chin quivering with emotion. 'You must speak to your daughter. I'm at my wits' end. I declare she'll see me in my grave before the year is out.'

Father and daughter exchanged an eloquent glance. In deference to his wife's insistence that they all change before sitting down to the evening meal, John Gillis wore a black frock coat over a waist-coat of embroidered satin, breeches with fashionable ties at the knee, silk stockings and black shoes with oval buckles. He looked thoroughly uncomfortable. But Tamara knew his unease was as likely caused by the manner and content of his wife's greeting as by what he termed his *fancy dress*.

Crossing to his wife's side he patted her shoulder as if she were a nervous mare of which he wasn't entirely sure. Which, Tamara thought, wasn't far from the truth.

'I hope not, my dear. That would be a very sad thing. Tamara, have you been upsetting your mother?' His expression was suitably grave, but as his gaze met hers Tamara saw mirrored in it her own wish not to be having this conversation, and to be somewhere – anywhere – else.

'No more than usual, Papa.'

'Oh!' Morwenna stifled a sob. Then moving so abruptly that he jumped, she turned to look up at her husband. 'Tamara says you sent her down to the beach.'

'No, Mama,' Tamara corrected quickly. 'I didn't say Papa sent me. It was my idea to go. I thought if I got there quickly enough there might be—'

'You see?' Morwenna demanded of her husband. 'How we can expect any decent man to make an offer for her when she insists on conducting herself like – like a hoyden!'

'But I don't *want* the men you consider suitable. They're either old and boring or young and stupid.'

'Now, now,' her father warned.

Jumping up, she hurried to his side, slipped her arm through his as she pleaded, 'Papa, there's only one man for me. I want Devlin Varcoe.'

Her mother squeaked then slumped back in her chair and fluttered her handkerchief.

'For heaven's sake, Tamara.' John Gillis frowned and stretched his chin and forced a callused finger down between his neck and the starched cravat that, despite his wife's urging, he refused to tie in anything but the simplest knot. 'Don't be ridiculous.'

'I'm not!'

'It's out of the question.'

'But *why*, Papa? If you are so anxious for me to marry, then at least let me have the man I—'

'You don't—'

'Papa, you've known the Varcoes all your life.' She would not be silenced. She had to make them understand. 'You've built boats for them.'

'That's different. That's business. Listen, girl, and hear what I'm saying. Devlin Varcoe is not for you.'

'Why?' Tamara demanded. 'Because he's a smuggler? Is that why,

Papa?' she repeated, trying hard to sound more reasonable. He looked, she thought, like a man already floundering and desperate not to sink any deeper.

'That one reason. There are others. And no, I do not intend to discuss them with you.' He rubbed his palms together, visibly embarrassed.

'That's not fair!'

'Enough! I mean it, Tamara,' he warned, as she opened her mouth. Clearing his throat and avoiding his daughter's flushed cheeks and stormy gaze, he moved across to the fireplace and studied the dancing flames. 'Listen to your mother. She knows far better that you what's best.'

'Best for who?' Tamara cried.

'*Whom*, dear. It's *whom*,' Morwenna corrected gently, sitting up straight once more.

'I don't *care!*' Tamara yelled. 'I love Devlin.'

'Love?' Morwenna tilted her head. Her patronizing smile made Tamara want to scream. 'My dear child, what would you know of love? You're far too young to—'

'I'm not a child. I'm nineteen,' Tamara cried. 'And if I'm old enough to be married off to a man of *your* choice, I'm certainly old enough to know about love.'

Her mother paled, darting a shocked and frantic glance towards her husband.

'That will do!' her father thundered, startling all three of them. Clearing his throat he continued in a quieter tone, 'I want no more talk like that. You'll upset your mother.'

Tamara threw up her hands. 'Mama's always upset about something. Papa, this is *important*. It's my whole future—'

'Not with Devil Varcoe.' John Gillis was grim. 'He's not for you.'

Hot tears of fury welled but she blinked them back. This was too serious. Besides, she had never resorted to weeping to get her own way. That was her mother's behaviour; it would never be hers. 'You care more for what other people might say than you do about my happiness.'

'Oh, *Tamara*.' Morwenna buried her face in her handkerchief.

Anger darkened her father's features. 'You listen to me, my girl. It's because we care about your happiness that we want to see you safely married to a man of—'

'I won't marry someone I don't love. I'd sooner not marry at all.'

'So what will you do instead?' her father demanded.

Tamara shrugged. Wanting Devlin, determined to have Devlin, she had never considered alternatives. 'I could – I could be a governess.'

'Oh yes? Where?'

'Here,' she retorted defiantly. 'In Porthinnis.' While Devlin stayed so would she.

'The only governess in this village is Miss Everson. She's been with Dr Avers fifteen years and will no doubt be with the family for another fifteen if Mrs Avers continues breeding.'

'Mr Gillis, please,' Morwenna gasped.

Ignoring his wife he raged on, 'Or will you work in the pilchard cellars among women with coarse clothes and coarser minds who stink of fish? How long would your pretty dresses last then?'

'John!'

'If you really want to drive your mother to her death-bed you could take a job at The Five Mackerel where you'll be leered at and pawed by drunken fishermen and farm labourers.'

'Oh!' Morwenna shrieked. 'The shame – I couldn't bear – quick, my smelling salts. I feel faint.'

'Now, now, my dear.' Guiding the vinaigrette clutched in his wife's hand to her nose, John glared at his daughter. 'See what you've done? Are you happy now?'

'But *I* didn't – why are you blaming *me*?' Hurt and furious, she went to the door.

'Tamara, wait. Your dinner—'

'I'm not hungry.' She raced upstairs, her eyes burning. Why wouldn't they *listen*?

CHAPTER THREE

Thomas Varcoe rode down the long incline of Lemon Street into the town of Truro. Crossing the bridge at the bottom he glanced to his right, his gaze drawn to the trading schooners, brigs and fishing luggers moored alongside quays on both sides of the river. Their hatches were open, decks swarming with men loading and unloading cargoes. Behind the quays, warehouse doors gaped like open mouths to receive sacks and boxes and baulks of timber.

Men shouted, iron-shod hoofs clattered against the granite setts, heavy carts creaked, winches squealed. The village could be noisy, but it was nothing compared to this. Unsettled, Thomas's horse tossed its head. He urged it on with a sharp kick, scattering barefoot children clad in filthy rags who, recognizing a stranger, darted between carts and carriages to run hopefully alongside.

'Gi' us a penny, mister. A ha'penny? A farthing? Go on, mister. Please?'

He ignored their grubby outstretched hands and rode past, disregarding the curses screeched after him.

'Tight as a duck's fert, you are, mister.'

'Skin a turd for the tallow, he would.'

He had left Porthinnis early yesterday, stopped for dinner and the night at the Norway Inn, and set off again this morning. Now after almost four hours on the road he was saddle sore and extremely hungry.

Reaching Boscawen Street, an even more imposing thoroughfare since the demolition of a row of houses down the centre had more than doubled its width, he glanced at the façade of The Red Lion. Four storeys high, with three gables at the front and pediments over the windows, the majestic building had once been the town house of a prominent family.

Thomas's chin rose. When he'd made his fortune he would have a town house. Nothing too large – one had to consider the cost of running such an establishment – but certainly grand enough to indicate his success. He'd show all those who still harboured doubts that he was more than equal to his father. His father was dead, for God's sake. He was in charge now. Had he owned such a house nothing would have induced him to part with it.

But instead of crossing the busy thoroughfare to take a room there he turned left. Impressive it might be but he'd had enough of coaching inns. They were exceptionally busy places with noise and bustle that lasted long into the night and began again in the early hours.

He preferred The Bull. Situated opposite the coinage hall, the inn was popular with mine owners, tin and copper smelters and free-trading businessmen like himself. The rooms were neat, the sheets properly aired, and the landlord kept an excellent table and wine cellar. Dismounting, Thomas waited for the boy to unfasten his bag from the saddle and hand it to him. Then as his horse was led round to the yard and stables, he entered the inn.

An hour later fortified by a hearty meal of cold beef, cheese and good claret he went out once more into the busy street. He had two calls to make. One he dreaded. The other – he patted his chest and was reassured. Tucked into a hidden pocket on the inside of his double-breasted waistcoat, the emerald lay snugly against his heart. It was a particularly fine stone. Certainly the best of the gems Trevanion had brought back from India.

Unfortunately it was also the last. Trevanion's announcement had come as an unpleasant shock. While Thomas was still coming to terms with all the implications, the colonel had dealt him a further blow. Despite the brandy fumes on his breath and the floridity of his complexion, Trevanion's instructions had been unequivocal.

He trusted Thomas would get the best price possible. But this time only half the sum would be invested in cargo. The remainder was for his daughter Jenefer's dowry.

This presented Thomas with not just one but several problems. He already owed his uncle for part of the last cargo. To buy time he'd sent a letter with Devlin to Roscoff citing late payment by a couple of his customers. But Hedley had his suppliers to pay and would expect the debt cleared when Devlin arrived to collect the next shipment. If it wasn't – Thomas's skin tightened in a shiver. He couldn't fail. He'd find the money. He had to, because if he didn't, all his plans, his whole future – he slammed a mental door on thoughts too horrifying to contemplate.

Following his father's death two other venturers had decided to retire. Both had told him it was nothing personal. But he knew better. They hadn't waited, hadn't even allowed him an opportunity to show that he was just as shrewd, just as able. If they had only given him a chance he would have proved it.

He felt a rush of anger, a fierce quickening of his pulse as he relived the memory. Overcoming his pride he had actually pleaded. And still they'd turned him down. He hated that they had seen his desperation. Their rejection was an insult he wouldn't forgive. Nor would he forget. He'd show them. His time would come. When it did revenge would be sweet.

Since their defection Colonel Trevanion had been his only source of finance. But with no more gems to sell, the next cargo would be his last investment. In addition, when an increased profit was vital in order to balance the accounts, the colonel was reducing his stake. It was imperative to find a new venturer.

But who? No one else in Porthinnis had that kind of money. Apart from the Casvellans: but Branoc Casvellan was a Justice of the Peace. Though his sentencing of smugglers was usually less severe than that of his colleagues, he flatly declined any involvement in free trading. Thomas's mouth twisted bitterly. Was the man blind or simply naïve? Did he really believe duty had been paid on his after-dinner brandy?

Yet even he could not be as much of a hypocrite as Sir Edward Pengarrick, who regularly sentenced Mount's Bay men to trans-portation when everyone knew he was the venturer backing the Cawsand smugglers.

Someone bumped his shoulder, jolting him into awareness of his surroundings. Startled, he realized he had reached the shop without any recollection of the journey. Taking a moment to clear his mind he focused on the negotiation that lay ahead. His dead father still cast a long shadow. But *he* ran the business now. Devlin was just a courier. It was *he*, Thomas, elder son and his father's heir, who held the reins and the power. He breathed deeply, felt new strength and determination infuse him, then pushed open the door.

Later that evening, replete with an excellent meal accompanied by more fine wine, Thomas sat beside a roaring fire in the coffee room, reliving once more the pleasurable part of his afternoon. He had secured an excellent price for the emerald. Unwilling to trust the landlord's strongbox, and far too wary to leave anything of value in his room, he had secreted the money in various secret pockets about his person. After another brandy he planned to retire to bed. The journey back to Porthinnis would require an early start.

'Why, damme, it's Thomas Varcoe!'

Looking up, Thomas saw a brawny figure he knew by sight and reputation. Standing over six feet, Harry Carlyon was a head taller than almost every other man in the room, including himself. Thomas found this doubly irksome as it reminded him of his

brother. Because thinking about Devlin always filled him with
anger and resentment he usually avoided doing so.

The most successful smuggler in Coverack, Harry wore his noto-
riety as comfortably as he wore his well-cut frock coat. Bitterness
burned in Thomas's stomach. *If Devlin possessed such a garment,
he'd fill it with the same careless ease.*

'Carlyon,' Thomas greeted with a smile, and snapped his fingers
at the landlord who was hurrying past with a bottle but appeared
not to see.

'Jack!' Carlyon roared above the rumble of conversation and
laughter. 'Two glasses of your finest cognac.'

'Coming right up, Mr Carlyon,' the landlord shouted back.

'So,' Harry folded himself into the high-backed settle, forcing
Thomas to move along and making him feel cornered. 'What brings
you to Truro?'

'Business,' Thomas said curtly, still smarting from the landlord's
snub.

'Me too.' Harry's expression was open, his grin expansive, but his
narrowed gaze was as sharp as a gimlet. 'I tell you, if my bank
manager had bowed any lower he'd have been sweeping the floor
with his nose. Does your heart good to see them grovel, doesn't it?'

Thomas responded with a wry nod, intimating shared experience
while his dinner curdled inside him. He had known the meeting
with Mr Daniell would be difficult, but it had been worse. It had
been a disaster. The banker was immovable. Until the current overdraft had been reduced a further loan was out of the question. He
hadn't even softened his words with an apology. Thomas had found
this deeply insulting.

Wanting to grab the man by the throat and shake him until his
teeth rattled, instead Thomas had inclined his head, saying he
perfectly understood. This acceptance was the banker's cue to relax.
When he didn't, Thomas found himself driven to further explanation. The situation had come about because money due to him had
been delayed. Unfortunately, this had compromised his own affairs.

'Indeed.' The banker's response was totally devoid of inflection.
But Thomas's shirt had grown damp as he masked his embarrassment and fury behind a casual smile.

'I did consider taking a mortgage on the property—'

'A *second* charge, Mr Varcoe?' the banker interrupted, his brows climbing. 'As I understand it, there is already—'

'You did not allow me to finish,' Thomas chided gently. *How in the name of all that was holy did Daniell know?* 'I said I considered it. But as I fully expect to clear the overdraft within the next few weeks. . . .' His gesture intimated that it wouldn't be worth the trouble. It was a wild impossible claim but he didn't care. The only thing that mattered was to escape with the few shreds of dignity remaining to him.

'I shall look forward to it.' The banker's tone made clear the meeting was over.

Thomas bowed and bade him good day, receiving in return a nod of minimal politeness. He left the bank fuming with rage and indignation. But beneath the anger lay cold numbing fear.

He smiled at Harry. 'It's always good to hear of someone else doing well.' Careful not to betray the slightest trace of envy his tone implied there was plenty of business for both of them.

Harry rubbed his palms together. The rasp of callused skin grated on Thomas's raw nerves like a blacksmith's file. The landlord set two goblets half full of golden-brown spirit on the table and hurried away. Harry picked up one and swirled it gently, then inhaled the vapours. 'Bit of all right, that is.' He raised the goblet in a toast. 'Fair winds for all but the revenue men.'

Saluting with his own glass, Thomas drank deeply.

Harry cradled the goblet between scarred hands that were twice the size of Thomas's soft pale ones. He shook his head. 'Got to admit I'm bleddy exhausted. Demand's so high it's hard to keep up. In fair weather I'm making a run every three or four days.'

Thomas was sceptical. 'You can't get to Roscoff and back in such a short time.'

After a brief and apparently casual glance round, the smuggler half-turned so his back faced the room, and lowered his voice. 'Not Roscoff, Guernsey.'

'Even so, no lugger could—'

'I sold my lugger. I've got a cutter now. Fast as a swallow she is. I can outsail anything on this coast.'

'Even the revenue boats?' Thomas challenged, an idea beginning to take shape in his mind.

Harry grinned. 'Especially the revenue boats.'

It was a risk, but life was a risk. It would solve all his problems.

What if it failed? – Why should it? *He was supposed to take the money back.* The colonel didn't need it immediately. No banns had been posted, so his daughter could not be getting married for at least a month. By then he would have recouped both the investment and a sizeable profit. Besides, most of the time Trevanion was too drunk to know what day of the week it was. It would be easy enough to fob him off. He'd say the jeweller wanted to take the emerald to Exeter to get a better price.

'Do you believe in Fate?' Thomas blurted, telling himself if Carlyon laughed he'd forget the whole thing.

The smuggler swirled his brandy again and raised it to his lips. He held the spirit in his mouth, savouring the bouquet and taste before swallowing.

'Funny you should ask that,' he murmured. His expression grew pensive but his gaze remained sharp. 'How long is it since I saw you last? Must be two or three months at least. Yet here we are, enjoying a drink and a yarn, both doing well and looking to do better. Would you call that Fate?'

Harry Carlyon had turned the question without actually answering it. But Thomas was only half-listening. Surely this was exactly the opportunity he'd been waiting, hoping for? It was too good to miss. Raising his own glass he swallowed deeply, allowing himself sufficient time to control swelling excitement. He had to give the impression of offering, not needing.

'Well,' he smiled, 'fate or not, our meeting like this could do us both a bit of good. As it happens I've got some spare funds to invest.' Just saying the words made him feel powerful. 'Would you be interested?'

Carlyon's gaze flicked up. 'Certainly would. Do you want to take delivery and arrange your own distribution, or—?'

'No. You handle all that. I'll settle for my stake plus the profit less your costs. What's your percentage rate?'

After a few minutes of haggling they agreed terms.

'How long—?' Thomas began.

'Two weeks.' Harry Carlyon grinned. 'Meet me back here and you can buy me dinner.' They shook hands on the deal and Thomas excused himself, going to his room to remove the money in private. Then he called for pen and paper and wrote out a receipt. After signing the document, which Thomas pocketed, Harry stuffed the cash inside his coat and called for more brandy.

The following morning Thomas mounted his horse carefully in deference to the dull throbbing in his skull. He was two hours later than he'd planned. Sitting talking late into the night with Harry, he'd drunk far more than he usually did and woke with a sour stomach and a pounding headache. But after a wash, a shave and several cups of strong coffee, he had managed to eat a decent breakfast.

The residue of his hangover faded as he pictured his return to Truro, and Harry handing over a bag of golden guineas or a thick wad of the new five-pound notes. His mind leapt forward to his next visit to the bank. It would give him great pleasure to put the supercilious Daniell firmly in his place. But that would be only a passing pleasure. What he really wanted, and was determined to have, was Tamara Gillis.

The ebbing tide had exposed a wide expanse of firm sand. Tamara loosened the reins and leaned forward in the saddle as the mare lengthened her stride and picked up speed. The cold morning air stung her face as they thundered across the beach. Hatless, her hair streamed behind her like a black banner.

Approaching the rocks she reined in, slowing to a trot then a walk. Exhilarated by the gallop, she patted the mare's neck, guiding her along beside the rocks while she looked at what was left of the schooner.

The morning after the storm Lt Crocker had arrived with a party of dragoons. Tamara had watched them loading bodies on to a cart borrowed from one of the farms. Only two had been strangers. She hadn't heard if they belonged to the schooner's crew, or were wreckers from Brague.

The others were local. One woman and three men, drunk on plundered rum, had died of exposure. One man's widow and the woman's two children were bound for the workhouse. Another man had slipped on the weed-covered rocks and fallen into a crevice. His leg broken, unable to move, he had drowned in the rising tide.

The lieutenant had examined the wreck, shaken his head, and ridden away with his men. Tamara knew from previous occasions that he would visit the local shops and inns, and post notices warning that anything taken from the wreck was stolen property and must be returned. She also knew, as he surely must, that it was a pointless exercise.

Closing mines had thrown tinners out of work. The fishermen were at the mercy of both weather and shoals. Last year's bad harvest meant that several farmers, unable to pay their rent, had been thrown off their land. So what the sea gave, the villagers kept.

The schooner had grounded three nights ago. The villagers, the tides and the knife-edged rocks had torn the ship apart. Another week and there would be nothing to show she'd ever been there. Only a marker in the graveyard.

Tamara halted the mare and glanced seaward, judging the state of the tide. Then she looked towards the cliff that marked the end of the beach and separated it from the rocky coves beyond. At the base of the cliff was a basin where, at certain phases of the moon, things lost from the beach or harbour were washed up by tidal currents.

She sat for a moment longer, reluctant. She could tell someone else. Who? Doctor Avers? He'd feel bound to tell her mother. As for Mr Carthew, the Methodist preacher, she definitely could not tell him. 'Holy' Moses Carthew believed half the village – the half that drank spirits and smoked tobacco – was condemned to hellfire and damnation. It was inevitable he would consider her gift a mark of the Devil. In any case telling someone would only provoke questions. Such as how did she know?

What could she say? She didn't know *how* she knew things, she just did. Anyway, she was here because if the knowledge was a gift it was also a responsibility.

Drawing a deep breath she clicked her tongue and gently kicked the mare with the heel of her boot. As they approached the basin the mare tossed her head and edged sideways but Tamara urged her on, soothing her with murmurs.

Her heart sank as she looked at the tangle of rope, seaweed torn loose by the gales, driftwood and smashed crabpots. But as she drew closer, able now to see the area hidden from view, there it was, just as she had 'seen' it, white against the dark rock, small and broken like a doll.

Her eyes burned and her throat tightened. Dismounting she flipped the reins over the restless mare's head and looped them over her arm. Untying the holly-green sash around the waist of her jacket, she shook out the folds and laid it on the sand. Blinking away tears and biting her lip hard she gently picked up the tiny battered corpse and wrapped it closely in the fringed muslin. Then, remounting the mare and holding the tragic little bundle in the crook of her arm, she rode up the beach and through the village to the parsonage.

The Reverend Dr Trennack was a scholar, happier with his books than with his parishioners who found him pleasant if slightly detached. But his wife was a kind woman of great understanding who had borne him seven children and buried three of them.

Caroline Trennack accepted the bundle, her gaze warm and sympathetic. 'Oh my dear, Thank you. It cannot have been easy. I will write to his mother. Knowing he's been found might make her loss a little easier to bear.'

Nodding, Tamara turned away. Remounting, she guided the mare up on to the moor and galloped her along narrow paths through the bracken and heather until they were both exhausted.

With her pointed stem and stern and an outrigger to hold the mizzen sheet that mirrored the bowsprit, the lugger was a 'double-ender' and typical of the Mount's Bay boats.

Devlin stood at the helm, the slim package wrapped in oiled silk stuffed down his boot and pressing against his ankle. He had brought back letters and dispatches in the past. But this packet, his uncle told him, was to be placed in the hands of Branoc Casvellan and no one else.

'Are you mad?' Devlin had whispered fiercely. 'I'm running contraband and you want me to take this to our local Justice?'

'It'll be all right,' his uncle promised. 'This is far more important than your cargo of brandy.'

'You're sure of that, are you? What is it anyway?'

'Better you don't know.'

'And if we're attacked?'

Hedley's fingers had tightened on his forearm. 'Weight it with an iron pig and throw it overboard. Mind me now, Devlin. It must not be found.'

Jared stood at the mizzen with the other crew forward near the mainmast: three to handle the big lug sail and the fourth to man the jib.

'Where do your uncle get all his information from?' Jared asked, shaking his head in awe.

Devlin shrugged. 'He keeps his ears open. Roscoff is always

buzzing with rumours.'

'D'you think this one's true?'

'That there are English agents working in France? Or that the French are desperate to catch them?'

'Both.'

'I'd say so. If we need to know where the revenue cutters and the dragoons are on the days we make a run, the British Government would certainly want to know if the French are planning another invasion.'

'After they lost all those men in Ireland?' Jared was sceptical. 'They'd be bleddy mad to try.'

'Still, it's hardly surprising there's a growing number in favour of restoring the monarchy.'

Jared grunted. 'Why, fer God's sake? 'Tis but a few years since they killed the king and queen they had.'

'True. But what they've got now is a corrupt dictatorship that rules by terror. People are even worse off than they were before the revolution. There's no work, virtually everything is in short supply, and the paper currency is worthless. Still, at least they have plenty of cheap flour.'

'Don't matter how cheap it is,' Jared said. 'If you got no work, you got no money to buy it.'

'True again. So with the French Government offering a reward in gold for the capture of enemy agents—' Devlin broke off, stiffening as he peered into the gloom. 'What—?'

Jared followed Devlin's gaze. 'God a'mighty, 'tis a revenue cutter.' He frowned. 'But 'e shouldn't be. . . .'

'No, he shouldn't.' Devlin was grim. 'The Penryn boat is out of the water for repairs, and the two Falmouth boats are supposed to be up around Fowey and Cawsand.'

'Well, that one isn't,' Jared growled.

'Hey, skip,' Ben Tozer had caught sight of the customs cutter. 'That's the *Lark*. What the 'ell's she doing down here?'

'Get ready to go about,' Devlin interrupted. This was a complicated manoeuvre as it required the heavy yard from which the lug-sail hung to be dropped to the deck, moved round forward of the mast then rehoisted on the new tack. Yet skill and practice meant the crew usually made short work of it, even in heavy weather. But this morning Charlie Grose kept fumbling the ropes, delaying the tack.

Sam and Andy cursed his clumsiness, and Danny swore.

'For Chris'sakes, Charlie, what are 'ee doing of?'

'Me 'ands is froze,' Charlie whined. 'I can't feel to grip.' He was certainly trembling, apparently racked by shivers. This struck Devlin as strange, for all of them – including Charlie – were dressed for the winter weather. Beneath canvas smocks they wore woollen shirts, Guernseys, or jumpers of heavy, off-white oiled wool, thick trousers and knitted socks inside wide-topped high leather boots.

As Charlie shook and fumbled, his gaze kept darting towards the cutter. This slowed him down even further, making him more hindrance than help.

Watching him through narrowed eyes, Devlin's impatience was suddenly swept aside as shocked realization was swiftly followed by icy rage.

'Jared, take the helm.' Plunging forward, Devlin seized a handful of the stained canvas covering Charlie's chest and jerked him close. 'You tipped them off.'

In the pre-dawn gloom Charlie's eyes widened in fear. Despite the knife-edged wind, sweat beaded his face giving the lie to his claim of being cold. His lips parted but before he could speak Devlin backhanded him across the mouth. A drop of blood bloomed darkly on the pallid skin.

'Lie to me and I swear to God I'll kill you where you stand.'

Tears ran down Charlie's cheeks and he began to gibber. 'Hammer said he'd break me legs. There wasn't no other way I could get the money.'

'So you sold us out? You treacherous bastard.'

Charlie flinched violently at the cannon's echoing boom. Devlin didn't even glance up. He knew it was merely a warning shot. The cutter was too far away to have any hope of hitting them.

'Looks like they want us to heave-to, skipper,' Sam said.

'Not a chance.' Though Devlin's gaze remained fixed on Charlie he raised his voice so they could all hear him. 'But they can have their informer. I've no use for him.'

There was a moment's utter silence as the crew realized what Charlie had done and what Devlin intended.

'Skip,' Jared's voice was pitched low. 'You sure 'bout this?'

'Oh yes,' Devlin dragged Charlie to the gunwale. 'He made his choice.'

'No,' Charlie gasped. 'Jesus, Skip. You can't.'

'You think not?' Devlin was implacable. 'Five years, Charlie. Five years you've been on this boat. A crew is closer than family. Trust is everything. Whether we're fishing or running contraband, trust can mean the difference between life and death. But you betrayed us. You sold us to pay your gambling debts.'

Trembling violently, Charlie wailed, 'But Hammer was going to break me legs—'

'Then you'd better hope he doesn't find you.' With strength born of anger all the more bitter because he'd liked Charlie, Devlin forced the struggling man backwards over the kegs that lined the ledge along the inner edge of the gunwale.

'I can't swim,' Charlie croaked desperately.

'Nor can Sam or Andy,' Devlin replied. 'They were your mates. If the cutter had got close enough to sink us, they would have drowned. You knew that, but you didn't care. Go to the devil, Charlie.' With a sharp thrust that pushed the crewman off-balance, Devlin seized his ankles and tipped him over the side.

CHAPTER FOUR

A splash cut short Charlie's scream. Devlin heard 'Bleddy 'ell', from one of the startled crew and someone else muttered, '*Devil* by name. . . .' He turned his back on the flailing figure whose choking screams were shredded by the gusting wind. The lugger bore away, the gap widening rapidly.

'Billy, help Joe shift the ballast.' Leaving Jared on the helm Devlin grabbed a rope. 'Ready, lads? Right, drop her.'

A few minutes later with the tack completed and sails reset, the lugger creamed through the choppy swell heading shoreward. Given the strength of the south-east wind Devlin knew they were in danger of being driven on to the jagged rocks. But it was a risk worth taking. Against the dark cliffs the boat's black hull and brown sails would be hard to see.

Laden with eighty tubs of fine cognac the lugger sat low in the water. Yet her flat bottom and shallow draught would enable her to sail far closer inshore than the deep-keeled cutter.

Devlin looked at his crew. Their lives were in peril on every run. They didn't do it for a thrill like the bored younger sons of the gentry; it was a matter of survival, especially when weeks went by and the shoals didn't come. Cornwall was a long way from the capital and a government knew little and cared even less about the desperate daily struggle with poverty.

The slim packets of tobacco, silk and lace stuffed inside the crew's boots were their personal ventures and not counted as part of the cargo. Some might be kept for a mother, sister, wife or sweetheart. But most would be sold to buy bread and meat, a length of cloth or a new cooking pot.

'You making for the cove, skip?' Danny enquired.

Devlin shook his head. 'We wouldn't have time to land the brandy. Besides, if Customs were willing to divert one of the revenue cutters down here from Fowey on the strength of whatever Charlie Grose told them, it's possible Lieutenant Crocker will be waiting for us with a welcoming party of dragoons.' He heard the soft hiss of indrawn breath as his crew recognized the depth of Charlie's betrayal.

'We'll drop the tubs and creep for them once the coast is clear. They'll come to no harm on the sea bottom for a few days.'

As the crew began checking the ropes that linked the tubs in groups of five with a sinking stone attached, Devlin was grateful for his uncle's foresight in having them already prepared.

Sunrise approached and, as the sky gradually lightened, the men worked hard and fast. Andy and Billy managed the sails while Joe shifted ballast.

Devlin took the helm, steering the lugger on a course parallel to the cliffs. This freed Jared to help Ben, Danny and Sam drop the tubs smoothly and quietly over the windward side of the boat away from any watching eyes onshore. Keeping the boat moving, and timing each drop so she was in the trough of a swell, meant that even with a glass trained in their direction, the revenue cutter's captain would be unable to see anything that might indicate suspicious activity.

As the last tubs went overboard, Jared dropped a crab pot with a small cork buoy attached as a marker. Joe dragged the fishing nets from the cuddy and piled them in the bottom of the boat while Andy hoisted buckets of seawater inboard and thoroughly wet the nets. Returning with dry gear after a night supposedly spent chasing a pilchard shoal had caused more than one boat crew to be hauled before the Justice on a charge of smuggling.

A brilliant white-gold sun rose over the horizon and lit rag-edged clouds with flame orange and shadowy purple. The black restless sea turned to wine, then blood, then bronze. As the sun climbed higher, blurred outlines hardened to reveal a coastline of foaming surf, black rocks, wooded valleys, heather and gorse-clad hills, and small fields bounded by stone hedges. Guiding the lugger into Porthinnis's tiny harbour, Devlin glanced back across restless grey water.

'D'you think they picked him up?' Jared kept his voice low.

Devlin shook his head. 'I doubt it. Better they didn't. Bloody young fool. He could never have come back to the village.' He turned to face his crew. 'Any man who wants to leave will be paid up and is free to go. There'll be no hard feelings.' He studied each man in turn. They gazed back unflinching. Not a single glance dropped. Not a man moved.

'You done what you had to, Skipper,' Billy said.

' 'Twas 'im or us,' Sam added, shaking his head.

'Charlie was a fool,' Joe growled. 'Andy warned him about Hammer, but he wouldn't listen.'

'What shall us say, Skip?' Ben asked. 'People is bound to ask.'

Devlin rubbed his jaw. His voice was as bleak as his expression. 'We say it was an accident. We had a rough crossing with a full cargo and everyone was tired. We spotted the cutter and in the scramble to put the boat about, Charlie slipped and went overboard.'

He watched as they exchange nods. 'The truth stays on the boat. Once you're ashore, for your own safety say as little as possible.'

'What about his brother?' Sam growled.

'I'll tell Willie exactly what I've told you.'

'D'you think he'll believe you?' Jared asked.

Devlin's smile was grim. 'That depends on whether he knew Charlie had informed on us.'

'Skip,' Danny pointed.

Realizing he'd been outwitted and further pursuit would be pointless, the cutter's captain had altered course and was heading out of the bay.

*

A watery sun was climbing a sky the colour of pearl when Devlin finally returned to the quay. He was tired to his bones. Willie's first response had been disbelief.

'No, he can't be dead.' He had pushed Devlin aside, peering up and down the street as if expecting his brother to jump out, grinning at the trick he'd played on them. He looked at Devlin again. 'Not Charlie.' It was a plea.

'I'm sorry.' Devlin spoke the truth. Charlie had been popular with the crew, even if his love of practical jokes had occasionally irritated. *Yet he'd betrayed them all for money, had been willing to see them all hanged or transported.* A lifetime's practice of hiding his feelings kept Devlin's face unreadable as he nodded in farewell and turned away. Willie's shock was genuine. No one could feign that waxy pallor or stunned expression.

Whether or not Willie knew what his brother had done, Charlie's death had shaken him to the core. The crew would stick to the accident story. Willie could not challenge it without implicating both his brother and himself.

Devlin sighed, then caught himself. Regret was a waste of time and energy. The past could not be changed. Charlie had reaped what he'd sown.

Devlin left the quay and turned into a cobbled alley alongside the building where he kept the gig and spare gear for both boats. The main entrance was at the front. Inside, wooden stairs led up to the net loft and sail store. At each change of season the nets were dropped through a trapdoor into wheelbarrows then taken along the quay to the barking shed. There they were steeped in a boiling liquid made from shredded oak bark to protect and preserve them.

Half way up the alley Devlin lifted the latch on a tall gate in the high wall. It led into a yard with a lean-to privy in one corner. Climbing a flight of stone steps to the building's third storey, he removed a key hanging on a cord around his neck, unfastened the hasp and padlock and opened the stout door. Once inside he shot the thick oak bar across. He was in no mood for company.

Then, despite exhaustion and the stress of the trip, the corners of his mouth lifted. Neatly arranged on the scrubbed sycamore table were a crusty loaf, a dish of butter and a jar of blackberry jam. The blue and white china jug was covered with a circle of muslin weighted with blue glass beads, which meant it was full of fresh milk. Beside it lay a parcel wrapped in a crisp white cloth. After cleaning up, Inez had left him a pasty for his dinner.

Pulling off his canvas smock he hung it on the back of the door and sank into the bentwood armchair by the hearth. Kindling sticks and furze were piled in the grate ready to be lit. Yawning hugely he tugged off his boots. Packages fell out on to the floorboards, among them the oiled silk. He gathered them all up and, silent in his thick socks, padded across to a battered oak chest, opened the lid and dropped the packages inside.

Ignoring the small keg that had been emptied of brandy several years ago, he lifted out a stone jar. Taking a pewter mug from the crowded shelf he poured a generous measure of cognac and tossed it down.

The spirit burned his throat. But as the heat spread through him he felt knotted muscles loosen and tension began to dissolve. He knew he should eat. But food would have to wait. His head ached and his eyes were sore from salt spray and lack of sleep. Stripping off his thick sweater he stumbled across to the neatly made bed that occupied one corner of the large room. Falling on to it he pulled up a blanket and fell instantly into deep sleep.

Dimly aware of hammering he tried to ignore it, hoping it would stop. But it didn't. Then someone called his name. Cursing as he recognized his brother's voice he forced his eyes open.

'Stop the noise,' he croaked. 'I hear you.' Lifting the bar he opened the door and turned away, padding over to the grate. There he crouched and used flint and steel to light the fire.

Thomas walked in, his caped greatcoat swirling around the ankles of his polished boots. 'At last.'

As the fire caught and crackled, Devlin added more wood. Pushing the brandis – an iron triangle on three legs – over the flames he set a large pot of water on it then stood up, yawning as he raked both hands through unkempt hair. 'What time is it?'

'Almost eleven. When did you get back?'

'Just after dawn.'

Thomas peered out of the small-paned window. 'I hear you had trouble. What happened?'

Devlin watched his brother. 'We were chased by a revenue cutter and I lost a crewman.'

Thomas turned round, gave a brief nod. 'I saw Willie. He's very upset.'

'He would be.'

'What about the cargo? Where—?'

'Overboard.'

Thomas frowned. 'When can you retrieve it?'

'When I'm sure the coast is clear.' Devlin took down the teapot and a tin caddy.

'I need that cargo, Devlin.'

'Then you go and get it.'

'There's no call to—'

'We could have been caught.'

'Yes, well, it's a risky business.'

'For some,' Devlin said drily.

Thomas's lips compressed. 'I must go. I'm extremely busy today.' He hesitated. 'Do you have any letters for me?'

Devlin stretched and scratched himself. 'Who from?'

Thomas sighed. 'Our uncle, of course.'

'No.'

Thomas crossed to the door. With one hand on the latch he scanned the room, his expression disparaging. 'I don't know how you can live like this.'

Devlin glanced from his rumpled bed to the food on the table. Above it a large brass lantern hanging from a hook in the ceiling beam gleamed like gold. Beneath the crowded shelf a long narrow bench held a large bowl and a neatly folded towel, and under that stood two buckets – one with a lid – and a stoneware ewer filled with fresh water.

'I'm perfectly comfortable.'

'I could let you have some pieces from the house.'

'I have all I need.'

'You don't have to stay here.'

'This is my home.'

Thomas snorted. 'You can't possibly—'

'Thomas, where I live, how I live, is none of your business.'

'People talk.'

'Let them.' Devlin shrugged. Then he realized. 'Oh, you mean they talk about *you*. Fame at last, Brother.' Devlin's mockery made Thomas flush.

'The business – Father's name – I have a position to uphold. But
you – this' – he waved a gloved hand – 'look, what I'm trying to say
is that now father has … gone we can put the past behind us. You
could come home.'

*Their father's house had never been home to him, and never would
be.* Devlin eyed his brother thoughtfully. 'What's going on, Thomas?'

'I don't know what you mean.'

'Why this sudden desire for my company? You've hated me since
the day I was born.'

Thomas flapped a hand. 'That's ridiculous. It's all in your mind.'

'Oh yes? And the boys you paid to beat me, did I imagine them
too?'

'I never paid – that's a lie.'

'Everyone lying but you, eh, Thomas?' Devlin's mouth quirked.
'The funny thing is, you did me a favour. Jared took me back to Arf
and Inez, and I found out what a real home was.'

'For God's sake, that was years ago. Anyway, Father offered to
have you back.'

'Only when he realized I could be useful to him.'

'You owed him—'

'I owed him nothing,' Devlin snarled. 'All my skills I learned from
Arf Sweet, and Inez was the mother I never had.'

She was still looking after him, bless her. She'd done so since he
moved in here, keeping the place clean, doing his washing, bringing
a pasty, or a thick warming stew several times a week.

He had begun paying her for his keep when he was thirteen and
Arf gave him his first wage. Understanding his fierce pride she had
accepted the money without protest. Though Arf had no quarrel
with free-trading, and enjoyed the brandy his son brought home, he
preferred to earn his living fishing where he was less of a target for
the press-gang than men of his son's age.

But this had been a hard winter with poor catches and low earn-
ings. While Inez accepted help from her son, she had refused
Devlin's offer of extra money – until he discovered additional jobs he
wanted done. Then honour was satisfied.

Thomas shrugged. 'Well, you can't say I didn't offer.'

'What exactly *are* you offering, Thomas? Any man shaking your
hand would be wise to count his fingers afterwards.'

Thomas swelled with indignation. 'How dare you—'

'Easily,' Devlin cut across the protest. 'I've known you a long time. By the way,' he continued, ignoring his brother's spluttering fury. 'Hedley sent a message.'

'Well? What is it?' Thomas demanded.

'Pay what you owe or find another supplier.'

Thomas seized the latch. 'You bastard.' Rage and embarrassment had turned his face dusky crimson. 'You think you're so clever.' Saliva sprayed from his lips. 'But I'll make you crawl.' The door slammed behind him.

'That will be a cold day in hell,' Devlin murmured.

After a wash, shave, and something to eat, he took the oiled silk packet from the chest, pulled on a clean pair of boots and a short seaman's jacket and set off for Trescowe. The wind had eased and backed round to the west. But though the day felt milder, low cloud threatened more rain to come.

Skirting the harbour, Devlin climbed the hill that led out of the village and took a short cut across two small fields to join the rutted track that led him across a stretch of moor between Porthinnis and the next village along the coast. Outcrops of granite pierced a dense carpet of heather and brown bracken. Patches of gorse were sprinkled with butter-yellow flowers that blossomed all through the year regardless of the weather. *Kissing is out of season when the gorse is out of bloom.*

As the old saying came into Devlin's mind, so did Jenefer Trevanion. Had she ever been kissed? Properly kissed, by a man who knew what he was doing? He doubted it. He only had to look at her and she blushed up. Which meant her careful indifference to him was thin as a fish scale. Yet she had accepted Erisey's proposal. Of course she had. Her father would have been delighted with Erisey's money and background, and Jenefer Trevanion was a dutiful daughter as well as a caring one. Not like Tamara Gillis, who was wild and headstrong and who looked as if she knew a damn sight more about kissing than a girl should.

Devlin shook his head to clear it of a thought that was as dangerous as it was tempting.

Trampled to a muddy mess by countless hoofs, the track was edged with deep water-filled ruts made by the carts that carried fish, tin or copper ore, animal fodder, and farmers going to and from the markets. A little further on Devlin saw two tall granite posts that marked the entrance to the Casvellan estate. The drive was lined with trees, now bare and stark against the lowering sky.

At the top, Devlin rounded a corner and stopped. He had never seen the house and knew nothing about architecture. But he was instantly smitten. Built of pale stone in the form of a square block with two smaller wings, an imposing entrance of squared columns and ornate moulding was flanked on each side by tall windows.

Ignoring the fork that led round to the tradesmen's entrance, Devlin crunched across the gravel to a front door painted dark green. It looked solid enough to withstand a siege.

Reminding himself he was the equal of any man, and that he was dispensing a favour not asking for one, Devlin rang the bell.

The door opened. An elderly man dressed in black looked him up and down then opened his mouth.

Devlin didn't give him the chance to utter the words his expression had already signalled. 'I want to see the Justice. I have a packet for him.'

'You may give it to me.'

Ignoring the extended hand, Devlin shook his head. 'I must put it into his hands.'

'I don't think—'

Stretched thin by the man's supercilious expression, Devlin's patience snapped. 'It's not your job to think. Go and find Mr Casvellan and tell him Devlin Varcoe—'

'Good afternoon, Mr Varcoe. Thank you, Bassett, that will be all.'

As the servant bowed and retreated, Devlin found himself face to face with a man of roughly his own age, height and build. But similarity ended there. Branoc Casvellan's frock coat and buckskin breeches were expertly tailored, his top boots gleamed and a discreet gold pin nestled in the folds of his snowy linen. Recalling his brother's attempts at elegance Devlin bit back a smile.

'Please come though, Mr Varcoe.' Casvellan opened a door. 'We will be private in here.'

Elegantly furnished, the room had blossom pink walls that gave an impression of warmth despite the unlit fire and north-facing windows. 'You wish to speak to me?'

'I have something for you.' Taking the oiled silk packet from inside his jacket Devlin passed it across.

Though Casvellan's expression didn't alter, a fractional widening of the eyes betrayed him.

'You know what it is.' Devlin said, the words a statement not a question as his mind raced. What was going on? How was his uncle involved? If Thomas knew nothing – and Hedley's demand for absolute secrecy indicated he didn't – then it wasn't related to the business.

'Where and when was this given to you? Don't be concerned, Mr Varcoe. I know you didn't steal it.'

'Yesterday, in Roscoff.'

'By whom?'

Devlin hesitated, then realized the pointlessness of it. 'My uncle.'

Casvellan nodded. 'We both know the reason for your trip to Roscoff.'

Devlin nodded. 'I was selling pilchards.'

Surprise softened Casvellan's austere features, and his gaze held a glimmer of amusement. 'Pilchards?'

Devlin shrugged. 'The French are starving yet the markets are closed to Cornish fish because of the war. I was simply—'

'Acting in the interests of humanity. How very good of you.'

Devlin made a brief ironic bow. 'The packet is safe in your hands. How it got there doesn't matter.'

'As you say. I'm grateful to you, Mr Varcoe. Will you excuse me? I must deal with this immediately.'

As he walked away from the house, Devlin reviewed his impression of the Justice. Despite knowing he was a smuggler, Casvellan had treated him courteously and without arrogance. The Justice's views on free trade were no secret. With grinding poverty the only alternative and widespread corruption in the customs service, running contraband seemed almost reasonable. But he had sworn to uphold the law, and in his court any man convicted of smuggling was sentenced accordingly.

Devlin had not expected the Justice to offer him refreshment, and appreciated Casvellan's tact in not sending him to the servants' entrance to ask for a drink. Perhaps, he mused, had their circumstances been different they might even have become friends. Mocked himself for a fool he turned his face to the cold wind.

He had no need of friends. An outsider since birth he had learned that separateness suited him. He was his own man owing nothing to anyone. He was closer to the Sweets than he had ever been to his father and brother. But Jared, Inez and Arf were not his family. He had no family except in name. It was better that way.

A mile from the village ahead of him on the track he saw a limping horse being led by a slender figure. The poppy red coat and black curls streaming from beneath a beaver hat told him it was Tamara Gillis. He didn't know whether to be glad or sorry. It didn't take him long to catch up with her.

'What happened to you?'

She whirled round. 'Devlin!' Her beaming smile was cut short by a wince as she lifted a gloved hand to her grazed cheek. 'What are you doing here? Were you looking for me?'

He shot her a dry look. 'No.'

'So where have you been?'

'None of your business. What happened?'

'Silly animal put her foot in a rabbit hole and I went over her head.'

'You were lucky she didn't break a leg.'

'Thanks for your concern.' She pouted at him. 'What about *my* legs.'

She knew exactly what she was doing for instantly his head conjured images his body itched to explore. He crushed them. 'You're not limping.' He would not tell her she was foolish to ride on the moor alone. If her parents could not curb her wanderlust it was certainly nothing to him where she went or what she did.

'No,' she sighed. 'But tomorrow I'll be black and blue. Still, Roz says that arnica is good for bruises.'

Reluctantly impressed by her refusal to bid for sympathy by simpering or dissolving into tears, he experienced the familiar powerful tug of attraction. And reminded himself once again, *you don't shit where you eat*. When a man married he wanted a woman who was sensible and obedient. Someone he could trust to run his house and raise his children. Someone like Inez. Or Jenefer Trevanion, who had shown such devotion to her sister. Tamara Gillis was a fire in the blood. But she was as untameable as the wind. No man with a grain of sense would marry such a girl.

CHAPTER FIVE

The knocker thudded heavily against the door. Jenefer glanced up from the list of provisions they needed. She knew Maggie was busy in the kitchen but surely Treeve had heard? The tattoo was repeated indicating otherwise. So where was he? *Rarely where he was needed.* Sighing, Jenefer hurried out into the hall. As she opened the front door her breath caught in her throat.

'Oh, it's you.' The words spilled out before she could stop them. He had been so much in her thoughts though she had tried hard to dislodge him, now here he was in person: formidable, unnerving.

'And a good morning to you too, Miss Trevanion.' Lifting one dark brow Devlin made a mocking bow.

Angry with herself, Jenefer tried not to think about her burning face, the hot colour that signalled his effect on her as clearly as if she were waving a flag. 'I beg your pardon. I thought – I wasn't expecting—' She bit her lip then took a deep breath. 'What can I do for you, Mr Varcoe?'

He smiled. 'Now there's an offer.'

Shock punched. She struggled to frame a suitably cutting response, but as she opened her mouth he lifted the big basket. Guessing what it held she felt her stomach tighten.

'Oh no,' she said, before he could speak. 'Please take it away.' As surprise lifted his brows she glanced quickly over her shoulder. Fortunately the hall was empty and all the doors closed. It was mortifying but she would have to explain. Though the way gossip raced around the village he probably knew already. 'My father's health is causing great concern.' She lowered her voice. 'Doctor Avers has advised most strongly that he must not have spirits.'

'Then it's a good job I didn't bring any.' He thrust the basket into her hands, forcing her to take it.

She was surprised at its weight. 'But – oh. Then, what?'

'A cod and two fresh crabs.' He paused. 'Plus a few yards of lace, some silk and a bag of wheat flour.'

Her gaze flew from the basket to his face and back. Some she had asked for, the rest she had not. With so much on her mind she had completely forgotten. Now he would expect payment and she had no money. She kept her gaze lowered and felt pinpricks of perspiration at her temples and along her upper lip. 'Thank you, Mr Varcoe. How much do I owe you?'

'Nothing.'

That brought her head up. 'I don't unders—'

'They are a gift, Miss Trevanion.'

Knowledge of what was proper fought relief and the desire to accept gratefully. Propriety won. As it must. 'That is most kind, but I couldn't possibly—'

'For your sister.' Devlin's tone warned against argument.

'Oh.' He had made it impossible for her to refuse. Horribly self-conscious because she had assumed – hoped – the gift was for her, *what foolishness*, Jenefer's grip on the twisted willow handle tightened and she forced a smile. 'How very generous. I know Betsy will appreciate the thought, and your kindness. As I do.' Nerves had dried her mouth. She moistened her lips with the tip of her tongue, saw his gaze flick to her mouth, and cleared her throat as heat surged beneath her skin. 'Mr Varcoe, about your brother.'

A shadow darkened Devlin Varcoe's gaze. 'What about him?'

'Is he in good health?'

'As far as I know.'

'It's just . . . we expected him to call last week, after his return from Truro. But we haven't seen him and Father is growing very agitated. As I said he isn't well and anxiety makes him . . . difficult. When next you see your brother would you ask him to visit as soon as may be convenient?'

As Devlin's features hardened Jenefer wondered if she should not have mentioned it.

'I will indeed.'

Had she offended him by asking him to carry a message? She knew – as everyone did – that the Varcoe brothers weren't close. But she could not call on Thomas herself. And the matter was urgent. She swallowed. 'I'm afraid there's something else.'

'Yes?' Still polite he was no longer smiling.

'Lieutenant Crocker has been spending a great deal of time in this area recently, far more so than usual. Betsy has observed him almost every day on the cliffs between here and the far side of the village.' Jenefer's grip on the handle whitened her knuckles. Aware of the basket's contents she had no wish to offend him and chose her words with care. 'Mr Varcoe, if there is any contraband hidden on our property I would appreciate it being removed as soon as possible.'

Her heart thumped uncomfortably against her ribs. She could feel the fire in her cheeks despite the fact that she had no reason to blush for what she was asking. *It wasn't the request; it was his nearness, and the ice in his eyes.* 'If the lieutenant or his dragoons were to find – my father would be held responsible.'

'Whatever Crocker finds – should he find anything – was not put there by me or my men.' Devlin was curt. 'You have my word on that.'

He was a smuggler. He lived outside the law. He had just given her French lace and silk for Betsy. Yet she believed him. *Was she mad?* Hysterical laughter bubbled in Jenefer's throat but she forced it down. He was watching her, his brows forming a black bar across his forehead.

'Are you all right?'

No, she wasn't, and wondered if she ever would be again. She could not answer for she would not lie. Making an effort she forced a smile. 'Good day, Mr Varcoe.' She lifted the basket. 'Thank you again. You won't forget to tell your brother?'

'You can be sure of it, Miss Trevanion.' His tone sent a shiver down her spine.

Sprawled in his father's armchair beside the blazing fire, Thomas drained his glass and levered himself upright to reach for the decanter. His hand trembled and fine cognac splashed on to the polished surface of the small table. *Bloody Devlin, telling him what to do. It was none of his damn business. Who did he think he was?* The scene played over and over in his head. He tried to convince himself he had handled it well. But all he kept seeing was Devlin's face, bleak as granite, *ordering* him to Trevanion's house.

The door opened and his housekeeper appeared.

'What?' he snarled. 'Go away.'

She ignored him. 'Someone to see you. Says it's important.'

'I'm not in the mood.' When she still didn't move, Thomas blinked at her. 'Well? Who is it?'

'Willie Grose.' She sniffed, letting him know her opinion of the company he kept.

'That's enough from you.' He glared at her. 'This is my house now

51

and I'll entertain whoever I like. Anyway it's business. Go on.' He waved her away. 'Do what you're paid for and fetch him in.'

'Paid is it?' She sniffed again. 'When am I going to see some money then?'

'I haven't got time for you now. I'm busy.'

'Is that what you call it?' she muttered under her breath as she waddled out.

A few moments later Willie sidled round the door and flinched when it slammed behind him.

'What's up wi' she?' When Thomas didn't answer, Willie stood where he was and rubbed his hands uncertain what to do next. 'Gone cold again,' he remarked.

'Have they found him?' Thomas asked suddenly.

Willie's shoulders drooped and he shook his head. 'Nah. Could be days, could be weeks. Depends on the currents.'

Thomas grunted. 'So what do you want?'

Willie brightened. 'A drop o' the old cousin jack would go down a treat. Bleddy freezing out there 'tis.'

'No, you fool. What are you doing here? Why have you come?'

'Thought you'd want to hear the news, didn't I?'

'What news?'

'About Harry Carlyon.'

Thomas swivelled round to stare at him. 'What about him?'

Willie gestured at the decanter. 'Go on, jest a drop. 'Tis bitter out.'

'There's a glass in the cabinet. Mind you don't drop it. What about Harry?'

Pouring a generous measure Willie took a gulp. 'Oh yes,' he smacked his lips. 'Bit of all right, that is. He been wrecked.'

Thomas jerked upright, spilling brandy on to his breeches and filling the air with sharp fumes. 'Wrecked? I don't believe it. Not Harry Carlyon. You've got it wrong.' He refused to believe it. Sobered by shock he could feel the liquor churning uneasily in his stomach.

Willie nodded emphatically. ' 'Tis true as I'm stood 'ere. Riding Officer was waiting for 'n, dragoons and all, up off Coverack. Word is that Harry guessed something wasn't right. Either there wasn't no signal, or someone gived 'n the wrong one. But he couldn't stand out to sea again.'

'Why not, for God's sake?'

'Another storm blowing up wasn't there? So he tried to sail in under the cliffs where they couldn't see 'n. Might have been all right if he'd still had his old lugger. But that new cutter of his got a deep keel. I reck'n in the panic he forgot what he was sailing. Struck the rocks and ripped the bottom out of her. Went down with all hands she did, and most of the cargo. Some of it was saved. But Customs got it locked away.'

Thomas was afraid he might vomit. Such detail meant there could be no doubt, and no hope of mistaken identity.

'Here.' Willie's face puckered. 'All right, are you? Gone white as a sheet you 'ave.'

Thomas barely heard him. Far from making his fortune he'd just lost every penny of his investment. The cargo Devlin had brought back last week was still underwater. God alone knew when it would be raised. Even when it was distributed it would not make anything like the sum he needed to pay Hedley. Colonel Trevanion was expecting his money and if he didn't get it he would demand the emerald's return. Thomas had neither cash nor jewel. What was he to do? Terror engulfed him. *Think.*

Trembling violently he tossed back the cognac, shuddered, and dragged the back of his hand across his mouth. He poured more, the lip of the decanter rattling against the glass as he fought the dread that turned his guts liquid. He needed time and he needed money. But first he needed to know for certain if Trevanion had been telling the truth. Was the emerald really the last of the gemstones? Or had that just been an excuse? What if the colonel was simply backing out of their arrangement like the other two venturers had? Even worse, what if he'd decided to invest with the Carters or the Rinsey boys instead?

Thomas cleared his throat. It took huge effort to hold his voice steady.

'Make yourself useful and find me two men. But I don't want anyone local.'

'No need to bring in outsiders. If you want a bit o' help I don't mind doing whatever 'tis.'

Thomas shook his head. 'No. You're known in the village. Besides, it could be dangerous. If only Charlie—' He shook his head.

'Always up for a dare, Charlie was,' Willie murmured, then lifted his head. His face was haggard with grief. 'And where's he to now?' he demanded. 'Feeding the bleddy crabs.' He drained his glass. 'Say I find someone, what's in it for me?'

53

'Same as for them, brandy and tobacco. Keep it or trade it, your choice.'

'Fair enough.' Willie nodded. 'Trouble, is it? I'll get 'e a couple o' tinners then. Good in a fight they are. What do 'e want 'em for?'

'Don't ask. If you don't know you can't tell.' Thomas swallowed the remainder of his brandy welcoming the burst of heat along his veins. Panic was replaced by growing excitement. He'd show them. He'd show all of them. He had a plan. By this time next week all his problems could be over and done with, out of his life for good. And that included his hated brother.

Jared pushed aside his empty plate and leaned back patting his stomach. ''Andsome, that was, Mother.'

'Nothing like fresh pilchards.' Inez rose from her chair. 'Want any more do 'e, Arf? Devlin?'

Both men shook their heads. Her husband pushed his chair round and reached for his pipe. 'Full as a tick, I am. Couldn't eat another bite.'

Devlin smiled at her. 'You're a fine cook, Inez. Will you marry me when I grow up?' It was a long-standing joke.

'Here, don't you go giving her ideas,' Arf growled, blowing a cloud of fragrant smoke. 'Took me years to get her trained.' He winked at his wife who tossed her head and hid a smile.

Tired and replete, Devlin stretched. Three days ago Becky Couch, who lived above one of the cellars, had heard the stones moving. These were round granite boulders used as weights to press oil and brine from the casks of salted pilchards. They each weighed roughly a hundredweight and were fitted with an iron hook to lift them into the casks.

No one had ever actually seen them roll about on the cellar floors, but tradition held that to hear them, especially in the evening, was a good omen. It was a month since the last good catch so word of Becky's *visitation* had rushed through the streets and alleys like a gale. That night hope made sleep fitful and restless for almost everyone in the village.

Shortly after dawn the following morning came the cry they had all been waiting for. Sighting a shoal, the boy posted as lookout in the small hut at the highest point on the cliff bellowed, 'Heva! Heva!' at the top of his lungs.

Within the hour every fishing boat was on the water. They worked for three days and nights. Arf's crew, Devlin's men and two more boats handled the seine. Other boats used hand lines to haul in scores of hake that ran with the pilchards to prey on them.

That evening when the first of the catch was brought ashore every woman and child in the village hurried to the cellars. There they piled the fish, layered with salt, in square heaps on the stone floor. It was hard exhausting labour. But no one complained for it brought in much-needed money. For ten days the heaped fish would be left untouched while the blood and brine drained out.

Devlin wasn't surprised when Jared rose to his feet and announced, 'I'm going up-long.'

'To see Miss Betsy I suppose.' Inez shook out a towel and folded it.

'Give 'e some shock if I said no,' Jared teased.

'Dear life, you're up there every week doing something.'

'One of the wheels on her chair is catching. I said I'd free it up.'

'Devlin,' Inez demanded, 'tell 'n he's wasting his time.'

Devlin raised his hands, palm out. He had no intention of intervening. Nor did Jared give him the chance.

' 'Tidn nothing to do with Devlin, Mother. And you can't call it wasting time to help someone who've lost so much.'

Inez put both hands on her hips. 'I didn't mean it like that.'

'Would you be worried about me seeing her if she wasn't the colonel's daughter?'

'I would,' Inez said at once. 'Though to my mind he idn much of a father to either of they girls, not the way he's drinking. No, Son, listen' – she raised a hand to stop him interrupting – 'nothing against Betsy. A sweet girl she is, and some brave. But fact is, and tis no use pretending different, she *is* the colonel's daughter. There isn't no way he'd give his blessing to any match. And even if she wasn't who she is – hark to me, my son, you're a young man. What kind of wife could she be to you, her being like she is, off her legs and all?'

'Mother!' Jared blushed scarlet.

After glancing from one to the other, Arf studied his pipe and said nothing. Devlin guessed he shared his wife's concerns.

Inez's cheeks grew pink. 'Dear life, boy. 'Tis all part o' nature. How d'you think you got 'ere? Look, even if 'tis possible for her to have children, how would she ever manage looking after them?'

Jared's embarrassment dissolved in a grin. 'Mother, if Betsy and me was blessed with a chield we'd have to bar the door to keep you out. Father would be wailing you're never 'ome. And getting the babby off you would be harder than chipping limpets off a rock.'

Arf gave a bark of laughter. 'He got you right, Mother.'

Tossing her head at her husband, Inez swatted her son with the towel. 'I just don't want to see you hurt.'

Jared laid a brawny arm across her shoulders. 'No more do I. But I love her, Ma. I want to wed her. If children come along, fine. If they don't,' he shrugged. 'Well, 't will be a pity for you. But I don't want no one else.'

'Where's Andy?' Devlin reached for his sou'wester. The rest of the crew stood in the cellar doorway, rain dripping from their oilskins to pool around their booted feet.

Ben peered out into the downpour. 'Coming now, he is. Dear life, I 'aven't seen he move so fast in years. What's on, boy?' he demanded as Andy splashed to a halt.

'Fire over to Mousehole,' he gasped. 'Only set the Custom House alight, they 'ave.'

'Who?' Sam demanded.

'The Rinsey boys.'

'Never!' Joe grinned.

'True as I'm stood 'ere. I was over to my sister Bessie's when the boy come for Tom. Told 'n he must report to the Riding Officer right away. Customs Officer at Mousehole do need reinforcements. I hung about till I seen 'em leaving, jest to make sure. Going like long dogs they were and none too happy about it. Can't blame 'em. 'Tis some long ride to Mousehole 'specially in this weather.'

Devlin clapped Andy on the shoulder. 'No fishing today, boys. We've got a cargo to raise.'

Devlin signalled to Jared and they threw the grapnels over the side. Immediately Andy, Ben, Danny and Sam bent to their oars, pulling the galley through the low swell. Driving rain stung their faces, pelted their oilskins and sou'westers, slid down their necks, seeped up their sleeves and trickled into their boots to soak their trousers and feet. But in spite of the chilly discomfort Devlin welcomed it. The liquid curtain veiled them from other boats and would keep most people indoors. Should anyone be on the cliffs or shore, the rain, low cloud and poor light would make it impossible for them to see what was going on.

Feeling the hook snag, Devlin signalled Billy who leaned over, grabbed the rope and began hauling it in. Silence was the rule when retrieving a cargo. Sound travelled further over water than on land. A word, a laugh, even a grunt of effort could so easily betray them. The Riding Officer and his dragoons might be miles away but still no one spoke.

A few moments later the grapnel broke surface with the rope linking the kegs caught over one of its hooks. Jared began hauling the kegs inboard. As Andy freed each one it was passed up the galley to be stowed in the bow. Finally the sinking stone was cut loose and the rope quickly coiled to be burned later. French rope had a different twist from English and its discovery would betray them.

When twenty kegs had been retrieved and the weight pressed the galley low in the water, Devlin pointed to the shore. Waiting at the top of the cove, dressed in boy's clothes, her hair tucked into a cap pulled low over her face, Roz Trevaskis held the halter of the lead mare. The rest of the pack animals were mules borrowed from outlying farms. To make it impossible for any revenue officer to grab hold of them, their manes and tails had been clipped and their coats greased. Roping them was unnecessary. They would follow the mare.

The landsmen – farm labourers who would be paid as much for three hours' work as they could earn in a week – quickly lifted the kegs from the galley. The crew turned in their seats, the galley was pushed off, and soon Devlin had the grapnel overboard once more.

Three hours later the heavily laden string plodded out of the cove and along the muddy path into the wooded valley.

'Fetch the nets, shall I, skip?' Billy indicated the opening near the top of the cove.

'No. Crocker isn't around so they can stay where they are.' Pulled by drenched and weary men the galley headed for the harbour. The wind was picking up again. Pushing against the tide it heaped the sea into waves topped with curls of foam.

'Not another bleddy gale,' Danny groaned.

'I never known a winter like it,' Sam grunted, straining at his oar.

' 'Tisn't just the wind,' Andy said. 'All this here rain is drowning the soil. The next blow will bring more trees down. Ground's so wet the roots won't hold.'

'I'm more worried about me roof.' Joe blinked water out of his eyes.

With the galley safely in her cradle and his crew bound for home, dry clothes and a much-needed hot meal, Devlin climbed the stone stairs to his own front door. The room was as he'd left it: bed unmade, his breakfast dishes on the table and last night's ashes in the grate. Once inside he shed the dripping oilskins, hauled off his sodden boots and socks. Leaving a trail of wet footprints he padded across to the table to light the candle and the two lanterns.

Crouching to pile kindling and dry furze on to the dead ashes he imagined opening the door and seeing a roaring fire, inhaling the savoury aroma of a hearty beef stew, and being greeted with a smile by a slender young woman with barley-gold hair. Snorting in self-mockery he shook his head. Jenefer Trevanion rarely smiled and never at him. All he got from her were blushes and a refusal to meet his eye. *What else could he expect from someone of her background and upbringing?*

As he added more wood to the hungry flames Devlin wearily rubbed the back of his neck. Jenefer Trevanion was engaged to be married. *To a man who appeared to have abandoned her.* She was out of his class. *That certainly hadn't deterred Jared.* He was successful, his own man, owing nothing to anyone. *He was a smuggler, an outlaw.* Everything he had he had earned himself. *This? You would bring her here?* He glanced around. Maybe not here. But the cottage – *was still unfinished.*

The wood caught and blazed. Devlin threw the poker down, poured himself a generous measure of brandy and swallowed it in three gulps. As welcome warmth spread along his chilled limbs he stripped off the rest of his wet clothes. Kicking them into a heap he stepped into dry trousers and began towelling his dripping hair.

A sharp rapping on the door brought his head up. 'Who is it?' There was no reply, just another quick tattoo. Lifting a soft woollen shirt from the chest he pulled it over his head, raking his hair back as he opened the door.

Beneath the black umbrella he saw a poppy red coat, the bottom six inches soaking wet and splattered with mud. 'What in the name of—?'

The umbrella tilted back. 'You might at least ask me in,' Tamara snapped, through chattering teeth.

CHAPTER SIX

He stayed where he was, holding the door and trying to ignore the quick clench in his gut. His attraction to her was wrong for both of them. He had plans for his future and they didn't include her. He frowned.

'Are you mad, coming here like this? What do you think you're doing?'

She swallowed. She had expected him to be surprised even irritated. But surely he realized she would never have called on him at home unaccompanied, not without a very good reason. 'Getting wetter and colder, and wondering why I bothered.'

'Tamara, if this is your idea of a game—'

'I don't play games, Devlin. Not with you.'

His expression signalled disbelief. 'Oh no?'

She tossed her head impatiently. 'Of course I tease you. How else am I to get your attention? But I'm here now because of something I heard. Something you should know about. It's important.'

'It could have waited until morning.' Damn the girl. What was he supposed to do? Shut the door in her face? Jenefer Trevanion wouldn't dream of pulling a trick like this. She was a lady. While Tamara – how in the name of sweet Jesus did you describe Tamara? Able to mimic decorum when it suited her, her behaviour the rest of the time was determinedly unconventional. Yet for all that there was nothing common or vulgar about her. He almost wished there were. For then she would be easy to ignore, forget. Instead she had worked her way under his skin like a barb. Nuisance, irritant, impossible to dislodge she was . . . herself, unique. *And should not be here.*

'Oh yes?' Scorn lifted her brows. 'I should call on you in broad daylight with all your neighbours watching? They'd enjoy that. Besides, how often are you at home in the daytime? If you're not on a run you're out fishing.' She shivered. 'Look, are you going to invite me in, or shall I just stand here and tell you? Of course it will be all round the village by tomorrow. But if you don't mind everyone knowing your private business . . .'

'God's blood, girl.' He wrenched the door wide. 'It's you they'll be gossiping about.'

She shrugged, tilting her chin defiantly. 'They've been doing that all my life.'

Ignoring the shadows in her eyes, telling himself they were caused by the wavering candle flame, he sucked in a ragged breath and clenched his teeth in frustration. Nobody had ever wrong-footed him the way she could – and did.

'If your parents had known what they were getting' – he stepped back, indicating with a jerk of his head that she should enter – 'they'd have drowned you at birth.'

'Just think what you'd have missed.' She sailed past him, her shoes squelching as she snapped the umbrella closed and leaned it against the wall. Instantly a puddle formed on the wooden boards.

Closing the door he raked a hand through tousled curls still damp from his own soaking. 'Do they know you're here?'

'Who?'

He shot her a warning glare. 'Your parents.'

Her brief wry glance gave him the answer. She fumbled the buttons on her coat, her fingers stiff and clumsy. 'They'd only worry. Besides, this has nothing to do with them.'

'It's late.'

'For heaven's sake, it's not even six o'clock yet.'

'But it's dark. Tamara, you shouldn't—'

'Do stop fussing, Devlin. I'm not a child.'

His gaze flicked from her heavy-lidded green eyes to her full mouth and down to the curves beneath her close fitting coat. He bit back an oath. She was young, not yet twenty. But she was right. That teasing gaze, husky voice and deliciously rounded body were certainly not those of a child.

She had come here of her own free will and more or less black-mailed her way inside. Trying to protect her reputation – such as it was – had won him no thanks. Indeed he had been ordered to *stop fussing*. So be it. She could go to the devil. Was probably well on her way already. Why should he worry? She was nothing to him. *Oh no? His inner self mocked with bitter amusement.* She fired his blood that was all. *No, that wasn't all.* She was wild and unpredictable and he had trouble enough in his life.

He'd been enjoying women since he was fourteen. He'd learned how to give pleasure as well as take it: a valuable lesson that made conquest easy and left smiles and sighs when he moved on. But none had touched his heart. *Nor would she.*

Finally managing to unfasten her coat she pulled it off and dropped it across the table. Her hair hung about her shoulders, sodden tresses dripping water down the creamy swell of her breasts and soaking the lace that edged her bodice. She raised one arm to lift the dark curls off her neck and in the lamplight raindrops glistened on her face like diamonds.

As she looked up he turned away, his teeth clamped so tightly that his jaw ached. Deliberately increasing the distance between them he crossed to the hearth and dropped another log on to the bright flames.

'You might at least offer me a towel.' She forced the words through cold-numbed lips.

Anger roared through him: at her for coming here, at himself for being unable to retain his habitual detachment. *She had invaded his home and when she had gone he would still see her here, still smell her delicate floral scent with its hint of lemon. So many of the women he went with smelled of fish.* Snatching up the towel he had used he tossed it at her. She flinched as she caught it then swayed.

Devlin cursed under his breath. Her cheeks were pale as candlewax. 'Here.' Grabbing her upper arm he pulled her forward. 'Sit down before you fall down.'

'I'm perfectly all right.' But the words lacked her usual bite and she sank without protest into the wooden armchair. She just needed a moment and she'd be fine. Coming here had seemed the logical thing to do. She had a genuine reason. And an opportunity to see him alone if only for a few minutes was not to be turned down. Yet though she would cut off her tongue sooner than admit it, stepping over the threshold had taken far more nerve than she expected.

With his back to her he poured a small measure of cognac into a pewter mug then pushed it into her hand. 'Drink this.'

She peered into the mug then up at him. 'What is it?'

'Poison, what else? Surely your mother has warned you about men and their wicked ways?' Hearing the sarcasm in his tone he took a deliberate breath. 'It's cognac. Think of it as medicine. It will stop the shivers.'

Raising the mug she swallowed a mouthful, coughed, and pulled a face. 'Ugh. It's like drinking fire.' She thrust the mug at him.

Devlin found her violent shudder oddly reassuring. He had expected her to be accustomed to spirits. Most of the villagers used them as a cure-all. Brandy was rubbed on the gums of teething babies, added to bedtime milk to make children sleep, swallowed to ease hunger pangs, relieve the grief of bereavement or blot out the wretchedness of poverty.

'But it does the job. Are you feeling better?'

'I'm perfectly well, thank you,' Tamara lied. She tipped her head sideways and began to rub her hair with the towel, drawing on every ounce of willpower she possessed to force back the horrible dizziness. She was wet and chilled despite having run nearly all the way. Her heart was racing and though warmth from the brandy was creeping through her limbs, her head still felt light and strange. She needed a moment, just a moment, then she'd be fine.

Devlin watched her, relieved to see colour gradually returning to her cheeks. He knew all the little tricks that women employed to attract men or convey interest. He'd been a target more times than he could count. But there was nothing of the flirt in her action. In fact she seemed so absorbed in her own thoughts he might not have been there. What was she doing? What game was this? *I don't play games with you, Devlin.* Exasperation flared – directed at himself as much as at her. Like hell she didn't. He tried to look away but found himself transfixed by the gleam of her skin in the fire's glow: soft curves and secret hollows, highlights and shadows. A log settled and flames rose. The soft sound broke the spell and increased his anger.

'Well?' His tone was brutal.

She looked up with a start. Her eyes were wide green pools, deep and mysterious. *Eyes a man could drown in.* 'This important information?' Even to his own ears he sounded unnecessarily grim. *It was safer that way.* 'Are you going to tell me, or am I supposed to guess?'

Dropping her hands to her lap she arched her spine. 'You couldn't, I don't care how long you tried.' She fiddled with the towel. 'I went to see Roz to get some salve for my horse's leg. She'd made a new batch after one of Davy Casvellan's horses scraped its knees out hunting.' Her expression brightened. 'Apparently his brother is so pleased with the results of Roz's salves and lotions he won't allow anyone else to treat their horses now.'

Branoc Casvellan and barmaid Roz Trevaskis? That was an unlikely alliance. 'Is there a point to all this, Tamara?'

Her smile became a glare. 'I'm just coming to it. I could see Roz was worried.'

'With a mother and brother like hers—'

'No,' she cut him short. 'She's used to that. This was different. To be honest, I don't understand why it bothered her so much. But sometimes Roz prefers to keep things to herself. I understand that.'

So did he. If Tamara's parents knew half of what she got up to he'd be very surprised. An image flashed across his mind of Roz disguised in her brother's clothes, leading the heavily loaded pack animals into the rain-drenched darkness. 'Yet she told you what was worrying her?'

Tamara nodded. 'We're friends.'

'What do your parents think about that?' Before she could respond he shook his head. 'They don't know, do they?'

Tamara shrugged. 'What purpose would be served by me telling my mother something that would upset her? She would order me to stop seeing Roz. I would refuse. We'd have a row.' She shrugged again, the subject dismissed. 'The point is, a couple of nights ago Davy Casvellan was in the Five Mackerel. He was with a group of friends and they'd all had a lot to drink. As usual Davy was the last to leave. He was so unsteady that Roz had to help him on to his horse. That's when he told her that he was planning to make a run to Guernsey.' Rubbing the ends of her hair between towel-draped hands she scooped the long tresses over her shoulder so they tumbled down her back.

Devlin leaned one elbow on the mantelpiece above the fireplace. 'So? Some young men have too much to drink and decide to play night-crow. Why would that interest me?'

Tamara tossed the towel on to the table. 'Branoc Casvellan is a Justice.'

'What of it? I know of at least four Justices who take an active part in the trade.'

'Not Mr Casvellan. He'd be furious if he found out his brother was involved. They're probably only doing it for excitement, or as a prank, but if they're caught it will certainly embarrass their families.'

Devlin's dark brows climbed. 'If Roz is a regular visitor to Casvellan's stables why didn't she tell him?'

'I don't know. Perhaps she has.'

'Then why are you telling me?'

Tamara smoothed her dress over her lap. 'If you were to tell Mr Casvellan you'd heard a whisper, he'd be in your debt. Which would certainly do you no harm. My point is that if Davy has bragged to Roz then more than likely other people know as well. Which means Lt Crocker is sure to hear about it. You won't want a party of dragoons lurking around on the cliffs night after night, will you?'

Thinking through the implications, the potential inconvenience, he shook his head. Indeed he did not. Her delighted smile hit him with the force of a punch to the gut. For an instant he couldn't breathe. *Get her out, now, before—*

'Well? Are you glad I came?'

Moving away from the fire he picked up her coat and held it open. 'Yes. Thank you. Now you must go home before you are missed.'

She shot to her feet unable to hide her anger and disappointment. 'That's it? That's all you have to say?'

'I said I'm grateful.' He shook the coat impatiently.

'No you didn't.'

'What am I supposed to do?' he snarled. 'Fall at your feet?'

Confused, she gazed at him. 'Why are you so angry?'

'For God's sake, Tamara. Just go, will you.'

'Why?' Ignoring her coat she folded her arms. She knew it looked belligerent but she couldn't help that. The pressure helped ease the grinding tension in her stomach. 'Why must I go?'

'Don't ask stupid questions. If anyone saw you come in—'

'But they didn't. Listen.' She turned her head towards the window. Rain spattered against the glass like hurled gravel while below waves thundered and crashed against the quay. 'No one will be out in this. It's bucketing down. Let me stay a little while longer. Just until it eases off.' Nerves fluttered beneath her ribs. It was like standing on the edge of a cliff unable to see the bottom. If her plea had surprised him it had certainly startled her. She hadn't known she was going to ask until she heard herself uttering the words. But destiny had brought her here. If Davy hadn't boasted to Roz, and Roz hadn't confided her anxiety, she wouldn't have come. She'd have had no reason, no excuse. But she was here, alone with Devlin, the only man she had ever wanted.

He swore softly, viciously.

'Please don't.'

Frustration drove one hand through his hair then he rubbed the

never revealing his deepest feelings. Those were the basic rules of survival. Ignoring them might reveal a weakness, an advantage others could and surely would exploit. Ignoring them was foolish and dangerous.

Needing to touch, Tamara slid her hands up beneath the loose shirt. His skin was damp, burning, slick and smooth, and the hard muscles bunched and quivered beneath her fingers. Caught like a leaf in the storm he had unleashed within her she clung to him as her legs trembled and her bones melted.

Control snapped and he plunged. His fingers curled in her hair, pulling her head back as he crushed her against him. His lips locked on hers, not gentle now but hard and hot and demanding.

His hungry mouth stifled her gasp as he pulled her down on to the tumbled bed, his fingers at her bodice. She felt cool air on her skin, then his lips, his tongue. His hand skimmed over her body as if learning every curve and hollow and her flesh leapt to his touch. She quivered, instinctively arching towards him in passionate yearning.

Beyond thought or reason, conscious only of need, she pushed his shirt open and pressed her mouth to his throat, his shoulder. She licked, tasting heat and salt, held him close, wanted him closer. She felt his hand on her thigh, and her body rose to his. 'Oh yes, oh please.'

His grip tightened and a tremor rippled through him as his mouth ravished hers. He lifted her, his breath hot and quick against her face. She gasped at the sharp pain.

He froze, shock tearing a harsh sound from his throat. But she pressed against him, seeking his mouth and he lost himself in the taste and scent of her, the velvet softness.

He began to move, a slow rhythm that turned warmth to heat, that swept her up and carried her with him and she knew she would die if he stopped. Inside her something spiralled, lifting her ever higher. Her breath caught in tiny gasps as the coil tightened. A strange tingling began in her toes and blossomed into a silent explosion that broke and wrecked her. As she cried out his arms tightened and she clung to him while his body bucked and shuddered.

She gloried in his weight, the sensation of his skin against hers, his ragged breath warm on her neck. This then was the joining of man and woman? This was what the marriage service meant? She had dreamed of him. He was always in her thoughts when she walked the cliffs and rode over the moors. But this was beyond anything she had imagined. Now she was his, body and soul.

But suddenly, abruptly, he rolled away. Bereft, she smothered a cry and reached out, seeking reassurance, an anchor while the storm quieted and she came back to herself.

Lithe as a cat he rose to his feet and, with his back to her, cursed with intense and bitter fluency as he buttoned his trousers. He hadn't known. How could he have known? Any girl as bold as she was, who teased and flirted like she did, knew what she was doing, knew what she wanted. So he had obliged.

But he had been wrong about her, totally wrong. She had come here a virgin, untouched. Shy yet ardent, naïve yet passionately responsive, she had given as he took, taking when he gave. She had reached him in ways he had not expected and did not know how to deal with.

It was impossible to undo what had been done, to return to 'before'. Impossible because this had been different. He had lost himself in her. That frightened him far more than any revenue cutter. Never again. He did not want – could not afford – distractions. A woman should know her place and stay there. Tamara Gillis obeyed no rules but her own. He wanted her gone. Out of his home and out of his thoughts.

Sensing something wrong, Tamara sat upright and drew her skirts down. Her throat was parched and her mouth felt swollen. There other aches too but they were her secret pride, her proof of womanhood.

He swung round, one brow arched. ' "I don't play games with you," ' he mimicked then his mouth curled. 'You tricked me.'

Shock blanked her face. 'What?'

He might as well have slapped her. He'd known she was intelligent and saw the instant she realized what he meant. What he hadn't expected, and what deepened his guilt and his anger, was the terrible hurt that widened her eyes.

'You thought – you believed that I – with someone else?' Her expression reflected her horror and disbelief. 'How could you even think that I would *ever*—?' Her mouth quivered and she bit hard on her lower lip as she fought for control. Her breath caught as she lifted her chin. 'Well, now you know differently.'

'Why?' It burst out against his will. It didn't matter why. He gestured abruptly, dismissing the question. He didn't want to know.

She sighed, bewildered and impatient. Why ask a question to which he already knew the answer? Why else would she have come? Why else would she have stayed?

'You know why. I love you.'

Stunned, he stared at her. Love? He'd never known it, didn't trust it. He shook his head. 'No, you don't. You might think you do. But it's just' – he waved an arm in frustration – 'girl dreams. You don't know me. No one knows me.' He jammed his fists into his pockets, wanting to kick something, or pound someone to a pulp. She didn't know what she was saying. How could she love *him*?

Scrambling to her feet Tamara buttoned her bodice with violently trembling fingers. *What had she done?* She had been so sure he would understand. How could she have been so wrong?

Tidying herself as best she could she reached for her coat. 'Don't presume to tell me what I feel, Devlin. If you don't want me that's your loss.' She paused to swallow the agonizing lump in her throat. She had made a terrible mistake. She felt sick and shaky and needed to get home. But she would pull out her own fingernails sooner than let him know how deeply his words had cut. Pride was a flimsy veil but it was all she had.

He looked away, keeping his distance as she struggled into her sodden coat. Loathing himself and furious with her he wished she would hurry up and go.

Shock and the cold weight of her coat made her teeth chatter. But she steadied her voice by sheer force of will. 'You're right. I don't know you. I thought I did. I believed you were different. I was sure you understood things that other men can't, or won't. But I was wrong. You're blind. And you're a coward.'

The scorn in her voice stung like a whiplash. His head jerked up. 'That's ridiculous,' he snapped. 'I face death every time I go to sea.'

She fastened her coat and picked up her umbrella. 'Yes, perhaps you do. But so does your crew. So do the miners who work underground. So does every woman who bears a child. People face death every day. But to embrace life, to share your heart and soul as well as your body' – she opened the door to the relentless rain – 'that takes courage.' She stepped out into darkness. 'And you don't have enough.'

CHAPTER SEVEN

Jenefer woke with a start. There was a time, before the accident, when she had slept deeply, rarely waking until morning. But now, always aware that Betsy might need her, she could never relax completely and her sleep was light and fitful.

She lay in the darkness listening to the wind outside and the waves crashing on the rocks as she waited for a repeat of whatever had disturbed her sleep. A few months ago she would have jumped out of bed immediately. But it had been warmer then, and the nights lighter. Nor had she been so desperately tired.

Was that a door creaking? *Please don't let it be her father up again*. After settling her sister for the night Jenefer had emerged from Betsy's room and heard muffled voices in the hall below. Looking over the banister she had seen Treeve, who was certainly not sober, with a supporting arm around her father who was so drunk he could barely walk.

She had known better than to offer help. She would get no thanks. Her father was more likely to curse her interference then accuse her of spying on him. Walking quietly along the landing to her own room she had closed her door and, leaning her back against it, listened to their erratic progress up the stairs.

A thud followed by a series of smaller ones told her one of them had dropped something, probably a bottle or maybe a decanter. It bounced to the bottom but didn't smash. She would make Treeve mop up the spillage in the morning. Maggie already had more than enough to do and Treeve was responsible for her father's condition. Yet as Treeve said when she tackled him about it, if master ordered him to fetch brandy and threatened dismissal for him and Maggie if he refused, what was he supposed to do?

Voices, one slurred and querulous, the other trying to placate and being shouted at, had indicated their advance along the landing to the master bedroom on the far side of the stairwell. Eventually the door slammed. It would have taken Treeve an hour to undress her father and get him into bed. Though she had searched, all the while fighting guilt at intruding, she had not been able to find any brandy in his room. But that meant nothing. If it were there it would be hidden.

Preparing for bed, Jenefer had dabbed her wrists with lavender water and closed her eyes while inhaling the fragrance. She recalled her mother claiming it soothed the nerves. But she doubted her mother's nerves had ever been scraped and battered like this.

Eventually all her anxieties had blurred into a multi-stranded tangle as exhaustion sucked her down.

Now, hardly breathing, straining to hear, she wished she knew what time it was. A muffled crash made her gasp and she sat up, her heart pounding. Throwing back the covers, shivering in the chilly air, she reached for the flower-patterned bedgown lying across the bottom of the coverlet and pulled it on over her nightdress, her fingers unsteady as she knotted the sash.

In the faint glow from the embers of her bedroom fire she fumbled for the saucer-shaped brass holder on her bedside table and lit the candle with a taper.

As she opened her door she heard Maggie scream. Then a male voice growled an order. It wasn't Treeve's voice. *Someone had broken in.* Who? Why? What did they want?

Fear and indecision paralysed her. Should she go downstairs? Or go and reassure Betsy? Or try to wake her father? She dismissed that thought immediately. Even if she were able to rouse him he'd still be fuddled and of little help. Where was Treeve? She could hear Maggie shouting and being shouted at in turn. Suddenly Jenefer realized: *Maggie was trying to warn her.*

Her father kept a pistol in the desk drawer in his study. Fearing his dark moods and knowing how clumsy and careless he could be when drunk, she had begged him to let her lock it away safely in a cupboard. Offended, furious, he had reminded her that he was a soldier and knew perfectly well how to handle firearms. At the time his refusal had added yet another to her list of anxieties, but now she was grateful for his stubbornness.

Shielding her candle with a trembling hand she crept quickly down the stairs, her nose wrinkling. The smell of brandy was strong. How much had spilled? It was too dark and the candlelight too weak for her to see.

If she could just reach the study. . . . She was halfway across the hall when her heart leapt into her throat at the imperious summons of Betsy's bell. She stopped, torn between reaching the pistol that would offer both protection and threat, and the equally desperate need to stop Betsy ringing the bell before the intruder heard it and realized others in the house were awake.

Too late. Two men appeared at the far end of the hall. Both had pistols. One held a lantern high. The other held a struggling Maggie.

'Run, miss, run!' Maggie panted.

'Shut up, you daft besom,' Maggie's captor shook her.

'You move one step and I'll shoot 'e down,' the man with the lantern warned Jenefer.

Seeing their filthy, red-stained coats and canvas trousers Jenefer knew at once they were tinners. Their boots were old and scuffed. Each wore a shapeless felt hat and a grubby kerchief that masked the lower half of his face.

Jenefer swallowed and forced the words. 'What do you want?'

'Gemstones,' said the one with the lantern.

'Money,' added his partner.

Jen darted an involuntary glance towards the stairs as the bell rang again and Betsy's voice called her name through the closed door.

'That the cripple, is it?' The man turned to Maggie. 'Go and shut 'er up.'

Jerking free, Maggie rubbed her arm. 'I'm some sorry, miss. I couldn't—'

'Never mind that,' the man snarled, shoving her violently with his pistol barrel. 'Get up they stairs.' As Maggie hurried up the staircase, the tinner turned back to Jenefer. 'Now tell us where your father do keep the stones and be quick about it.'

The candle was shaking in Jenefer's grasp. 'There aren't any stones.'

'Want me to shoot you?' the man threatened, raising his pistol. His hand, she saw, was rock steady. 'Better still, I'll shoot the cripple and you can watch.'

Jenefer swallowed again. Her mouth was dust-dry and her lips felt stiff. 'Do you think I'd risk my sister's life by lying to you?' Mortified, her skin hot and damp with perspiration, she told them the truth she had done her best to hide from everyone but her father. A truth he had simply refused to face. 'There's no money and no gems.'

The second man stepped forward and punched her shoulder hard with a clenched fist. 'Bleddy liar. Your father brought 'em back from India.'

How did they know? 'Yes, he did. But they've all gone. My father is a venturer. The gems were sold and the money used to buy cargoes of contraband. Thomas Varcoe organized it all. His uncle is a merchant in Roscoff. Mr Varcoe took the last of the gemstones to Truro over two weeks ago.'

The men exchanged a glance. Then the one with the lantern threatened, 'If we search the house and find anything—'

'You won't find anything because there isn't anything to find.'

'Maybe the cripple knows something you don't.'

'Stop calling her that!' Jenefer shouted, her fear swamped by sudden fury. 'My sister was injured in an accident. She can't walk. So even if something had been hidden in the house – which it hasn't – she wouldn't know anything about it. I can give you food and clothes, but that's all. There isn't anything else.'

'Think we're stupid, do 'e?' The tinner spat. 'We been lied to by mine owners, gentry and politicians. Why should us believe *you*? Where's your father's study?'

Arguing was pointless. 'This way.' If she could just reach her father's pistol. But she would need to divert their attention. How on earth was she to do that? Raising her candle she opened the door. The smell of brandy was even stronger in here.

The back door crashed open, making Jenefer jump. Booted feet pounding down the flagged passage.

'Maggie? Wha'd'e think you're doing of leaving me out there? 'Tis bleddy freezing in that bleddy barn,' Treeve bellowed.

Startled, distracted, both tinners turned towards him.

'Stop or I'll fire,' one shouted.

While they had their backs to her, Jenefer seized the moment. Setting the candleholder on the paper-strewn desk her father would not let her touch even though he could never find anything, she wrenched open the drawer. Trembling violently she grabbed the pistol. It felt cold and heavy. She remembered to pull back the hammer but needed to use both thumbs. Holding the pistol with both hands she ran towards the door, gasping with fright as one of the tinners loomed in front of her and swung his lantern high.

Her finger jerked on the trigger. The noise was deafening. Shocked, she screamed as he stumbled backward and fell sprawling.

The lantern flew from his hand and smashed against the bottom stair. Treeve and the other tinner turned.

'Jesus, miss!' Treeve croaked. 'You bleddy shot him!'

Jenefer dropped the pistol, her hands flying to her mouth. 'I didn't mean— Oh God, is he dead? Have I killed him?'

The candle from the smashed lantern rolled into spilt brandy that had pooled beneath the bottom stair. A shimmering blue line snaked into the study and up the stairs and erupted in bright white flame.

'Get back!' The uninjured tinner waved his pistol, motioning Jenefer and Maggie away. 'You,' he snarled at Treeve. 'Open the front door.'

'No, you mustn't—' Jenefer cried desperately.

'Shut your mouth!' As he hooked an arm around his unconscious partner, Jenefer saw a dark red stain spreading down the fallen man's filthy sleeve. Blood dripped steadily from limp fingers. *Please, please, let it be just a flesh wound.*

Treeve opened the door and the tinner stumbled out bowed under the weight of his burden. Fuelled by the blast of fresh air, hungry flames leapt up the carpeted stairs and billowing smoke began to fill the hall.

Panic swamped her. Should they try to fight it? No, get Betsy out first. What about her father? Trembling with shock and cold she clasped her arms across her body.

'Treeve, *Treeve*! Push Betsy's chair outside then try and wake my father. Maggie, we have to get Betsy.'

'What about the door, miss? Leave'n open, shall I?'

Jenefer wanted to scream. If she closed it the smoke would soon make it impossible to breathe, but the freezing air was fanning the flames. 'No, close it. Treeve, when you've put Betsy's chair outside, get water from the kitchen and throw it up the stairs as high as you can reach.'

'We'll never get up there, miss,' Maggie turned her panic-stricken gaze from the burning staircase to Jenefer, 'let alone bring her down.'

Jenefer could hear Betsy screaming. 'We'll use the back stairs. If Treeve can soak the carpet it might stop the fire reaching the landing before we can get Betsy out.'

The front door slammed. Leaping flames lit the hallway and cast dancing shadows. Thick smoke billowed and coiled upward, burning her eyes and catching in her throat. Coughing, Jenefer held her nightgown and robe tight against her legs as she ran down the hall and through to the kitchen with Maggie panting along close behind her.

Slamming the door, praying it would hold back the flames, she skirted the big scrubbed table and lifted the latch on the door concealing the narrow wooden staircase that led up to the first floor where Treeve and Maggie had their room. As she hurried along the landing, smoke thickened the air making it hard to breathe. She heard Treeve clattering up behind her.

Bursting into Betsy's bedroom, Jenefer saw her sister's eyes huge with fear in the orange light of the flames.

'Jen? What's happening? I heard a shot and—'

Jenefer heard a clank and rattle then the gush of water as Treeve emptied his bucket down the stairs, then the thud of his boots receding. She shut the door. 'We have to get you outside.'

'But what—?'

'Two tinners broke in but they've gone now.'

'But the shot—'

'Later, Betsy, I'll tell you later.'

Maggie was already at the closet pulling out clothes. 'C'mon, my bird, let's get you dressed quick as we can.'

As Betsy pushed back the bedclothes, Jenefer reached into the chest for a clean sheet, shook it open and laid it on the floor. Crossing to the chest she pulled the top drawer open, scooped out the folded underwear and tossed it on to the sheet, almost colliding with Maggie as she turned again to the chest.

'Look, miss, us'll be tripping over each other. I'll get Miss Betsy ready and the rest of 'er clothes. Go on, you see to yourself.'

Reluctant to leave them, Jenefer knew Maggie was right. She hurried to the door. 'Drop the bundle out of the window. I'll be as quick as I can.'

'Maggie, my needlework.' Panic drove Betsy's voice higher. 'All my silks – there, on the chair.'

'All right, my bird. Calm down now. I've put'n in with the rest.'

Jenefer ran to her own room and emptied the contents of her own closet and chest on to a sheet ripped from her bed. Knotting the corners, she heaved up the lower sash window and pushed the bundle out. Pulling pillow and bedding from the mattress she rolled them up and tossed them out as well, sucking in deep breaths of cold clean air before she closed the window again. At least it wasn't raining.

Turning she saw flickering orange light at the bottom of the door. Puffs and tendrils of smoke curled into the room. *She didn't want to go out there.* She had no choice: Betsy needed her. Grasping the doorknob, trying to ignore the roar and crackle of the fire beyond, she took a breath and pulled the door open. On the landing the smoke was thicker and the flames had almost reached the top of the stairs. Panic gripped her throat along with the choking smoke and her heartbeat drummed in her ears as she coughed and gasped for breath.

Keeping close to the wall she stumbled along the landing to Betsy's room. Her sister was sitting on the edge of her bare mattress.

'Maggie, get your clothes and go outside,' Jenefer ordered. 'Don't try to save anything else.'

'Never mind about me. Let's get the both of you out first,' Maggie urged. 'How do 'e want 'er?'

'Jen, you can't carry me. I'm too heavy. Where's Treeve?'

'Helping your father,' Maggie said. 'We'll get on without'n.'

Jenefer could only hope she was right. 'Come on, Betsy, I'll carry you piggy-back, like when we were little.' She drew her sister's arms over her shoulders then bent forward while Maggie boosted Betsy on to her back. Normally she and Maggie worked as a team carrying Betsy from bed to bath or chair. But there wouldn't be room on the narrow staircase. She could feel her sister trembling and though every muscle protested, she gritted her teeth, determined not to pile guilt on to Betsy's fear.

Maggie opened the door and Jenefer staggered as fast as she could along the landing. The smoke was thick and choking. Her eyes streamed and her throat burned. She couldn't breathe and began to cough. Betsy was coughing and sobbing in her ear. Behind them the fire roared.

Jenefer took the stairs one at a time, her hands against the wall on each side, her legs trembling uncontrollably. The back door stood open and she stumbled out into the fresh air, her lungs heaving.

Blessing Treeve for having the foresight to bring Betsy's chair round, Jenefer twisted so she could drop her sister into it. It was several moments before she could stop coughing. Then she straightened up, pressing both hands to her strained and aching back.

Above the fire's roar she heard breaking glass and a loud thud. Still gasping, Betsy grabbed Jenefer's arm. 'Father.'

Whirling round Jenefer stumbled back into the kitchen. Her voice sounded cracked and hoarse as she shouted. 'Maggie! Treeve?' Smoke was curling under the door separating the kitchen and hall-way. *How long before the fire burst through?* She had to reach her father. Surely Treeve should have got him out by now?

She crouched low as she climbed the wooden staircase and tried to keep her breathing shallow. But her chest ached and burned from the smoke. Coughing, blinded by streaming tears, she reached the top of the stairs. In the light of the leaping flames she saw Maggie staggering backwards as she dragged an unconscious figure along the landing.

'Father?' Jenefer croaked, stumbling forward and falling to her knees.

Glancing over her shoulder as she coughed, Maggie shook her head. ' 'Tis Treeve, miss.' Her voice was raw, her face blackened and smeared.

Jenefer grabbed one of Treeve's arms and helped Maggie haul him towards the back stairs.

'Coughing fit to burst a lung, 'e was,' Maggie gasped. 'Fell and hit his head on that there carved chest by the top of the stairs.' She broke off, coughing and retching from the smoke. 'I couldn't leave'n there.' She sobbed for breath. 'If we can get'n outside, the fresh air might bring'n round then he can go for help.'

'My father—'

Maggie shook her head as another spasm of coughing shook her. 'Dunno, miss. Didn't see'n.'

Jenefer helped her drag Treeve down the stairs and out into the back yard.

'Jen!' Betsy cried. 'Are you all right?'

Jenefer bent forward her hands on her knees as she gasped for air. Her head was spinning. But Betsy was safe. She could hear her sister's voice. But it was muffled by her pounding heartbeat.

'I was so afraid. Where's Father? Oh God, he's not still in there?'

Jenefer forced herself upright and turned towards the door. *How was she to get him out?* He was taller and far heavier than she, *but she couldn't just leave him there to die.*

Her arm was grabbed and she was pulled backwards. 'You can't do nothing.' Maggie croaked.

'Treeve can help me.' Jenefer struggled but Maggie's grip tightened.

'Heaving his guts up, he is,' Maggie rasped. 'You go back in there and you won't never come out.' She choked on another racking cough. 'Miss Betsy need you now.'

Jenefer looked at Betsy huddled in her wheeled chair, her stricken face orange in the flickering light. Above them a window shattered and flames leapt out.

'Father!' Betsy howled.

Jenefer's hands flew to her mouth in uncomprehending horror.

'There idn nothing you can do, my bird,' Maggie said quietly. ' 'Tis all up with him.'

How had the fire spread so fast? Jenefer shook her head, refusing to accept the immediate, obvious answer. No, surely he wouldn't have: not in the house. But what else would have caused the fire to spread so quickly and burn with such ferocity? *He had risked their good name, the shame of a court appearance, possibly imprisonment, or worse.* She didn't want to believe it. In any case it was no longer relevant. If contraband had been hidden it had burned in the blaze. The doctor had warned that brandy would kill her father, and so it had.

She glanced across at her sister. After their mother's death, while Betsy was so desperately ill, she had bargained with God. *Let Betsy live and I'll take care of her.* But with what? There was nothing left. The fire had consumed everything except a few clothes and Betsy's wheeled chair.

Jenefer's legs gave way suddenly and she sank to the ground. 'Maggie? What am I going to do?'

CHAPTER EIGHT

'Hey! Anybody there?' A male voice, breathless and frantic with anxiety, bellowed.

Raising her head, Jenefer saw her sister's anguish turn to relief. 'Jared!' Betsy screamed. 'Jared, we're round at the back.'

Pounding footsteps came closer. Skidding round the corner in his heavy boots, Jared fell to his knees and grasped Betsy's hands. 'All right, are you? Not hurt?' He gasped the words out, his chest heaving.

'No, no, I'm fine,' Betsy's voice wobbled. 'Oh Jared, thank heaven you're here. Papa—' She stopped, unable to finish.

Rising to his feet Jared turned to Jenefer who shook her head.

Maggie patted her arm. 'C'mon, miss, we'd best pick up they bundles.' Treeve stumbled towards them wiping his mouth on his sleeve.

'I'm sorry, miss. I got in, but I couldn't wake'n. I reck'n he was already gone. I tried to pull'n out, but the smoke made me cough fit to burst me lungs. I dunnaw what 'appened then. Next thing I knew I was out 'ere.'

'Miss Jenefer and me carried you out,' Maggie told him. 'Some great lump you are too.'

'You did?' Startled, Treeve looked from his wife to Jenefer and gestured helplessly. 'I'm sorry, miss.'

What could she say? 'You tried, Treeve. I'm grateful for that.' She ached all over and was utterly exhausted. But sleep would be impossible. Which was just as well considering she no longer had a bed. Laughter swelled like a bubble in her chest and she started to shake. Tears burned the back of her eyes and she swallowed hard, fighting hysteria.

'Miss?' She forced herself to look up. Pushing the chair he had made for her sister, Jared paused beside her. 'I'm taking Betsy back to my place. Mother'll look after her.'

It was clear from his tone, his use of her sister's name and the set of his shoulders that he was stating his intent, not asking permission. Jenefer stiffened. He had no right. Betsy was *her* sister, *her* family, not his.

'You're welcome too,' he added.

She shook her head. 'I can't. Thank you. But there are – I have to—'

'Maybe later then.'

'Jen?' Betsy lifted her hand and Jenefer grasped it. 'I'll stay if you want.'

'No.' Jared and Jenefer spoke simultaneously as their eyes met over Betsy's head. In that moment Jenefer knew her relationship with her sister had irrevocably changed. She hadn't the energy to grieve for it, much less to engage in a fight she would surely lose.

'No.' *What would be the point? What could you do?* She managed to bite back the words before they reached her lips. None of this was Betsy's fault. 'If I know you're safe then I won't be worried about you.'

'Don't you fret, miss,' Jared tried to reassure her. 'Mother'll see her right. Others'll be here soon.' Having got his way his manner was more conciliatory. Had he expected her to argue? They both wanted what was best for her sister and Betsy had made her choice. 'Half the village will have heard by now I shouldn't wonder. I'll come back as soon as I've got Bets – your sister settled.'

'Thank you.' Jenefer cleared her throat, trying to shift the choking lump. 'Betsy, you'd better take your things with you.'

Jenefer walked ahead of them round to the front of the house. Clothes and bedding lay where they had been flung from the upstairs windows.

Picking up Betsy's bundles Jenefer placed both on her sister's knees, bent and kissed her cheek, then stepped back. 'On your way then.'

With a nod Jared pushed the chair towards the gate and the track leading down to the village.

Jenefer picked up her own belongings and carried them out of range of flying sparks and falling debris towards the low hedge that bordered the garden and separated it from the track. The whole house was ablaze. Flames leaping out of the broken windows were hot on her face and the bright golden light cast long shadows. Jenefer clasped her upper arms and shivered as she watched her home burn.

After her mother's death she had accepted betrothal to a man she didn't love so she would be able to take care of Betsy. She had made herself think of it not as a sacrifice but as a gift: gratitude for being well and whole and not disabled as her sister was. But by going with Jared Betsy had discarded that gift and made it worthless.

When she had believed herself responsible for both her father and her sister the burden had weighed heavily. Now in the space of a few hours everything had changed. Her father was surely dead and Betsy was moving into the Sweets' cottage to be looked after by Inez.

She couldn't blame her sister. Betsy loved Jared and he loved her. They wanted so much to be married. And now there was nothing –

and no one – to prevent it.

For the first time in her life Jenefer was alone. Instead of feeling free she felt totally lost.

'Here they are,' Maggie said beside her. 'Come to gawp.'

Glancing round Jenefer saw villagers arriving and was touched to see how many carried buckets. But the fire was unstoppable. It would burn until there was nothing left for it to feed on. Unable to get near, they congregated near the hedge talking in lowered voices.

'What are they waiting for?'

'Whatever's left, miss. I'd better tell Treeve to put a padlock on the barn door else they'll be in there. If it isn't nailed down, they'll have it.'

'Miss Trevanion.'

Jenefer looked round. Her heart thumped hard against her ribs as Devlin Varcoe strode across the grass towards her. Seeing him reminded her suddenly that she was clad only in her night attire. Automatically she reached up to the single untidy braid hanging over her shoulder.

In the firelight she saw her hand was streaked with soot and dried tears. Her face must look even worse. Shame and self-consciousness dewed her skin with perspiration as she tucked the bedgown more tightly into its sash then folded her arms.

How could she even think of her appearance while her father lay trapped inside the burning house? *Please let him have passed away without ever waking up.* That he might have come round and found himself alone, surrounded by flames and unable to see a way out – she blocked the thought, unable to bear it. *What was she to do? Where could she go?* She would manage. She had no choice. Sucking in a shaky breath she drew herself up. She was Colonel Trevanion's elder daughter and would – must – conduct herself accordingly.

Behind Devlin she glimpsed Willie Grose standing apart from the crowd. He was staring towards them, his face contorted with naked malice. Despite the shocks she had already suffered it gave her an unpleasant jolt. But before she had time to wonder what she could have done to warrant such enmity, Devlin reached her.

'I passed Jared and your sister on the track. I'm sorry about your father.'

She forgot about Willie Grose. 'Thank you.'

'What happened? How did the fire start?'

'Spilt brandy and a smashed lantern.' She drew a steadying breath. 'I heard a noise then Maggie shouting. Two tinners had broken in. They threatened me with a pistol and demanded money and gemstones.' She looked up, saw him frowning, and was suddenly overwhelmed by anger at everything that had happened that evening.

'They were very specific, Mr Varcoe. Someone must have told them what to look for.' In the light from the flames she saw his eyes narrow.

'All thieves demand money and jewellery.'

'But they didn't ask for jewellery. They asked for *gemstones*. When I told them there weren't any they accused me of lying and said my father had brought them back from India. How would they know that, Mr Varcoe, unless someone had told them?'

He stared at her for a long moment. 'Clearly someone had told them. But it wasn't me, Miss Trevanion.'

'I never said—'

'You didn't need to. Your meaning was plain enough. But you've had a shock so I won't take your accusation personally.'

Glad he could not see the flush she could feel burning her face, Jenefer looked down and moved one foot away from the sharp stone pressing through her slipper.

'A word of advice.' He glanced round before turning back to her and lowering his voice. 'It might be wiser not to tell anyone about the break-in or that tinners were responsible.'

Her head flew up. 'Oh really? That's your advice, is it? I should just allow people to believe my father started the fire? Because that's what the gossips will say.' She ticked off points on trembling fingers. 'He was drunk; he knocked over a candle; and it served him right.' She held herself again, her arms pressed tight against her body.

'But that isn't the way it happened and I won't allow his name to be smeared.' She couldn't control the tremors that were making her teeth chatter. 'Besides, as I shot one of them—'

'You *what*?'

'I didn't mean to. It was an accident.'

He smothered an oath. 'Did you kill him?'

'No! I don't think so. I hope not. I'm sure I didn't. He dropped the lantern as he fell. It smashed and that was what started the fire. His friend dragged him out. There was blood all down his sleeve. A

82

lot of blood. It was dripping—'

'Then you probably just winged him,' Devlin broke in as she shuddered. 'Do you have any relations nearby?'

Still fighting vivid memories Jenefer shook her head.

'What about Erisey?'

She stiffened and her chin rose as she repeated what Martin had told her the last time she had seen him. 'Mr Erisey is abroad at present, in America. He's part of a diplomatic mission, something to do with a treaty granting British vessels the status of most-favoured nation.'

'Taking long enough, isn't it? He's been gone months,' Devlin remarked, his speculative gaze bringing another wave of heat to her face.

'Apparently,' she replied, her wretchedness increasing, 'there were problems about American sailors not being guaranteed protection against the press gangs.' She had gleaned this information, not from Martin, who had warned her he would have little spare time in which to write, but from the *Sherborne Mercury*. She saw no reason to mention either fact to Devlin Varcoe. 'I expect him back any day now.'

'Well, until he does turn up, does he have any family who might be willing to take you in?'

'There is only his father. But he's a widower and spends much of his time in London. In any case I could not impose on a virtual stranger.' Mortified by his questions, she was humiliated by the knowledge that despite being betrothed she had no protector and no one to whom she could turn for aid or advice. Angry and hurt, she felt very much alone. *It wasn't supposed to be like this.*

Pride drew her up. 'You need not concern yourself on my account, Mr Varcoe.'

His mouth tightened and she saw a muscle jump in his jaw. 'By Christ, you're hard to help,' he growled.

'I don't recall asking you for help. In any case, I will not leave here until my father's – until my father is found.'

'For God's sake!' He raked a hand through his hair. 'That fire could smoulder for days. When it stops burning what's left will be unsafe. It might be a week or more before his remains can be recovered. What were you planning to do? Sleep on straw in the stable?'

She turned away, looking at the blaze rather than at him. He saw too much, knew too much. It was none of his business. From the corner of her eye she saw Maggie and Treeve coming towards her. Heads bent, they appeared to be arguing.

'Look' – Devlin gazed past her – 'I've got a place in the village – I don't mean the workshop or my loft,' he said, as her head jerked up. 'It's a cottage I'm rebuilding. It's watertight and the roof is sound. You can stay there if you want.' He nodded at Treeve and Maggie. 'With a bit of help you could make it liveable.'

'Wish we could stay, miss,' Treeve's voice was hoarse from coughing, 'but now master's gone – and no money – well, we can't live on fresh air. We'll go downlong to brother's farm at Marazion.'

'Yes, of course.' How many more losses was she to suffer this night?

Maggie folded her arms. 'We aren't going nowhere till I seen miss got a safe place to lay 'er 'ead.' She glared at her husband daring him to argue then turned back to Jenefer. 'If I had my way I'd stay here along wi' you. But—' She shrugged helplessly.

'It's all right, Maggie.' It wasn't all right. Nothing was *all right*. But it was important not to make Maggie feel any worse. Good manners demanded she put others' well-being before her own.

Jenefer couldn't remember a time when Maggie hadn't been part of the household, part of her life. None of this was Maggie's fault any more than it was Betsy's. Her life was disintegrating and there was nothing she could do to stop it.

There was a fist-sized lump in her chest and she pressed the heel of her hand against it. Her eyes stung. But she couldn't break down. Not here, not now, and especially not in front of Devlin Varcoe.

An image of her mother's face sprang vividly into her mind, delicate brows arched in reproof. *A lady does not indulge in emotional displays. Such behaviour is common.*

'Of course you must go.' She touched Maggie's shoulder. 'There'll be work for Treeve on the farm and you'll have somewhere to live.'

'Yes, but what about you, miss?'

'Miss Trevanion can use my cottage in Hawkins' Ope for as long as she needs it,' Devlin said.

Maggie's eyes widened then she beamed. 'Why, that's some good of you, Mr Varcoe. Worried sick I was 'bout what miss would do. But that's 'andsome. I go that way sometimes. Be lovely it will once 'tis finished. I heard you 'ad a range put in.'

Jenefer knew about the range. She had overheard Rose who came every Monday to do the laundry telling Maggie about it. Nothing happened in the village without someone seeing. The brief ironic twist of Devlin's mouth told her he was thinking the same, and the awareness of something shared kindled a tiny glow inside her.

'There's no furniture,' he warned.

'Don't you worry 'bout that.' Maggie was brisk. 'There's a great pile of stuff in the barn. Some of it 'ave been there years. Master wouldn't throw nothing away. Said you never knew when there might be a use for it. God rest the poor soul.' She tucked her arm through Jenefer's and drew her gently away. 'C'mon, my bird. Let's go and see what us can find. Treeve, you get the cart out and harness up the cob. Got a lantern out there, 'ave you?'

'Miss Trevanion?'

Glancing over her shoulder Jenefer saw Devlin watching her.

'You needn't fear anyone will bother you.'

Not trusting her voice, Jenefer gave a quick nod. She knew she should be grateful. In fact, she was terrified. She had never lived alone. But as of this moment all she possessed of her former life were two knotted sheets containing her clothes and some bed linen, and a small wooden box that held a few pieces of jewellery, some of it her own, the rest inherited from her mother.

She had nowhere else to go. Jared's suggestion had been kindly meant but was impractical. There would only just be room at the Sweets' for Betsy.

She had to accept Devlin Varcoe's offer. Beggars could not be choosers. *People would talk.* Not if she paid rent. *With what?* She would sell her jewellery. Regret stabbed, sharp and painful but she ignored it. It was the only way. If only – *things were different?* But they weren't. Her father had employed the Varcoes. To be in debt to a smuggler was unthinkable. He was what he was. And she . . . was engaged to be married.

But the fire had altered everything. Betsy would marry Jared and no longer needed a home with her and Martin. What had not changed was that Martin's proposal had been a generous offer made in good faith. He was far from home, his work vital to England's security and trade. For her to break their engagement would expose him to rumour and gossip. Unpleasant for any man, but doubly so for someone blameless and whose career depended upon a spotless reputation. How could she justify such an act? And anyway what would it gain her? *Devlin Varcoe?*

Her heart leapt and fluttered and she tried to swallow but her mouth was dry. *She should decline his cottage.* And go where? *He was watching her.* She cleared her throat. 'Thank you, you're very kind.'

Wrapped in her coverlet Tamara sat on the window seat in her bedroom and hugged her knees as she watched the flames and the bobbing lanterns of villagers still making their way along the track to join others clustered in front of the burning house. She knew a few would be there to offer help, others simply to watch, but most in case there might be any pickings.

She was desperately tired. She had always taken sleep for granted, drifting off within minutes of her head hitting the pillow, waking seven or eight hours later refreshed and ready for the day. But that had been . . . before.

For almost two weeks she had made herself to do all the things she had always done. Each morning she greeted her parents with a smile and asked if they had any errands for her. She commiserated with her mother over the little catastrophes that were a daily occurrence: a pulled thread in her kerchief, the wind rattling the window, Sally being late with the coffee. To distract them from her lack of appetite she told them bits of village news. But she never mentioned Devlin. She did not dare. And as soon as breakfast was over, she escaped.

Each night she prayed it would get easier. But it didn't. If anyone found out they would say she deserved to suffer. That what she had done was a sin. But she would never believe that. Love was not sinful, and she had loved Devlin. Loved him still, fool that she was.

She wondered how much longer she could maintain her pretence. But she had no choice. Give the village gossip to chew on? Allow them to see how badly he'd hurt her? Put up with gloating sympathy because she, who knew herself different, was no better than half-a-dozen other village girls: just another of Devlin Varcoe's cast-offs? *Never.*

She was desperately tired, exhausted by lack of sleep and by the war raging inside her. She kept reliving every moment she had spent with Devlin in his loft and in his arms. She had always trusted her instincts and sensed in every fibre of her being that he had been as deeply and profoundly affected as she.

So what had happened? Why had he rejected her? She felt no shame at what they had done. It had been a transcendent experience, beyond imagination. The memory of it still turned her insides liquid, leaving her weak with longing. What gnawed at her, sapping her strength and her confidence, was bewilderment. How could she have been so *wrong*?

That first night she had been fired by rage. Fury at his cowardice, and for being so much less than she had believed, had filled her with nervous energy. But she hadn't been able to hang on to it. Yet without that anger she had no support: nothing to cling to while she struggled to regain some emotional balance.

Lying awake in the darkness she could not escape the memories or block her thoughts by keeping busy. It was during these night hours that her emotions swung from incomprehension to grief as raw as an open wound. Then tears, hot and unstoppable, trickled down her temples to soak her hair and her pillow.

But each morning when daybreak pearled the sky she left her bed and bathed her eyes so Sally would not notice anything amiss.

Days passed. Somehow she got through them, her performance so convincing that not even her parents noticed she wasn't herself. Though the ache did not lessen, it was pushed deeper by a scar tissue of pride and necessity.

Tamara watched the glow of the fire pale to insignificance beneath an angry dawn of orange and purple cloud pierced by shimmering golden rays against which the smoking ruins were starkly silhouetted. As the sun rose, the sky changed from milk to primrose then turquoise and the underside of the clouds blushed rose pink.

Crows circled, wheeling and diving on the rising breeze, while seagulls headed inland. There was more bad weather on the way. Then Sally knocked, bearing a cup of hot chocolate and hot water for her wash.

Craving the open moor and solitude, Tamara put on her forest green riding habit and, after brushing her hair, tied it back in a matching ribbon. Only then did she look in the mirror. Her pallor emphasized bruise-like shadows under her eyes. But this morning she had a ready excuse.

She paused outside the breakfast parlour and pinched her cheeks to give them some colour. She could hear her mother talking animatedly. Inhaling deeply she lifted her chin and opened the door.

'Ah, there you are, Tamara.' Resplendent in a thigh-length caraco jacket and matching petticoat of floral painted cotton with a neckerchief of puffed white gauze at her bosom and a frilled cap covering her hair, Morwenna glanced up from the piece of bread-and-butter she was holding. The twin grooves between her brows deepened.

'You're looking pale this morning.' It sounded like an accusation.

Tamara smothered a sigh. So much for her cheek-pinching. 'I'm just a little tired, Mama.'

'I hope that's all it is, and you're not sickening for something. Mrs Blamey was telling me yesterday that there's a putrid sore throat in the village. Several of her acquaintance have caught it.'

'My throat is fine,' Tamara said, sliding into her chair. 'I was watching the fire.'

'I took a peek myself. Your father had ideas about going up there, but I wouldn't let him.' She turned to her husband who was working his way through two thick slices of ham. 'I don't know what you were thinking of, to suggest leaving us here unprotected in the middle of the night.'

'I was thinking of the Trevanions,' her father said.

'Yes, well, I'm sure it is a great misfortune for them. I must say I was astonished that the fire took hold so quickly.'

Anxious to prevent her mother making the obvious connection with stored brandy and mentioning Devlin, Tamara turned to her father. 'Is the family safe?'

John shook his head. 'Apparently the colonel died in the fire.' He glanced up as their cook came in with a fresh pot of coffee. 'That's right, isn't it, Mrs Voss?'

Setting the pot down carefully she nodded. ' 'Tis what my nephew heard, sir. Andy went up along with Ben Tozer and Danny Pawle, but they couldn't get near the place. Fire took hold so fast. Some fierce blaze it was.'

'Thank you, Mrs Voss. That will be all.' Morwenna waited until the door closed. 'Sally happened to mention that Jared Sweet took Betsy Trevanion away in that wheeled chair he made for her.' Morwenna sniffed. 'I'm sure Mrs Trevanion would not have approved of such a connection. Things were never the same up there after the accident. Anyway, I was about to suggest to your father that we offer to put Jenefer up. Just until she can contact relatives. It would be an act of Christian charity.'

Tamara knew that while Christian charity might have figured briefly in her mother's reasoning, a far greater incentive was the boost to her social status of having Colonel Trevanion's daughter as a house guest. She set her cup down carefully. 'I don't think Miss Trevanion would accept, Mama.'

'Oh? And why not, pray?'

'She doesn't approve of me.'

'Indeed?' Morwenna's expression veered between indignation and frustrated acknowledgement of an irritating but undeniable truth. 'So who will live up to her approval? Doctor Avers might, I suppose. But he won't have room. John, you go and find her and tell her she will be most welcome in our home.'

John Gillis sighed and cut into the ham.

'Where are you going?' Morwenna demanded as Tamara pushed her chair back.

'I thought I'd take a ride on the moor before the rain comes in.'

'But you haven't eaten a thing.'

'I'm not hungry.'

'Tamara! You cannot go out without a proper breakfast. In any case, if Miss Trevanion is coming to stay I shall want you to—'

'Leave the girl be. The fresh air will do her good.'

Surprised, Tamara flashed her father a smile of gratitude as she made for the door.

'John, I wish you wouldn't interfere—'

Tamara heard her father's cutlery clatter on to his plate then the scrape of his chair as he rose. 'It's time someone did.'

CHAPTER NINE

'Oh, 'tis you,' Maisy Roberts's frown softened and she opened the door wider. 'Proper stranger you are.'

As his brother's housekeeper moved back, Devlin stepped into the gloomy hallway. Immediately he was overwhelmed by memories, none of them happy.

After escaping the tyranny of his father and his bullying brother he had vowed never again to be beholden to any man. His was the power now. He gave the orders. He lived as he pleased and did as he wished. He owed nothing and needed no one.

He certainly didn't need Tamara Gillis. So why could he not shut her out of his thoughts and dreams? She haunted him. He kept seeing her face, first dark-eyed, heavy-lidded, *vulnerable*, her mouth swollen from the bruising pressure of his: then pale with shock, chin high, her gaze blazing contempt as she called him a coward.

Had she been a man he'd have killed her for that. But no man worthy of the name raised his hand to a woman, even one as provoking as she.

What had happened had happened and that was an end of it. His intention had been to call her bluff, teach her a lesson. Only it had got out of hand. It was never supposed to *mean* anything. He would not allow it to. Need was weakness. He had learned that lesson as a child: learned fast and vowed never to forget.

Now he made the rules and held the power. His life was busy and demanding. It was the life he had chosen. If he wanted company of either sex he could find it at the Five Mackerel.

He had always been content alone. But now he couldn't settle. Now he came home, not to the peaceful solitude of a place he had made his own, but to vivid memories and loneliness so deep he ached. *Damn her*.

Another woman would banish the taste and smell of Tamara Gillis. He wouldn't even have to flash the silver. There were plenty willing to do whatever he wanted so that later they could boast of bedding Devil Varcoe. He was not vain, but he knew the power of his reputation. Yet he could not block the echoes of her soft sighs and scathing condemnation. He jammed a hand through his hair and ground his teeth, wanting to roar his frustration.

'Is my brother at home?'

Closing the door, Maisy jerked her head towards the breakfast parlour further down the hall. 'In there he is. I made'n breakfast. But I dunnaw if he'll keep it down.' She clicked her tongue. 'Some mess he made. Blood all over the towels. I've put 'em to soak in salt water but t'will be some job to get the stain out.'

Devlin frowned, his thoughts racing. Jenefer Trevanion had shot one of the tinners. *They asked for gemstones. Someone must have told them what to look for.* Thomas? Though Devlin didn't trust his brother, he couldn't imagine Thomas risking so much for so little. But he couldn't be sure. It was those doubts as much as the need to know Thomas's plans for the next run that had brought him here for the first time since his father's death.

'Blood? What happened?'

Maisy shrugged. 'Cut hisself shaving. No wonder, the way he's shaking.' She clicked her tongue. 'I never seen the like of they towels. Zachary didn't make that much mess when he butchered the pig.'

Devlin was sure of one thing. No tinner wounded or otherwise, had set foot in this house. Thomas indulged himself but was close-fisted with everyone else. As for tending a wound he was far too squeamish. Nor would he trouble himself, especially for anyone he considered an inferior.

Still the doubts persisted. Varcoes had never worried about breaking the law. With times so hard and prices so high survival was all that mattered. Yet as their father's heir Thomas had inherited fishing cellars he leased out, a barking shed and shares in a couple of fishing boats as well as the house. If he needed money he had assets he could sell. He had spent his entire adult life trying desperately to fight free of his father's shadow and build a reputation as an important man of business. Surely he wouldn't jeopardize that?

'I just took in another pot of coffee. That's the second this morning for all the good it'll do. Bring another cup, shall I?'

'No, I'm not staying.'

She nodded. 'Well, you know your way. I must get on.' Picking up the wooden box of cleaning materials she had set down to answer his knock, she trudged heavily up the stairs still muttering to herself.

Opening the parlour door Devlin paused on the threshold and studied his brother. The fawn frockcoat, green and yellow striped waistcoat, brown breeches, snuff-coloured stockings and black leather shoes with pewter buckles were the clothes of a gentleman. The pallid sweaty skin, trembling hands and puffy bloodshot eyes belonged to a drunk.

Thomas's violent start spilled coffee over his hand and he cursed as he clattered the cup on to its saucer then wiped his fingers on the crumpled napkin.

'What are you doing here? The fire at Trevanions' I suppose. I saw it from my window. But in case I hadn't' – he sighed heavily in irritation – 'Willie Grose arrived at sparrow-fart this morning to tell me about it.'

'Why?'

'Why what?' Thomas picked up his cup again and tried to stop it shaking by resting his elbows on the table.

'Why did Willie come to tell you?'

'Why do you think? He'd have known from Charlie that the colonel put up the money for the contraband cargoes. I daresay he thought that telling me about the fire would earn him a tip. He says Trevanion didn't get out. Is that true?'

'Yes.'

Thomas shrugged and lowered his face to the cup. 'Oh well. It's fortunate I've found another investor.' He sipped carefully.

Devlin's tone was dry. 'Your humanity does you credit.'

Thomas set the cup down and wiped his mouth. 'Everyone knows Trevanion was drinking heavily. A brandy nightcap, a burning candle beside his bed.' He shrugged one thickly padded shoulder. 'The real surprise is that it didn't happen sooner.'

Thomas's reaction was exactly as Jenefer predicted. 'So Willie didn't tell you about the break-in?' Devlin enquired, watching his brother.

'Break-in?' Lifting the cup again, Thomas grimaced, swallowed audibly and closed his eyes. Setting it down hard he dabbed greasy sweat from his forehead and upper lip. 'What break-in?' His face was grey-green.

'Two tinners, demanding gemstones and money.'

'Did they get any?'

'No. But one of them was shot.'

Thomas eyed Devlin over the crumpled cloth that hid most of his face. 'Killed?'

'No. They both got away.'

Saying nothing, Thomas wiped his forehead again.

'Are you ill?' Devlin enquired.

'I've had a shock.'

'You just said the fire was—'

'Not the fire. Harry. Harry Carlyon.'

'He's dead.'

'I know he's dead!' Thomas shouted. 'But to go like that – the entire crew lost, and his cargo. Such a waste.'

Which bothered Thomas more, Devlin wondered? 'I wasn't aware you were that well acquainted.'

'Why should you be?' Thomas wiped his mouth. 'I know lots of people. Important people.'

'Indeed.' Whether this was just another of his brother's empty boasts Devlin neither knew nor cared.

Thomas's tongue snaked out to moisten paper-white lips. 'Harry was staying at the Bull the last time I was in Truro. We spent a very convivial evening together.' He mopped his face again. 'Now he's gone.'

'You should be careful.' Devlin turned to the door.

'Why? What do you mean?' Thomas jerked round, gripping the arms of his chair.

'Either stop drinking so much or let Zachary shave you. Otherwise the next time your hand slips . . .' Devlin made a slicing motion across his throat.

Thomas's hand flew to his carefully tied neckcloth and he inserted a trembling finger between collar and skin. 'When I want your advice I'll ask for it.'

'That'll be a cold day in hell.'

Thomas pushed himself to his feet. 'Oh go to the devil! No one asked you to come. I'm not myself today.'

'Indeed you are, Thomas. You are exactly yourself.'

'Get out! You've no business here.'

Devlin cocked an eyebrow. 'I need to know when I'm making the next run.'

'What?' Clearly flustered by the question Thomas waved his brother away. 'I can't think about that now. I'll let you know.'

Devlin left the room and strode to the front door. If he never entered this house again it would be too soon.

Thomas remained in his chair until he heard the front door close. When he was certain his brother had gone he pushed himself unsteadily to his feet, crossed to the bureau-cabinet standing against the wall and took out the brandy decanter. Crystal clattered against china as he poured a generous measure into his cup. He swallowed deeply.

He had handled that well, diverting attention from the break-in. He poured more, gulped it down and waited with closed eyes for the heat to slide through his trembling limbs. That was better. As the tremors eased and his head cleared he felt himself relax.

Pouring a third measure into his cup he replaced the decanter in the cabinet and closed the door. He straightened, steadying himself as the room swayed. Then carrying his cup he walked carefully out of the parlour and across the hall to the study.

No one knew about his deal with Harry. But unless he could find the money to pay his uncle, the business would collapse and he'd be a laughing stock. Damn Harry to hell and back. Running his boat on to rocks, how could he have been so bloody stupid?

He sucked air through his teeth. No use dwelling on that. Harry was dead. So was Trevanion. According to Willie the fire had started soon after the tinners broke in. Trevanion's daughters had escaped with nothing but a few clothes and blankets. Any cash or brandy would have been lost in the flames. Searching the wreckage was impossible. It would attract too much attention. Not that there'd be anything left to find. The villagers would be in there before the ashes were cold.

Thomas sat in his father's chair behind his father's desk. *Yours now*, a voice in his head reminded. Somewhere in the distance he could hear knocking. Ignoring it he raised the cup and gulped down more brandy. Yes, by God they were his now, and no one was going to take them.

The knocking continued. His vision blurred as images filled his head: Daniell the banker who knew about the mortgage and had probably guessed about his debts; his father's colleagues saying he'd never been man enough for the job; and Devlin, bloody Devlin, always mocking and sneering. *So get rid of him.*

The words were so clear that he looked round to see who had spoken, and was startled to find himself alone. He slumped back in the chair. How exactly had Devlin accumulated the money to buy his boat and the building that housed his workshop, net store and loft? He'd even bought that burned-out cottage.

Devlin owned all that while he, a businessman and his father's heir, was in desperate straits. How had it happened? *He cheated you.*

Thomas drained the cup, and nearly choked as the door opened and Willie Grose peered round it.

'What are you doing here? Who let you in?'

'No one. I been out there ages. Me bleddy knuckles is black and blue.' Willie rubbed his hand.

'You've no business just walking in here—'

'Yes I have, see?' Willie raged. 'Said it was an accident, didn't he? Bleddy liar. T'wasn't no accident at all. Only pushed'n off he did. Threw'n overboard like he was so much rubbish.'

'What are you babbling about?' Thomas snapped, massaging his forehead where a dull ache pulsed.

'Your bleddy brother!' Willie's eyes were wild and spittle had gathered at the corners of his mouth. 'Billy May told his wife who told her sister who told her husband who told me. T'wasn't no accident at all. Mister Devlin-bleddy-Varcoe tipped Charlie off the boat. Left'n there to drown, he did. Only I can't do nothing about it, can I? Not on my own. Not when half the village think the sun do shine out of your brother's arse.'

Satisfaction kindled warmth in Thomas's belly that eclipsed the brandy's heat. He felt a smile spread across his face. *Yes.*

'What you grinning at?' Willie spat furiously. ' 'Tisn't funny.'

'No, it isn't. I take it you've come to me because you want revenge?'

'Bleddy right I do.'

Better and better, Thomas rubbed his hands briskly. 'So do I, Willie. So do I.' Once rid of Devlin he, as next of kin, would inherit all his brother's possessions: the lugger, the galley, the new boat John Gillis had on the stocks, the building on the waterfront, and the cottage in Hawkins' Ope.

With all that to call his own, even after paying off his debts he would be set up for the rest of his life. He'd be a man of substance commanding the respect he deserved. He would get rid of that virago Maisy Roberts, have this place painted, hire properly trained staff, and buy some elegant furniture to replace what he'd had to sell. Tamara Gillis wouldn't turn her pretty nose up at him then. Her mother would make sure of that.

Morwenna Gillis had always fancied herself a cut above the rest of the village. How delicious it would be to see her curtsey and simper to him, anxious that he offered for *her* daughter and not someone else's.

'So what you going to do, then?' Willie challenged. 'Want me to find a couple more tinners?'

Thomas shook his head. 'No, I have a much better idea. The next time my brother makes a run to Roscoff, the Riding Officer and the Customs cutter must be informed.'

'If they catch'n you won't get the lugger,' Willie warned. 'Smugglers' boats is always forfeit. Saw 'em in three they do, so they can't be used no more.'

Thomas tapped his fingers on the grubby surface of the paper-strewn desk. 'There is always a price, Willie.' But to finally be rid of his hated brother losing the lugger was a price worth paying.

With her old cloak hiding night attire now soot-stained and filthy, Jenefer sat shivering beside Ernestine Rowse's hearth. She was cold to the marrow of her bones. Behind her Maggie talked to Ernestine, their voices too soft for Jenefer to hear what they were saying. She guessed Maggie was recounting the events of the night, events that once again had turned her life upside down.

Maggie placed a cup of hot milk into her trembling hand and gently closed her fingers around it. A plate containing a slice of soft white bread spread with butter was placed on a wooden stool beside her. Jenefer looked at it. She guessed the flour had been salvaged from the wrecked schooner, or smuggled over from France. But it was so much nicer than coarse dark barley bread. She looked up into Maggie's concerned face. 'Thank you.'

'You drink that while 'tis hot,' Maggie urged. 'I'm going back with Treeve and pull out some of that there furniture in the barn. Mrs Rowse is boiling up a kettle of water so you can 'ave a nice wash. Mr Varcoe already opened up next door. He've left the key on top of the mantel. Me and Treeve'll be back soon as we can. Be all right will you?'

Maggie's anxiety pierced the fog of shock and grief clouding Jenefer's brain. Straightening her back she drew in a deep breath and forced herself to smile. 'Thank you, Maggie. I'll be fine. As soon as I'm tidy I'll go up to the parsonage and see Dr Trennack. You get along now.' She turned to the woman whose home she had no memory of entering. 'This is very kind of you, Mrs Rowse.'

Ernestine bobbed a brief curtsey as Maggie closed the door behind her. 'That's all right, miss. 'Tedn no trouble. I'm some sorry 'bout your father and all.' Using a thick folded cloth to protect her hand she lifted the kettle from the triangular iron stand and poured steaming water into a large basin on the scrubbed table then set the kettle down on the hearth. Taking a dish with a piece of soap in it from the windowsill she placed it beside the basin, then pulled two clean linen towels from the airing frame above the open fireplace.

'I'm going up the shop, miss. I'll be a bitty while so you take your time. Just pull the door when you go out.'

Half an hour later, strengthened by her breakfast and refreshed by a thorough wash, Jenefer buttoned a lavender coat-dress over a frilled while petticoat, tied the ribbons of a woven straw hat beneath her chin and set off for the parsonage.

Surrounded by more books than Jenefer had ever seen in her life, Dr Trennack stood with his back to the fire, his hands clasped beneath the long tails of his dusty black frock coat. Tall and slightly stooped, he reminded her of a heron.

'The day after tomorrow? Is that not perhaps a little hasty?'

'I don't think so, Mr Trennack. My sister and I are the only family. And considering the circumstances of my father's death—'

'Ah, yes, I see.' The priest nodded. 'I'll send Mr Semple up to prepare the grave.'

'Thank you.'

'Er.' He rubbed pale long-fingered hands. 'You are quite sure that' – he coughed – 'that your father's mortal remains will have been retrieved?'

Nausea rose at the back of Jenefer's throat. She swallowed hard and gave a brief nod. Devlin Varcoe had promised.

'In that case, let us discuss the details of the service.'

Afterwards she stopped at Jack Hammill's workshop and chose a coffin she could ill afford. Then, her head throbbing from the clam-our of things needing her attention, she hurried down the street and saw the cart, piled high with furniture, pull up at the entrance to the lane. Treeve jumped down and helped Maggie off.

Aware of villagers stopping to watch and murmur, Jenefer slipped quickly down the narrow passage on to the cobbled yard that fronted the row of four cottages. Maggie hurried in behind her carrying a china basin and matching jug.

'There's a table, two chairs and a chest of drawers,' she panted. 'Treeve got to go back for the bedstead and a wardrobe. I couldn't b'lieve all the stuff I found. I got a kettle, half a dinner service – some of it's cracked but least you'll have decent plates – and an old drawer with all sorts of knives and such. Oh, and an earthenware pot like we use for pickling pilchards, a couple of nice big stone jars, and a saucepan.' She glanced round then whispered, 'And a po.' She set the basin and jug down, bustled across to the range and opened the fire door. 'The whole lot do need a good wash. 'Tis all filthy dirty and covered in cobwebs. Now, first thing we—'

She was interrupted by a knock on the open door. 'Oh, 'tis you, Lizzie.'

'All right, Maggie? I seen you come back and I— Oh, beg pardon, miss.' A plump, rosy-faced woman, wearing a frilled cap and a hessian wrapper over her brown wool petticoat, pressed a hand to the kerchief crossed over a patterned bodice faded from repeated laundering.

Jenefer smiled. 'Mrs Clemmow, isn't it?'

'That's right, miss. I aren't on the nose,' she added hurriedly. 'I just thought you'd be wanting a bit of kindling for the slab. Teasy to start they are.'

'Lizzie, that's 'andsome.' Maggie took the bundle of finely chopped wood.

'Want a hand do 'ee?'

'I wouldn't say no,' Maggie beamed.

'What shall I do?' Jenefer enquired, adding as the two women exchanged a glance, 'I'm not going to sit and watch while you work. So, shall I help Treeve unload the cart?'

'No!' Maggie yelped. 'No, miss. That would'n do at all. Look, soon as we got the fire going and some water boiled—'

'I'll go down the pump while you light the slab,' Lizzie said. 'There's an old keeve up the shed.' She indicated with a jerk of her head. 'He'll do for a wash tub.'

Changing into an old gown, Jenefer rolled up her sleeves and with one of Lizzie's hessian wrappers tied around her waist, washed dust and cobwebs off the furniture Treeve and Maggie unloaded from the cart and carried round to the cobbled area outside the cottage.

Her move to this cottage would be all round the village by now. So what if Devlin Varcoe owned it? She was a tenant just like any other. He had never lived here.

Living by herself would be strange. She couldn't deny she felt apprehensive. But better to be alone than an object of pity or condescension in someone else's house. She liked Mr Gillis, and had thanked him sincerely for his kind offer. She knew the invitation had not been his idea. Nor had she felt any regret in declining.

Betsy liked Tamara. But Betsy liked most people. Being the younger she had never borne the weight of responsibility or their parents' expectations. Was that why she had been able to accept Jared as an equal, caring nothing that he was merely a fisherman with no education?

Was this, Jenefer wondered as she scrubbed and wiped, the reason – apart from her betrothal – she had tried to deny her attraction to Devlin Varcoe? The fact that when he wasn't smuggling he was a fisherman? Yet there was a world of difference between him and the rest of his crew. For a start he owned property as well as his boat.

It suddenly occurred to Jenefer that there was little to choose between her own thinking and that of Morwenna Gillis, whom she considered an appalling snob.

Shame brought hot colour to her cheeks. If she were not already a topic of village gossip, she soon would be, just like Tamara. The difference was that while Tamara had chosen to be different, she had not.

At midday Jared arrived with three pasties cooked by Inez, a jug of ale for Treeve, and a twist of paper containing some tea leaves. Jenefer shared the brew with Maggie.

By 4.15 daylight was fading to dusk, and another kettle of water was boiling on the range. Treeve returned with the cart carrying several sacks of coal retrieved from the bunker at the back of the house.

'Best I brung it up 'ere to you, miss. If I'd 'ave left'n overnight some thieving bugger would 'ave been in and took it.'

'That was thoughtful, Treeve. Thank you.' Grateful for help already given, and only too aware of how she would depend on her neighbours in the coming days, Jenefer asked him to take a bag to each of them. It still left three for her.

The table, chairs and chest, now clean and dry, had been carried inside. When Treeve returned, Henry Tozer, who lived with his son Ben in Number 4, helped him manhandle the bedstead up the stairs. As they came down, the rain that had threatened all day finally started.

Maggie was rinsing out the cloths they had used to wash and dry the crockery and cutlery. Jenefer, aching from unaccustomed physical effort, rested in one of the chairs when a knock on the door made them both look up. Maggie opened it and Jenefer heard Lizzie Clemmow's voice.

'Here's three eggs, a loaf and a pat of butter.'

Light-headed with tiredness, Jenefer pushed herself to her feet. 'Please come in.'

'No, miss. Thanks all the same. I aren't stopping. Tipping down it is.' Lizzie wiped her palms down her apron. 'Tis just a bit of something for your tea. Sam said I shouldn't come bothering you, but Maggie won't have had no time for baking, and we're some grateful for that there coal. Got a lovely fire going we have.'

'You've been so kind. I don't know how we'd have managed without you,' Jenefer's gratitude was heartfelt. The day had been difficult in so many ways. Yet it would have been even harder but for the generosity of people whom previously she had only nodded to in passing.

A tide of crimson climbed Lizzie's throat and flooded her face. 'No such thing, miss. Nor I don't want you thinking I'll be on the doorstep every whit and stitch. But if'n you do need anything, well, you know where I'm to. Right, I'm gone.'

'Good as gold she is,' Maggie said. 'You mind what she said, miss. She'll help you best she can, and she isn't no gossip neither.'

That night Maggie insisted on sleeping in the chair by the range while Treeve took the cob and cart back to the stable.

'Better fit I'm up there, miss. Fire was almost burnt out this afternoon. With this 'ere rain damping'n down there's bound to be someone on the prowl. Anyhow, can't leave master up there all alone.'

Pressing her fingertips to her mouth Jenefer nodded, unable to speak.

'You stay in the dry, mind,' Maggie warned her husband. 'I can't be doing with you catching cold.'

'Don't fuss, woman,' Treeve growled. But he stood still while Maggie fastened a piece of old sail canvas around his shoulders.

Next morning as dark full-bellied clouds slunk across the sky driven by a cold wind, Jenefer stared at the devastation and shivered inside her warm coat. The acrid smell of wet soot caught in her throat as she waited. She was glad Betsy wasn't here.

'She wanted to come,' Jared said. 'But Mother said 't would only give you more worry. She said to ask you 'bout the funeral.'

'Tomorrow.' Jenefer had had to clear her throat, unable to tear her gaze from the blackened ruins of what had once been her home. 'Jared?'

'Miss?'

'You will look after her?'

'Long as I'm breathing. Think the world of her I do.' With a brief nod he had moved away to join Treeve, Jack Hammill and Devlin Varcoe inside the ruins where they were searching for whatever was left of her father.

She clasped her hands tightly as Devlin and Jared appeared, Jack and Treeve behind them, each carrying one corner of a piece of canvas on which lay a bundle wrapped in sacking. Jenefer started forward but Maggie caught her arm with surprising strength.

'No, miss. There's no helping him now, and 't would do you no good.'

Lowering the canvas to the ground, the men gently lifted the bundle and laid it in the coffin on the back of the cart. Jack put the lid in place. Then all four men turned to Jenefer and briefly dipped their heads.

CHAPTER TEN

As the parson spoke the words of committal by the graveside, Jenefer gazed at the freshly turned earth. She hadn't expected to see so many people. Yet by funding cargoes of contraband that ranged from wheat flour and cognac to silk and tobacco her father had touched the lives of virtually everyone in Porthinnis.

Betsy held her hand tightly. Jared stood on the far side of Betsy's chair, his parents behind him. Devlin and his crew, a pale and sombre Thomas Varcoe, and a crowd of villagers clustered at a respectful distance. John and Morwenna Gillis stood with Dr and Mrs Avers. But she didn't see Tamara.

She tossed earth on to the coffin, trying not to think of what it contained. Then at last it was over. She saw Jared bend towards Betsy. Maggie took her arm and steered her gently away.

'Come on, my bird. You can't do nothing more.'

With no money to pay Maggie and Treeve their wages for the quarter, Jenefer decided to let them have the cob and cart.

'You won't arrive empty-handed and they'll be useful on the farm,' she said, as Maggie clapped her hands to her cheeks and her eyes brimmed.

'That's brave kind, miss.' Treeve twisted his hat between scarred hands. 'Much obliged to 'ee.'

Next morning, when they reached Helston, she climbed down from the cart, trying hard not to notice or care about the stares of passers-by. She hated being an object of curiosity, yet it was inevitable when her mode of transport was so out of keeping with her blue coat-dress and feathered hat. 'Thank you both for all you've done.'

'You make sure you're down by the farmer's market for ha'past three, miss,' Treeve reminded her. 'Janner Laity will be watching for you. You can ride home with he.'

Jenefer nodded. 'Have a safe journey.'

As he flicked the reins and clicked his tongue, Maggie looked back over her shoulder, her chin quivering. 'Miss you awful, I will.'

Feeling her eyes prickle, Jenefer waved then turned away. Tightening her drip on the drawstring purse containing her jewellery, she set off up the street towards the offices of her father's solicitor.

Seated behind a vast oak table on which lay three large leather-bound volumes bristling with page markers, a brass inkstand and several piles of folded documents tied with red ribbon, Mr Renfrew's helpless gesture betrayed both embarrassment and irritation.

'My dear Miss Trevanion, I wish it were not so. Indeed I do. I wrote several times to your father impressing upon him the importance of putting his affairs in order. But I fear he responded neither to advice nor entreaty.'

Rigidly upright, her hands clasped in her lap, Jenefer moistened her lips. 'So there is *nothing*?'

Clad in black, his head covered by a grizzled wig with two rigid side curls and a short pigtail, the lawyer steepled soft plump fingers over his straining waistcoat and shook his head. 'I believe you were already aware that the house and grounds are entailed and are now the property of your father's cousin, Mr Charles Polgrain? I shall be writing to inform him shortly.'

'You had better tell him that his inheritance is currently a burnt-out ruin,' Jenefer said. 'However, it is a very pleasant location. No doubt when he receives the insurance money he will rebuild.' Hearing the bitterness in her tone she immediately felt guilty. It was not Mr Polgrain's fault that the laws governing inheritance gave him a property he had never seen while leaving her and Betsy dependent on the kindness of strangers.

'Ah.' Something in Mr Renfrew's tone tightened the knots of tension.

'It wasn't renewed?'

'I'm afraid not.'

Brief sympathy for her father's heir was lost beneath a wave of anger. For months she had been trying to talk to her father about their finances. Every attempt had met with ill-tempered rebuff. Now he was dead and she was alone and penniless. Fighting the urge to scream and stamp her feet at the unfairness of it all, she stretched her mouth into a polite smile.

'Mr Renfrew, may I trouble you for the loan of a pen and some paper? As I explained, my sister and I escaped with nothing but our clothes and there is someone I need to inform of all that has happened.'

Twenty minutes later, leaving her letter to Martin with Mr Renfrew who assured her his clerk would take it to the post office with the rest of the day's mail, she shook hands with the lawyer and walked out on to the street.

While in his office it had occurred to her to ask him to recommend a jeweller. Further reflection had kept her silent. Though Mr Renfrew hadn't mentioned it, perhaps because her bereavement was so recent and the circumstances so horrible, her father probably owed him money. If he knew she had assets, no matter how small, he would expect her to settle at least part of the account.

But she still owed Mr Hammill for her father's coffin, as well as tradesmen in the village. A lawyer of Mr Renfrew's standing was far better able to absorb the loss.

It shocked her that she could reason in such a manner. But moral behaviour was far easier when you were cushioned by the comfort and security provided by money. When you had little or nothing such decisions became far more complicated.

After walking up one side of the main street and halfway down the other without seeing a single jeweller's shop, realization left a hollow in her stomach. She was in the wrong place. People who could afford to buy jewellery, or have pieces specially made, would not come here. They would travel to the wealthy cosmopolitan towns of Truro or Penzance.

Panic fluttered beneath her ribs. It would soon be time to meet Mr Laity for her ride back to the village. She peered desperately up a side road. She must have seen the sign earlier, but it hadn't registered then.

The window was grimy; the broad shelf inside crowded with oddments. She glimpsed boots, an inlaid needlework box, an ivory-headed walking cane, decorated vases, and a small circular table on which lay several dusty ostrich plumes and a rainbow-hued pile of ribbons.

Crushing her misgivings she opened the door. Her plan had been to sell her jewellery. But perhaps this was better because she would be able to get it back. Martin would know what to do. When he received her letter he would come home at once. Then she would no longer have to cope all by herself.

The man behind the counter was over-polite and she hated the sly look in his eyes. He offered her far less than the pieces were worth. They both knew she would accept; that she would not be there unless she needed the money. With burning cheeks she put the gold and silver coins into her purse and pulled the strings tight.

She hurried outside, her heart thudding as relief battled with guilt, and retraced her steps to the main street breathing deeply to rid her lungs of the shop's pervasive smell of mustiness and despair.

She shopped carefully for necessities she could not buy in the village. Then, recalling the hours Betsy had spent embroidering new seat covers for the dining-room chairs, all lost in the fire, she bought canvas and skeins of coloured wool. She arrived down at the market on time, out of breath, and laden with parcels.

Sitting beside Janner Laity, grateful that his taciturnity meant she was not obliged to talk, Jenefer's brief euphoria was swamped by renewed anxiety. Yes, she had money now. But how much would be left after she had paid Devlin Varcoe a quarter's rent and settled accounts with the village tradesmen? She had nothing else to sell or pawn. She would have to find work of some kind. But what? What could she actually *do*?

*

Tamara pushed her silk-stockinged feet into cream kid slippers and picked up her gloves. As she drew them on, tugging the soft kid up to her elbows, she turned and caught sight of herself in the long glass.

She had chosen a round gown of apple-green figured muslin with short puffed sleeves and a wide neckline trimmed with lace and matching ribbon. It was her own design based on the new fashion for high waists shown in the ladies magazine for which her mother paid a yearly subscription of three guineas. The colour suited her and it was important that she looked her best. Held back from her face by a broad bandeau of the same green ribbon, her hair tumbled in loose curls down her back.

This past week she had felt more than usually tired. But as she was not sleeping well that was hardly surprising. At least her appetite had returned. In fact her rides or long walks made her ravenously hungry, though strangely she could no longer bear the smell of coffee.

She thought little of it. She was rarely ill and whatever had ailed her had passed. Which was fortunate, because this evening she would need all the strength she could summon.

The Christmastide Dance was being held in the long room at the Five Mackerel. The entire village would be there. Even those who followed Wesley and abhorred spirits would set aside their scruples tonight. She *had* to attend. If she cried off, her mother would want to know why. And what could she say?

She would *never* believe that he had felt nothing, that it had meant nothing. Yes, he was hard and ruthless. But during that magical hour she had glimpsed a vulnerability few would ever suspect.

Though he had little patience with the law, he possessed a strong sense of justice. She had been true to her feelings and honest with him. Why then had he behaved so cruelly?

With no answer and no comfort she told herself the loss was his. She would not hide from him. As for the grievous wound his rejection had dealt her, it would heal, eventually. Meanwhile she would say nothing, even to Roz. Roz never gossiped. But Roz had problems of her own. Better to remain silent and carry on as normal. No one but she would know the effort it cost.

Devlin prowled the room behind people clapping and laughing as the small orchestra at one end perspired and played for all they were worth and dancers whirled, skipped, linked and parted. The long room was crowded. Thirst had driven some to the taproom. Others sought escape from the crush and noise in the saloon and dining parlour.

The heat generated by sweating bodies and the ovens in which sufficient roast beef and plum pudding had been cooked to feed the entire community had forced a few outside to catch their breath in the chilly night.

Devlin had eaten, drunk and laughed with his crew and their womenfolk. Usually he enjoyed Feast Days. This one held no pleasure for him. Nor, it appeared, for Jared. Devlin had heard him telling Sam and Lizzie Clemmow that being in mourning and unable to come, Betsy and Miss Trevanion were keeping company for the evening.

A head taller than those in front of him, Devlin watched the dancers. A smile touched his lips as he caught sight of Arf and Inez breathless and laughing as they circled. But it faded as his gaze moved on, seeking, finding, instantly shifting away but inevitably drawn back.

Knowing Jared would leave soon, Devlin toyed with the idea of going with him. He could offer to escort Miss Trevanion back to the cottage. With the streets crowded and noisy with drunken revellers, no well-bred girl should be out alone. Instantly he recalled a rain-filled night, another girl, and events best not remembered but impossible to forget.

He had spent most of this evening as far from her as possible. All his life he'd been aware of an emptiness in his heart, something missing. When he was younger he had tried drinking to escape from it. But the effect was too brief and its aftermath both painful and unpleasant. Risk and danger filled the void.

His reputation had grown out of his daring, his fearlessness. Only he knew how hard it was sometimes to resist the lure of death, the promise of escape from a loneliness no amount of company could assuage.

Sexually experienced, he had never loved. But in Tamara Gillis's arms, for the first time in his life he had *belonged*. For an all-too-brief moment he had known peace. He craved more and hated her for that. He relied on no one but himself. Even Jared, once closer than a brother, was drawing away. Once married to Betsy Trevanion things would never be the same.

Standing apart he watched Tamara laugh and flirt. He saw wives and mothers whisper together and click their tongues; heard husbands scold them, arguing she was just a pretty maid enjoying herself and doing no harm.

He heard murmurs of sympathy for Morwenna Gillis at the impossibility of controlling such a flighty piece, and others criticizing her for not trying harder. Most agreed it was a wonder Tamara hadn't got herself into the kind of trouble no pert smile or flashing eyes would get her out of.

He listened to it all as he stalked up and down the room, outwardly relaxed, pausing now and then to exchange word or laugh at a joke, and told himself he'd been right to back away. So what if he couldn't sleep, jumped at unexpected sounds and his guts felt as if he'd swallowed fishhooks. He'd get over it. If he wanted company tonight he'd be spoiled for choice. That's what he should do. But he knew he wouldn't.

He watched her banter and flash teasing smiles. How dared she? Those women were right. She had the morals of an alley cat. *She had come to him a virgin. What then of his morals?* It was different for men. *She had been innocent yet without coyness or pretence. She had met him as an equal: passionate, tender, wild and gentle. He had never felt, never imagined—* He shook his head to stop the incessant argument and shut off the memory. Instantly another took its place: her face, wounded, defiant, *valiant*.

She didn't know him. For if she did, how could she talk of love? As he watched his anger flared again. She was a mother's nightmare. Morwenna Gillis was a foolish woman but Tamara would try the patience of a saint. With her passion for life and impatience with society's restrictions, she was a danger to herself and others. Yet while her mother clung to rules and standards set by others, Tamara followed her own path. He knew better than most what courage that required.

A brief hiatus opposite caught his attention. His brother, resplendent in evening dress, his shirt points so stiff with starch he could barely move his head, made an elegant bow to Morwenna Gillis who fluttered her fan and greeted him with smiles and simpers.

Oblivious to the throng milling around him, Devlin's gaze was riveted on Tamara as Thomas bowed to her and gestured towards the floor where people were lining up for the next dance. Tamara hesitated. Her mother urged her forward.

Raising her head Tamara looked directly at Devlin. *Coward*. He heard her voice as clearly as if she had spoken, yet her lips hadn't moved. Then she turned and gave Thomas her hand. He murmured something to which she responded with a polite nod as he led her out on to the floor.

The orchestra struck up with an opening chord and the dance began. Devlin strode towards the door. People looked up, saw his expression and stepped aside. No one tried to stop him.

As she and Lizzie approached the quay Jenefer heard women's voices, raucous and uninhibited as they laughed and chatted. Built at the rear of the quay a few yards from the harbour wall, the pilchard cellar had huge wooden double doors mounted on iron wheels. Rolled back as they were now, they revealed granite walls glistening with salt and fish scales.

The instant the women saw her they fell silent. Schooled in social etiquette Jenefer knew how to put strangers at their ease, but instinct told her that party manners would not work here. Self-conscious, acutely aware of being out of place, she cleared her throat.

'Good morning.' Her voice sounded tight and a flush climbed her throat. One or two mumbled a greeting then fell silent. They were as uncomfortable as she was. She should leave, go back to the cottage. But then what? She needed money and this was the only place she could earn any.

The stone floor ran with a mixture of salt water, blood and oil oozing from the large square piles of gutted pilchards layered with salt stacked against the back wall. The stench was overpowering. Jenefer felt her stomach contract. She swallowed hard.

'This 'ere's a towzer,' Lizzie Clemmow handed Jenefer a rough apron. 'He'll keep the worst off.'

As she tied the coarse sacking over her oldest bodice and petti-coat, Jenefer shivered. Even her thick woollen shawl, crossed in front and knotted behind, wasn't enough to keep out the cold breeze that ruffled the grey water with white caps that slapped against the quay.

A stocky woman wearing several ragged kerchiefs over a brown bodice and serge petticoat shoved her way through the silent group to stand directly in front of Jenefer.

'Well?' She planted her hands on broad hips. 'What d'you want? There idn nothing 'ere for the likes of you.'

Jenefer was startled and bewildered by the woman's open hostility. 'I've come to work.'

'Ha! What would you know about work?'

'Shut your gob, Mary-Anne,' Lizzie retorted, steering Jenefer towards a pile of fish stacked against back wall. 'Always making trouble you are.'

'She got no business 'ere,' Mary-Anne insisted, looking to the other women for support.

'She got as much right as you or anyone else,' Lizzie snapped.

'Always on the drip you are, Mary-Anne,' someone added wearily.

'Poor soul just lost her father,' said a voice at the back.

Mary-Anne whirled on the speaker. 'She idn the only one. Least he died in his own bed. Weeks it was before my Charlie was found. Or 'ave you forgot that?'

'Some chance,' a voice muttered. 'Wi' you always throwing it up to us.'

The women returned to their work and the buzz of conversation resumed. But Jenefer was aware of sidelong glances and whispers.

'Make no mind, miss,' Lizzie murmured. 'Mary-Anne is always craking up 'bout something.'

'Was Charlie her husband?'

Pursing her lips Lizzie gave a brief nod. 'Drowned, he did. Washed up down Rinsey way a couple of weeks ago, what was left of'n.'

'I'm sorry,' Jenefer said. 'Does she have any children?'

Lizzie shook her head. 'Good job too. Charlie Grose was a 'andful on 'is own. Mind your feet now, 'tis some skiddery.'

Lizzie explained that the pilchards had been gutted and bulked to allow the layers of salt to soak all the blood and moisture out of them. Now they needed to be packed in barrels.

'Lay the pilchards in a circle, heads to the edge, tails to the centre, see?' Lizzie demonstrated, her movements quick and sure. 'Each hogshead do hold about three thousand. When 'tis full, he's moved back there,' she gestured, 'and the pressing stone is put on top. The train oil comes out of they holes down the sides.'

'What happens to the oil?' Jenefer asked, dreading having to touch the wet, cold, salted fish.

Lizzie glanced up. 'We do keep some to use for lamps. The rest is saved in barrels and took by sea to Penzance. Then it go by schooner up to London. Mind the salt now. Brush'n off to the side. 'Tis scarce so we have to use'n again. All right? I'll leave you get on.'

'Mrs Clemmow?' Jenefer tore her gaze from the oozing pile. 'How – how much will I be paid?'

'Same as the rest of us,' Lizzie replied. 'Fourpence each hogshead.'

Thomas Varcoe crossed his legs and looked at the man on the far side of the desk who wore the king's coat denoting his rank as a Collector.

'You're new to this area, Mr Eddy. You want to make your mark and clear this part of the coast of smugglers. I can help you achieve that.' He flicked a speck of lint from his breeches.

The Customs Officer leaned back in his chair. His expression was sceptical, but Thomas saw the gleam of interest in his eyes. 'Indeed, Mr—? I didn't catch your name.'

'I didn't give it. My name doesn't matter. My information does.'

'What information is that?'

'You've heard of Devlin Varcoe?'

The officer's face darkened. 'Who hasn't?'

'How would you like to be the man who catches him?'

Eddy snorted. 'Plenty have tried.'

'But they didn't have your advantage.'

'What's that then?'

'What if I were to tell you that he will shortly be making a run to Roscoff.'

'You're sure about this?'

Thomas suppressed a smile. 'I am absolutely certain.'

'How—?'

'Mr Eddy,' Thomas interrupted. 'You and I both know that despite your best efforts, and those of your colleagues at Penzance and Falmouth, you will never be able to stop the trade in contraband. The rewards are too great for all involved. There will always be some brave or foolhardy sailor willing to risk the rope in order to turn a profit, just as there will always be men of substance willing to invest in those cargoes. A man of good sense would not waste his time trying to achieve the impossible.'

'So what are you offering?'

'In exchange for information that will guarantee you the capture of a notorious smuggler, you might be prepared to relax your vigilance on certain days of the month, for which you would, of course, be amply rewarded.' Thomas paused, watching the Customs Officer whose frown indicated rapid thought.

'Are you offering me a bribe?'

Thomas smiled. He saw through the bluster to the underlying interest and clamped down hard on his growing excitement. 'I wouldn't be so foolish, Mr Eddy,' he said smoothly. 'I had the pleasure of dealing with several of your predecessors, men whose salary rarely reflected the demands and unsociable nature of their work. They appreciated being able to spend two or three evenings a month in the bosom of their family while enjoying several glasses of fine cognac. I'm told their wives and daughters were delighted with the gifts of silk and lace. This war has made such luxuries dreadfully expensive.'

'My predecessors here?'

'Indeed,' Thomas lied. 'Men who understood the natural right of Cornishmen to buy what they want as cheaply as possible. I'm sure you will not expect me to name names.'

'No, of course not,' Eddy said hastily.

Thomas pressed home his advantage. 'We are the only two people in this room. What is said between us remains between us.' He sat back.

The officer tapped his fingers on the table while he thought. Then he bent forward. 'When?'

Thomas mirrored his quarry's position, leaning forward and lowering his voice. 'I'll send word to you of the exact date. Obviously it will be dependent on the weather. Now, as I understand it, to secure a conviction the boat must be carrying contraband loaded and paid for in France. However, if I am to lose not only my investment but also the profit I would have made, then I think it only fair that you should provide the cash to pay for the contraband.'

The officer's brows shot up, then he frowned. 'I don't—'

'Think for a moment,' Thomas interrupted. 'No Preventive Officer has managed to catch Devil Varcoe. But you can. You will. Your name will be spoken with awe. You'll be famous as the man who captured the most notorious smuggler in the whole of west Cornwall.'

Thomas watched Eddy's ruddy face, and saw the instant the

prospect of fame, reward and possible promotion triumphed over anxiety about finding the money and the dubious legality of the enterprise.

'Mrs Eddy would surely like that.' He sounded wistful.

'Imagine how proud she'll be,' Thomas urged. 'How happy.'

The expressions that passed across the officer's face revealed more than he realized about his domestic situation. 'I'll do it.'

'I knew I was right to come. Mr Eddy, you are destined for great things.' Thomas rose.

The Customs Officer pushed himself out of his chair then frowned. 'What if he has time to drop the cargo overboard? I'll have paid—'

'Don't worry,' Thomas soothed. 'I'll see to it you're not out of pocket.'

'Yes, but the way I hear it, Cornish juries never convict smugglers.'

'If a signal fire is lit on-shore, it won't matter if he's dropped the cargo. And with Sir Edward Pengarrick on the bench. . . .' Thomas smiled. 'He's waited years for this.'

'What about you? What do you get out of it?'

Thomas flicked his nails across his sleeve. 'Devlin Varcoe cheated me. He took what was mine.'

'You know he'll hang?'

'I hope so, Mr Eddy. I hope so.'

CHAPTER ELEVEN

'Don't take on, miss,' Lizzie murmured, as Jenefer fought tears. 'They don't mean nothing by it. 'Tis just – well. . . .'

'I'm too slow.' Never in her life had Jenefer felt so wretchedly cold and tired.

'You'll be quicker once you get the hang of it. We been doing it years.'

Jenefer shivered, pulling her shawl closer. 'You're very kind,

Lizzie. But I've been here a week now. Mr Tonkin has moved me from one job to another and I've been hopeless at all of them, especially the packing.' Though she had done her best, the other women had each filled a hogshead before she had managed to set half a dozen layers.

'Well, 't isn't no wonder. You never done nothing like this before.' Lizzie dropped her voice to a whisper. 'I tell 'e what. You pass 'em to me, I'll pack 'em, and we'll split the money. All right?'

Jenefer accepted gratefully. But Lizzie's generosity provoked comments that varied from mocking to spiteful.

'Shut yer yap, the lot of 'ee,' Lizzie snapped. 'No one asked you for help so you got no call to complain.' As the mutters subsided she turned to Jenefer whose face was burning. 'Make no mind,' she advised quietly. 'They do tease anyone new.'

Jenefer knew perfectly well that the women resented her presence among them as much as she hated having to be there. She also realized that she had put her new neighbour in a very uncomfortable position. Yet without Lizzie's assistance it would take her all day to fill one hogshead: hours of backbreaking labour for fourpence.

She would never get used to such work. It was boring, repetitive and disgusting. 'How do you face this every day?' she asked quietly.

Lizzie's expression reflected surprise at the question. 'Glad of it, we are. Usually the shoals come between harvest and hallowe'en. 'Tis rare the fish coming December-time so we been lucky that way. But there won't be no more now. Still, we've made good money. Good job too. What with the poor 'arvest and the bleddy war, prices 'ave gone up dreadful.'

'If the pilchards have finished what will you do now?'

'Once the nets been dried they'll be put up in the lofts and we'll mend 'em ready for next year. It don't pay much, but 'tis nice to have a bit of company and a chat.'

For the first time Jenefer understood how her birth and position had cushioned her from the harsh reality of life for most women in the village. Her hands were numb with cold and stung from the salt. Despite the thick protective apron, every day the bottom of her petticoat was splattered and her shoes soaked with the stinking liquid continually running across the stone floor. No wonder the women all wore thick woollen stockings and wooden clogs or heavy half-boots that laced up the front like those of farm labourers. She breathed deeply, inhaling dank chilly air that stank of fish. Would she ever get the foul stench out of her nostrils?

By the time they left the cellars to walk home, Jenefer had come to a decision. 'Lizzie, I'm really grateful, but you can't go on helping me. It will cost you too much.' Lizzie opened her mouth but Jenefer wouldn't let her speak. 'I don't just mean money. Apart from the fact that you're really good at what you do and I'm useless, if you spend any more time with me you'll lose your friends. I don't want that to happen. I'm going to look for something else.'

Lizzie's forehead puckered. 'Like what? If you don't mind me asking,' she added hurriedly.

'Of course I don't mind,' Jenefer smiled. 'You've been so kind. I don't know what I'd have done—'

'No such thing!' Lizzie blushed.

'Anyway, it's painfully clear I'm more hindrance than help in the cellars. I've been trying to think of alternatives. There must be something I can do to earn money.'

'Good with a needle, are you?' Lizzie suggested.

Jenefer shook her head. 'No, that's Betsy's talent. She's wonderful. She does all sorts from dressmaking to embroidering cushion covers. And she can paint.'

'I 'spect it helped after the accident,' Lizzie said. 'Took her out of herself. After I lost my youngest to fever I'd 'ave gone mad if it hadn't been for Ernestine. Had me making new shirts for Sam and William. Good as gold she was. Any'ow, if you can't sew, what can you do?'

Jenefer shrugged. 'Figures. I was always good at figures. After the accident I took charge of the housekeeping. My mother had taught me how to manage the household accounts. Then Papa was in such a state I had to take on his business accounts as well.'

'There you are then,' Lizzie gave a satisfied nod.

'Yes, but where—?'

'I tell you where you could try. Percy Tresidder been in the bed for near on two weeks. Started off with a cold, he did. But when I went up the shop yesterday, Hannah was saying 'tis gone to 'is chest and he've got some awful fever. She've even had the doctor to'n. 'Tis taking all 'er time to run the shop. And Perce isn't in no fit state to do nothing.'

'It's the end of the month. All the accounts should be sent out and there'll be suppliers to pay,' Jenefer felt hope rising like a tide.

'Tight as a gin, Hannah is,' Lizzie warned. 'She don't like parting with money.'

'That's all right. I'd be willing to accept part of the payment in groceries,' Jenefer said.

Lizzie grinned. 'You would? Just you remember, she need you as much as you need the work.'

'Miss Trevanion!'

As both women glanced over their shoulders, Jenefer saw Devlin Varcoe coming up the street.

'Wish me luck,' Jenefer said, as Lizzie moved away, then wished she hadn't in case Devlin had heard.

'You'll be fine.' Nodding a greeting to Devlin, Lizzie headed towards the cobbled lane that led to the cottages.

Though Devlin's stained canvas smock, thick trousers and long boots showed he'd been working, Jenefer was horribly aware of her shabby, splattered skirt and ruined shoes as his long stride shortened the distance between them. Still, at least this encounter spared her the embarrassment of seeking him out.

'Good afternoon, Mr Varcoe. I wonder if you could spare me a few moments?'

'It would be my pleasure, Miss Trevanion.'

Her blush deepened at his mockery. She knew the stiffness in her manner was totally out of keeping with her appearance and her new situation, but it had been automatic, an attempt at self-protection.

'Settled in all right?'

'Yes, thank you.' She walked ahead of him down the narrow alley and, pulling the key from the pocket inside her skirt, opened the door and went directly to the table where she had left the two lanterns and tinderbox.

'Please come in.' Unaccountably her hands were shaking, but after three attempts she managed to strike a spark. Within moments mellow light replaced the gloom. As she hung one lantern over a nail in the beam she saw him looking around, saw the room through his eyes: sparsely furnished with shabby mismatched items salvaged from a heap of discards piled in the barn.

'You've made it very comfortable,' he said.

She glanced up quickly. Was he serious? It could hardly be more basic. Yet he sounded as if he meant it. Though with Devlin Varcoe one could never be sure.

He turned to face her, one dark brow climbing, and the room seemed suddenly smaller. His physical presence was overpowering. She moved away towards the range, widening the distance between them. Reaching up she took her purse from the mantel-shelf.

'I was hoping to see you.' As soon as the words were out she wished them unsaid. She caught the glimmer of surprise in his gaze and bent her head quickly as she tipped coins into her palm. She held her hand out towards him. 'I'd like to you to accept this.'

Glancing from her hand to her face he folded his arms. 'Why?'

The tone of that single word was enough to tighten Jenefer's skin and a sensation like icy water trickled down her spine. 'It's a quarter's rent.'

His expression hardened. 'I don't want your money.'

'I appreciate your kindness, Mr Varcoe.' She swallowed, forcing herself to hold a gaze that had become cool and unreadable. 'But I cannot allow you to be out of pocket. Nor would it do for people to get the wrong idea.'

'Wrong idea?' He tilted his head. 'And what would that be, Miss Trevanion?'

'Please don't play games with me.' He flinched, Jenefer was sure of it. But his gaze was so steady, so coldly implacable that she knew she was mistaken. It had been a trick of light and shadow. 'I must pay you rent, otherwise—'

'Otherwise what?' he interrupted brusquely. 'How will the village know whether you do or you don't? It's not my custom to spread my private business around the village. Is it yours?'

Jenefer flushed. 'Of course not. But you are being wilfully blind if you cannot see that the change in my circumstances is bound to be a topic of conversation.' She took a deep breath. 'I'm engaged to be married, Mr Varcoe. Now more than ever my behaviour will be scrutinized. People love to gossip. I prefer not to give them ammunition.'

Devlin shrugged. 'I don't give a toss what people say.'

Angry, embarrassed, and resenting his refusal to appreciate her difficulties, Jenefer erupted. 'You don't have to! You're a man. Men are allowed a freedom forbidden to women. I, as you see, am not a man, and you must know that my situation is a difficult one. I am doing my best. My life has changed beyond all—' To her horror she felt the hard knot in her chest climb to her throat as scalding tears pricked her eyes. She forced them back. 'Please understand,' she entreated. 'I must observe standards of proper behaviour.'

'Do as you please, Miss Trevanion. But I won't take your money, so find another use for it. I offered you this place because you had lost your father and your home. The offer was made without conditions. I want nothing from you, and you insult me by suggesting otherwise.' As he reached the door he looked back, his eyes blazing. 'Ever since your father came back from India your family has lived off the profits of smuggling. How does that fit with proper behaviour?' He strode out, slamming the door behind him.

Jenefer stood frozen. Insult him? She hadn't meant – hadn't intended – a wave of fury engulfed her. How dare he be angry when her only intention had been to keep their relationship on a businesslike footing? Her hand trembled as she poured the coins back into the purse. He had no right to speak to her so. She was not responsible for her father's venturing.

Too tired to hold on to her rage, she felt it ebb, and found herself viewing her offer of payment through his eyes. She had simply been trying to do what was right. He had seen it as rejecting a kindness, turning it instead into a business transaction.

He didn't understand. Pulling the wooden chair from under the table she sank on to it and buried her face in her hands. But the reek of fish forced her head back. She dropped her hands to her lap and closed her eyes.

Their relationship? There was none, never had been, never would be, and she had been foolish to think otherwise. Her suspicion that he felt some attraction to her had been mere wishful thinking. He didn't. He had made that only too clear. Which was exactly as it should be.

Devlin Varcoe was undeniably an attractive man who, when he chose, displayed surprising charm. But there was a darker side to him that hinted at danger. He was too ruthless, too outspoken: too careless of convention.

Rules, obligations and the demands of her position in society had shaped her life, made her the person she was. But the realization that in his eyes she was somehow *less* both unnerved her and sapped her confidence. Her self-image based on how others perceived her was all she had left. Yet such things meant nothing to him.

Suppose, just suppose he actually had been interested. She shook her head. Loneliness and Martin's prolonged absence lay at the root of such notions. But they were just foolish dreams. It would never have worked.

Marriage to such a man would mean living in fear: fear he might drown, or be shot, or captured. *Fear he would tire of her*. She had neither the resource nor the courage for such a life. It was different for Betsy. Jared adored her and she loved him. Jenefer wondered if Devlin Varcoe was capable of loving anyone.

Devlin stormed towards the harbour and his loft. But after unlocking the door and banging it shut behind him he stood still. Why was he angry? By offering to pay him she had intended no offence. She had explained her reasons. And now he thought about them they made good sense, at least from her point of view.

So why was he so angry? As he faced the truth his temper cooled. While he had been standing in his cottage kitchen, observing the efforts she had made to turn an empty shell into a passably comfortable home, his attraction to her had dissolved like morning mist in sunshine.

She was a pretty young woman; her old clothes and the stink of fish could not hide that. And she was doing her best to adjust. But she would have to let go of the past. As the colonel's daughter she'd had status. That had died in the flames. Given her current situation, he doubted even Erisey's return would restore it.

A break in the weather brought brisk mild breezes, fast-moving cloud and occasional glimpses of wintry sunshine. Discarding their guernseys, Devlin and his men rolled up the sleeves of their woollen shirts. They lifted the pilchard nets out of the lugger and draped them over the harbour wall to dry. All along the small harbour other crews were doing the same. Some hung their nets on ropes slung between the masts, or across spars jammed into crevices in the rock face. Others spread them on south-facing moorland above the cliffs.

In the barking sheds fires were lit under vats filled with water and shredded oak bark. Mackerel nets were brought down from the lofts and steeped in the liquid to preserve them.

While Danny and Billy, Sam and Joe hauled the dripping nets out of the vats and over a roller to allow them to drain, Andy and Ben dipped the sails. The tanning liquid restored their distinctive brown colour while strengthening the coarse fabric against the harsh effects of wind and salt-spray.

While Devlin made minor repairs to the hull, Jared was in the workshop making new blocks for the mainsail rigging. Then he joined Devlin on the lugger where he spliced and whipped frayed ropes.

'Arf and Inez getting on with their new lodger?' Devlin teased. Once Jared's home had been his as well. Even after he moved into the loft, calling in on them had felt familiar and comfortable. But it wouldn't be like that now. Betsy Trevanion had taken his place. Yet seeing Jared's happiness how could he begrudge the change?

'Settled in lovely, she have,' Jared grinned. 'Some clever with a needle, she is. She've started making a cushion for Father's chair.'

'She's a clever girl,' Devlin agreed drily.

Jared caught his eye. ' 'Tidn' like that. She've got a kind heart. Mother think the world of 'er.'

'Over her doubts, is she?' Devlin asked, bent over the hatch coaming he had just replaced. He glanced up as Jared started coughing again.

'God's blood, Jared! You'll bring up your toenails next. You shouldn't have come down today.'

Thumping his chest, Jared rolled his eyes. 'Don't you start.' He sat gasping for breath, arms resting on his bent knees. ' 'Tis a bugger though,' he spluttered, his eyes streaming.

Devlin sat back on his heels. Jared's cough and the wheezy rattle in his chest had worsened since yesterday. 'What was that stuff Inez used to give us when we were young?'

'Treacle and vinegar,' Jared replied between coughs. 'Bleddy near afloat with it I am. When I come out this morning she was going up the village to get goose grease and camphor. 'Tis all right you laughing,' he said gloomily as Devlin tried and failed to hide his grin. 'I got two of 'em on to me now.'

Dismissing the tiny pang, for it would drive him mad to have women fussing around, he reached for the pitch pot, checked it was still hot and began to brush thick black pitch around the joint between the new coaming and the deck.

'No wonder, when you sound like that. Go home and go to bed.'

'I'm all right.'

Devlin sat back on his heels: noticed the hectic flush, the glittering eyes. 'No, you're not.' Leaning forward he touched the back of his hand to Jared's forehead.

'Get off!' Jared jerked back. 'Bad as mother, you are. 'Tis just a cold.'

'You're burning with fever and Inez will blame me.'

Jared grinned weakly. 'Scared of her, are you?'

Devlin nodded. 'Too right I am. I've seen her temper. Go on, you're not fit to be out.'

'What about. . . ?' Jared's gesture encompassed the ropes he'd been working on.

'One of the others can finish them. Go home, dammit!'

After Jared left Devlin worked on for a couple more hours and completed the repairs. His crew came by on their way home. The treated nets and sails would be left to drip-dry overnight then brought to the lugger the following morning. He was returning his tools to the workshop when a movement in the doorway caught his eye. He glanced up and saw Roz Trevaskis.

'Mr Casvellan would be obliged if you'll call on him.' Her voice was soft, pitched low. Very different from her shrewish mother's whose shrill ranting could shatter glass.

Devlin straightened, 'Did he say when?'

'Tomorrow, early.' She turned away, slim as a wand. He knew little more about her now than he had two years ago when she first led the string laden with contraband out of the cove to safe hiding places inland. Perhaps, like Jared, she was more talkative with her friends.

Mist lay like a soft blanket in the valley as he followed the narrow track across the moor. Gauzy cloud streaking the pale blue sky told him strong winds were coming. But now the still air was cold against his face. In the mellow light of the morning sun, dew glistened like diamonds on cobwebs that lay like fine lace on the heather and gorse.

He rapped twice with the heavy knocker, wondering why he had responded to Casvellan's request. A Justice and a smuggler lived in opposing worlds. Yet there was a bond. Not friendship – their lives were too different. Respect perhaps?

The door opened. 'Mr Casvellan is expecting you,' the butler said.

'This way if you please.'

Leading Devlin into the same room as last time the butler retreated, closing the door.

Devlin's gaze drifted over walls painted warm pink, gilt-framed mirrors, small tables and elegant armchairs upholstered in cream silk damask to a tall bureau-cabinet. Behind a glazed door the top part held four shelves of leather-bound books. The lower section had a fall front and four drawers with brass handles and keyholes. The honey tones of the wood drew him. He leaned down to examine it more closely, running his fingertips across burled walnut polished to satin smoothness.

'Beautiful workmanship, isn't it?' Casvellan said from behind him. Devlin froze, fighting the instinct to whirl round. He straightened slowly, turning as the Justice closed the door and came forward.

'I appreciate you coming, and so promptly.'

Devlin inclined his head in acknowledgement. Casvellan did not invite him to sit, nor would he have felt comfortable doing so. He didn't belong here.

'I have a commission for you.'

'Why me?'

'It's dangerous and demands absolute secrecy,' Casvellan said drily. 'Who else would I ask?'

'What do you want me to do?'

'Carry a letter to Roscoff. I should warn you, if you are caught I can offer no assistance.'

'So the risk is all mine?'

Casvellan met Devlin's gaze. 'Exactly so.'

'What's in this letter?'

'You expect me to answer that?'

'Expect? No. Clearly it's important. You would not ask my help otherwise. But I'd like to know whose side I'm on.'

Casvellan moved to the window and gazed out over the gravelled carriage drive.

'Last year a relation of mine was sent to Switzerland on a confidential mission of such significance that it was not made known to his colleagues in the Foreign Office. Instead he reported directly to the Foreign Secretary through a trusted intermediary. The information he sent back proved accurate and extremely valuable.'

Casvellan paused. 'Unfortunately something went wrong. We do not know the exact circumstances. But he died of gunshot wounds.' He was silent for a moment.

'What of the others?' Devlin asked.

Casvellan glanced back at him. 'Others?'

'Yes, the others, the network, the people who supplied the information.'

Casvellan's urbane expression did not alter but Devlin saw increased respect in the level gaze. 'We cannot be sure. The death caused a considerable fuss in both British and French diplomatic circles. It was impossible to replace him through normal channels.'

'But he has been replaced?' Devlin guessed.

'It is vital our government knows what effect the crushing of the Paris uprising has had on the royalist movements in La Vendée and Provence.'

'And this letter?'

'Information that may keep him alive. The decision is yours, Mr Varcoe.'

Devlin's thoughts raced. The Justice was one of the few men in public life whose honesty had never been questioned. He had offered no inducement, promised no reward. Instead he had shared information known to only a handful of men in the country. The letter was vital, its delivery urgent.

But it was past the dark of the moon. The lighter the night sky, the greater the risk. Plus he would be two men short: Jared's cough ruled him out, and he hadn't replaced Charlie. But he could rely on the others to take up the slack.

Having heard nothing from Thomas, Devlin guessed his brother had been unable to raise the money he needed to pay off their uncle and purchase a cargo. As the letter's urgency meant he couldn't wait, he would make the trip worthwhile and buy a cargo on his own account. Casvellan was no fool. He would not expect a boat sailing to Roscoff to return empty.

This time though, the danger would be as great on the outbound voyage as on the homeward run. The demands of wind and tide, of steering a course while keeping clear of all other ships, would require his total concentration. He would have no time to think of anything else.

'I'll do it.'

The Justice gave a brief nod, as if the response were a foregone conclusion. But Devlin sensed a release of tension and wondered at the scope and weight of Casvellan's responsibilities.

'How soon?'

'Tonight. Who do I give it to?'

'Your uncle.' Reaching inside his frock coat he withdrew a slim packet of oiled silk fastened with a red seal. He handed it to Devlin. 'God forbid you are stopped. But should—'

'I'll destroy it. It won't be taken,' Devlin promised, secreting it in an inside pocket the existence of which would have surprised the tailor who made the waistcoat.

Casvellan extended his hand and Devlin took it.

'Farewell, Varcoe. God speed.'

CHAPTER TWELVE

Awake since before dawn, knowing she would not sleep again, Tamara got out of bed and wrapped the cover around her. Sitting in the window with a cushion at her back, she had watched the sky change from pearl grey to turquoise then primrose and finally rose-pink as the sun climbed out of the sea and turned it to liquid bronze.

Sally came in with her morning cup of chocolate. 'What you doing up? All right are you?'

'I'm fine. Really,' Tamara assured. 'I just woke early.' She smiled, expecting the maid's worried expression to clear.

Sally hesitated as if about to speak, then went to the door. 'I'll fetch your hot water.'

As she washed, Tamara's mind drifted back to the dance and the scene with her mother beforehand. She had asked to be excused from going. But after admitting she was not ill, her hope of being able to avoid it was doomed.

'I will not hear of you staying at home, Tamara. The very idea! Tonight is an important occasion. Not just for the ordinary people. All the best families will be attending. Of course, the Trevanion girls must miss it this year as they are in mourning. But even the Casvellans have been known to put in an appearance. I daresay Mr Casvellan supplied the ox for the roast. He is the most generous of men. I know for a fact he has donated blankets and coal to the Poor House. Besides, I have it on good authority that Dr Avers' nephews are visiting. They will look for the prettiest girls as dancing partners. And for all your odd ways, Tamara, you have vivacity as well as one of the neatest figures in the village. So let us have no more nonsense. You will accompany your father and me, and you will behave just as you ought.'

So, unable to escape, she had gone. Once there, pride as well as good manners had demanded she pretend to enjoy herself. She did what in the past had been effortless and pleasurable: she laughed, teased, flirted.

If Dr Avers' nephews were present they did not come forward to be introduced. While dancing she resolutely devoted her attention to her partner yet remained oblivious to his blushes and stammered compliments. Frowning matrons murmured together behind their fans and their husbands beamed at her and clapped.

Without turning her head or raising her eyes she knew the instant Devlin entered the room and felt a wave of heat engulf her from toes to hairline.

Returning to her seat beside her mother, she was catching her breath after the Barley Mow when Thomas Varcoe approached and made his bow.

She sensed Devlin's gaze. She did not look, would not look. But in her mind she saw the harsh planes of his face, the lock of dark hair that always fell across his forehead and the intensity in his eyes. Her body remembered his hands. Scarred, weathered, rough hands: their gentle touch, their brutal rejection.

Her mother's voice jerked her out of her reverie. Arch and syrupy as she twittered at Thomas, it held warning as she gave Tamara's forearm a sharp tap with her closed fan.

Fighting renewed anguish, Tamara welcomed an upsurge of anger. Using its strength she raised her head, her gaze drawn unerringly to Devlin's. His expression was thunderous.

She tilted her chin a fraction, defying him even as she defied her own aching grief. Closing her eyes to break the contact, *to shut him out*, she turned her head and placed her hand in Thomas's. They took their places and the orchestra struck up the opening chords of the dance. She responded to his fulsome compliments with an absent smile. And wondered why, when Devlin had derided and rebuffed her, his glare had held such fury.

Turning from the washstand she pulled on a clean shift. Hooking up her stays then rolling fine knitted stockings to her knees and securing them with embroidered garters, she took her green riding habit from her closet and finished dressing.

She picked up her hairbrush and moved to the window to look out on the harbour and quay, tipping her head sideways as she swept it through her glossy curls. A trading schooner had arrived.

The hatches were open and a block and tackle had been rigged. Men swarmed over the schooner and quay like ants: unloading sacks and crates, rolling barrels up to the cistern to be filled with fresh water, making minor repairs and bringing hogsheads of train oil from the cellars. Even through the closed window she could hear the rumble of the barrels, the squeak of iron wheels and the men's shouts.

Inshore fishermen sculled small boats out to their crab pots. She knew cutters would be working on the beach and in the coves gathering oreweed. The Casvellans owned most of the farmland to the west of the village and bought seaweed to enrich the poor soil.

Automatically she scanned the harbour. Several luggers were still tied up, their crews stopping to chat as they manhandled nets.

Was he fishing today? Which boat was his? Hearing her mother shriek she froze, the brush suspended. More demanding cries, a babble of excuse or explanation, then a door slammed. Tamara felt the all-too-familiar sinking beneath her ribs. *What was it this time?*

Replacing the brush on top of the chest, she picked up the ribbon that matched her riding habit and tied her hair loosely at the nape of her neck.

There was a quick tap on the door and Sally whirled in. Closing it quietly she looked at Tamara over her shoulder, her face puckered with anxiety.

'Miss, I'm some sorry. I didn't mean no harm, I swear. Only I wasn't expecting it. So when mistress asked I never 'ad time to think and it just slipped out.'

Baffled, Tamara stared at her. 'Sally, I've no idea what you're talking about.'

'Your rags, miss,' she hissed, and jumped out of the way as her mistress flung open the door.

Ducking her head, Sally folded her hands over her apron and hunched her shoulders as if trying to make herself smaller.

Morwenna glared at her. 'What are you doing in here?' Swathed in a bed-gown trimmed with ruffles of lace, her hair covered by a voluminous frilled cap, she inhaled from her vinaigrette, wincing at its acrid pungency.

'Mama—'

'Hush. I'll deal with you in a moment.' Leaving Tamara smarting and even more bewildered, she turned to Sally whose expression revealed a fear Tamara didn't understand.

'Leave us. No, wait. Fetch me some hartshorn and water. And if you speak a word of this to a living soul I'll – I'll put you out of this house without a character.'

Sally squeaked in distress.

'Mama, that's enough!'

As Morwenna pressed a lace-edged handkerchief to her heaving bosom, Tamara went to the maid who was wringing her hands as tears streamed down her cheeks. 'Don't worry. She doesn't mean it. Just go and get the hartshorn.'

Sally bobbed a curtsey, nodding frantically. 'Right away, miss. I'm some sorry.' She hesitated then whispered, 'Bring the laudanum as well, shall I?'

'Please.' As Tamara closed the door on Sally's retreating figure, Morwenna sank on to the side of the bed.

'I never imagined you would do this to us. Though I suppose I should not be surprised. How *could* you, Tamara?'

'If you would—'

'Don't!' Her mother held up a hand. 'No excuses. Just tell me who is responsible.'

'For *what*, Mama?' Tamara gestured helplessly. 'What are you talking about?'

'Don't you dare play the innocent with me! Sally says you have not used your rags since October. Well? What have you to say for yourself?'

Her rags? Tamara watched suspicion and dread chase across her mother's features and finally grasped what it was that she feared. Her hands went to her belly.

Catching the movement and the realization Tamara was too stunned to hide, Morwenna let out a shriek. 'I knew it, I knew it! You wicked girl! How could you do this to me? I tell you now, miss, there'll be no bastard child born in this house! Oh the shame of it!'

As her mother wailed about the disgrace, Tamara stumbled to the window seat and sat. Her head felt oddly light and black spots danced in front of her eyes. *A child?*

With so much on her mind days had merged into weeks and weeks into one month, then two. She had assumed her unusual physical discomforts were simply due to the shock of Devlin's rejection. When they ceased she thought no more about them. Her emotions were still all over the place. But surely she had reason enough for that? As for missing her courses, she simply hadn't noticed. The effort of pretending everything was fine had demanded all her concentration. She had focused on getting through each day without giving anyone cause to ask questions she could not answer.

'Well?' Morwenna demanded between sobs and inhalations of her smelling salts. 'Say something! Why didn't you tell me? Did you think to keep it a secret?'

'I didn't realize,' Tamara said softly. She was carrying a child. *Devlin's child.*

'Didn't *realize*? Well, you realize now. Have you any idea the trouble you have brought on us? Who is responsible?'

Not listening, Tamara relived the sensation of being in Devlin's arms: those wondrous moments when he had been part of her and she had given him her heart and soul. In those moments they had made a child. Awed by this revelation Tamara caught her breath and turned her head, jumping as her mother shrieked.

'You don't *know*? What happened? Were you set upon? Have I not warned you time and time again against riding out alone? Who was it? There'll be no prosecution. I will not have our family name dragged through the mud.' Closing her eyes she wafted her vinaigrette and shuddered. 'But he needn't think he'll get away with it.' She drew herself up, quivering with emotion as she rearranged the folds of muslin at her bosom. 'Your father will have him horsewhipped.'

'I wasn't attacked.'

'You weren't?

Tamara saw her mother's last hope vanquished by disappointment then horror.

'No, no, I cannot believe – do you mean to say – are you telling me you were *willing*?'

The revulsion that distorted her mother's face allowed Tamara a brief glimpse into her parents' marriage. Even as she wished she had not seen it, she knew a moment's sadness and renewed sympathy for her father.

'Have you no shame at all?' Tears sprang to her mother's eyes. 'I've done my best to bring you up a lady, and what is my reward? I have reared a slut!'

Tamara flinched as shock drained the blood from her face. Nausea tightened her throat and she swallowed convulsively. 'How can you say such a thing?'

'What am I supposed to say? What am I supposed to think? Oh how *could* you, Tamara? Heaven knows what this will do to your father. Well, he can't blame me. I warned him about allowing you to go wandering off by yourself. Oh, it's all too dreadful.' She collapsed on to the bed sobbing hysterically. 'Where's that girl? I need my drops.'

Sally peered round the door. Tamara beckoned her in and pushed herself to her feet. Crossing to the maid she took the small brown bottle and removed the cork.

'Miss, I don't want to make no more trouble,' Sally kept her voice low, 'but Mrs Voss 'ave just come back from the shops and she said she could hear mistress out in the street.'

'She'll be calmer in a minute.' Tamara measured several drops of the opium tincture into the glass of hartshorn and water.

'All right, are you?' Sally's eyes were huge, her forehead creased with concern. 'Looking awful pale you are.'

Tamara bit her lip, not sure if she wanted to laugh or cry. She gave a little shrug. 'We've all had rather a shock.'

'Bleddy right.' Immediately the maid clapped a hand over her mouth. 'Oh, miss, I'm some sorry. I didn't mean—'

'I know you didn't. Hold the glass while I lift her up.' But it took both of them to get her mother propped up on the pillows.

Tamara picked up the glass from her bedside table. 'Here, Mama. Drink it all. It will make you better.'

Draining the glass, Morwenna pushed her daughter away. 'Better? Are you mad? How can I feel better? What am I to do? It will be all over the village—'

'It will if you don't lower your voice,' Tamara said with quiet firmness. 'They can hear you out in the street.' She handed Sally the glass. 'Ask Mrs Voss to make a pot of tea, will you? Does she know?'

'I 'aven't said a word, miss. On my mother's life, I 'aven't.'

'I'd be grateful if you keep it to yourself for now. Mrs Voss is bound to ask why my mother is upset. Tell her I went riding on the moor yesterday instead of paying a morning visit to the Avers. My mother was anxious for me to meet their nephews. But they left this morning and now it's too late.'

That at least had the advantage of being the truth. Nothing remained secret for long in the village. Tamara knew she was only postponing the inevitable. But she needed time to think.

Morwenna looked up from the handkerchief she was shredding and demanded piteously, 'What will people say?'

'Mama, it's no one else's business.'

Morwenna's voice cracked on a bitter laugh. 'That won't stop the gossip. Unless. . . .' A thought occurred to her and she clutched at it. 'Rozwyn Trevaskis! She knows about herbs and such like, doesn't she? No doubt that mother of hers has taught her how to get rid of . . . inconveniences. You must ask her—'

'No!' It was instinctive and immediate, out before she had even had time to think. Tamara stared at her mother, shaken yet not altogether surprised by her suggestion. 'Roz is a healer, Mama. She wouldn't—'

'How do you know? How can you be sure unless you ask her?'

'No.' Tamara placed a protective hand over her stomach. 'I can't. I won't.' Whatever Roz's mother had done, Tamara knew Roz. She would never use her knowledge to cause harm.

Morwenna beat her hands on the bedclothes and rolled her head against the carved wood behind her. 'Have you no pity? Will you take pleasure in seeing me scorned and your father a laughing stock?'

Watching her mother, Tamara knew her distress was genuine but suspected her concern was for herself and her standing among the village's well-to-do families. Moments later her suspicion was confirmed.

Wiping her eyes and nose, Morwenna drew a deep shaking breath. Her eyelids looked heavy as the laudanum began to take effect. 'I have to know who is responsible, Tamara. I assume this man is not yet aware? Indeed, he cannot be if you were not.' She didn't wait for an answer. 'There is nothing else for it. He must be informed and you will be married as soon as it can be arranged.'

Moving across to the window Tamara looked out beyond the harbour to the sea. She still loved Devlin, had loved him for as long as she could remember. Marrying him, making a life with him had been her secret dream. But not like this. She didn't know which would be worse: if he married her believing she had set out to trap him, for which he would never forgive her, or if he refused to marry her.

He cared nothing for public opinion. And he had rejected her once. That wound was still raw. She had been so sure he would understand: would recognize her gift of herself as proof of her love and her commitment to him. She had been certain that though he was fighting it, what he felt for her was as powerful and deep-rooted as her love for him. Even now she still found it hard to accept how wrong she had been. His reaction had shaken her to the core. She could not go through that again.

'I can't.'

'What do you mean, you can't? Oh dear God, he's not already married, is he?'

'No!' Startled and hurt, Tamara stared at her mother. 'Do you really have such a poor opinion of me?'

'And if I have, whose fault is that? Such shocks I've had this morning. My heart is beating fit to burst.' She pressed her handkerchief to her breast. 'So don't you dare look to me for sympathy. You have brought this on yourself. But it's your father and I who will have to deal with it. Now, tell me his name. You owe me that.'

It was a fair point. Turning from the window Tamara sat on the bed and took her mother's hand. 'I did not intend this, Mama. I've never set out to cause you trouble. You see, I believed—' She stopped. It was pointless trying to explain. Her mother would never understand. 'I love him, Mama.'

Fighting the effects of the laudanum Morwenna blinked slowly and pursed her lips. 'Who?'

'Devlin Varcoe.' She watched her mother's face, hoping for a softening, some glimmer of sympathy or understanding.

'Dev—' As Morwenna's eyes widened, her face flushed brick red.

Snatching her hand free she slapped Tamara's face with all her strength. 'After what your father said, this is how you defy us? How dare you! How *dare* you! Well, he had his way, now he must do his duty and marry you.'

Rising to her feet, Tamara swallowed tears as she smoothed the skirt of her habit. Her cheek stung and burned. She tasted blood and realized she had bitten her tongue. 'No, Mama. He is not to be told. And if you go against me I will deny it.'

After a moment of blank shock, Morwenna's face twisted with misery. Wailing, she flung herself sideways across the pillows. Then while Tamara watched, the laudanum finally took effect and her mother's sobs changed to snores.

CHAPTER THIRTEEN

'Ah, there you are. I'm in a hurry and cannot stay long.'

Having worked hard all day preparing the lugger, Devlin was in no mood for his brother's pomposity. He spoke without looking up. 'Goodbye then.'

'What?'

Devlin sighed. 'What do you want, Thomas? Why have you come?'

'To arrange your next trip.'

Putting the last of his gear away, Devlin ushered his brother out into the dusk and locked up.

'You're very quiet.' Thomas made it sound like an accusation as he followed Devlin up the stone steps and into the loft.

Ignoring him Devlin opened the door, and saw at once that Inez had been in. He lit the lamp and hung it on a hook. Kneeling to put a light to the kindling he lifted the lid on the pan sitting on the brandis ready for reheating, and smelled mutton stew. His mouth watered. A bit of meat would be tasty after all the fish he'd eaten lately. He hadn't expected her today: not now she had Betsy Trevanion to look after and Jared ill as well.

'You didn't make that,' Thomas pointed to the pan.

'No.'

'So who?'

'None of your business. How are you going to settle your account with Hedley *and* pay for a cargo?'

'Don't you worry about that. I have the money.' Reaching into the inside of his frock coat, Thomas removed a soft leather bag and hefted it in his palm. Devlin heard the clink of coin.

As the sticks crackled, he laid a couple of larger logs on the fire and turned a sceptical eye on his brother. 'Oh yes?'

'See for yourself.' Thomas untied the cord and tipped gold pieces on to the table.

Devlin rose to his feet. 'Now where did that come from?'

'None of your business,' Thomas smirked.

'You still owe me the boat's share for the last trip,' Devlin reminded him. 'And, as I'm not making any more excuses for you to our uncle, that purse had better be enough.'

'It's more than enough,' Thomas snapped. 'I made a handsome profit from selling off the brandy you raised. Harry Carlyon's cargo being impounded meant there were shortages. I was able to double my price. Harry would have appreciated that.' Thomas swept the coins back into the bag, tied the cord, and left it on the table. 'So when will you go?'

A feather of unease brushed Devlin's skin. He frowned, trying to find a reason for it, then gave up. Concern about delivering Casvellan's letter was making him see shadows where there were none. He focused his thoughts on the run. 'Tonight.'

Thomas couldn't hide his surprise. 'Tonight?'

Devlin shrugged. 'Unless you want to wait three weeks for the moon to wane.'

'No. No. Tonight it is then.' He rubbed his palms briskly. 'Will you have time to arrange the string and—?'

'Thomas, you mind your affairs and let me take care of mine.'

'No need for that. I was only asking. You haven't had much warning. How will you let everyone know?'

'I'll manage.' Devlin had no intention of telling Thomas that the crew, the landsmen and Roz had all been making preparations since mid-morning. The less he knew the better. 'We'll be ready to sail by nine tonight.'

'When will you be back?'

'Depends on the wind and if we can make the tides.'

'I know that. But roughly which day?'

Devlin went to the shelf and took down a large plate and a pewter mug. 'All being well, Thursday night or early Friday morning.' As his brother nodded, still rubbing his hands, Devlin took a ladle, knife and spoon from the table drawer. He glanced up. 'Close the door, will you?'

Thomas looked over his shoulder. 'It's already closed.'

Devlin stirred the stew, then replacing the lid and resting the ladle on his plate he straightened. 'On your way out.'

Wiping up the last of the gravy with a hunk of fresh bread, he sighed with satisfaction, leaned back in his chair and stretched his feet, clad in thick wool socks, towards the blaze. He still had a couple of hours before leaving for the boat. Sailing short-handed meant that every man would have extra duties, and maintaining a sharp lookout was imperative if Casvellan's letter was to reach its destination. He would try to get some sleep.

Levering himself to his feet, he stretched. Reaching over the table to pick up his plate and the pan, he heard a quiet tapping on the door and froze. *Surely it couldn't be . . .* No, it couldn't. She would never come back. Not after the way he had— The repeated tapping conveyed urgency. One of the crew? Surely not his brother again?

Removing the bar, Devlin lifted the latch and opened the door, startled to see Morwenna Gillis wearing a dark blue greatcoat and a bonnet-style hat with a long poke that hid her face from all except the person directly in front of her.

'I must speak to you privately,' she said quickly in a lowered voice, and walked past him into the room, leaving Devlin no choice but to close the door.

'It is not my habit to make calls at this hour.' Her tone was still harassed, but Devlin noticed her gaze darting around the large room, and felt his irritation growing.

'I am glad to hear it,' he said drily. 'Now that you are here, perhaps you'll tell me why?' He indicated the chair he had just vacated. But she shook her head, smoothing her leather gloves over her knuckles.

'I won't sit. I do not intend to remain here a moment longer than necessary.'

Devlin waited. What would have brought her here? Was there a problem at the boatyard? No, John would have come himself. Was it John? Was he ill? Were there money problems?

Morwenna took a deep breath. 'Mr Varcoe, Tamara is expecting your child, and what I want is for you to do your duty and marry her.' She glared at him, her bosom heaving with agitation.

Used to masking his emotions, Devlin stared back, knowing she could see nothing of the tumult inside him. Of all the things she might have said, he had never expected this. Tamara? A child? *His* child?

'Why should you assume it's mine?' Guilt stabbed, but he bitterly resented this overwrought woman's intrusion into his home and his affairs.

Morwenna's chin jutted. 'You are offensive, sir!'

'Perhaps. But I ask again, why do you assume it's mine?'

'Because my daughter told me so. Despite all Tamara's other sins – and God knows they are legion – she is not and never has been a liar.'

Turning away, Devlin raked a hand through his hair. A child? If it existed it was his. Tamara had come to him that evening, full of news, soaked from the rain, and a virgin.

'You cannot blame me,' Morwenna began, misinterpreting his silence. 'I have done my best. But she is completely unmanageable. She believes herself in love with you.' Morwenna's irritated gesture and down-turned mouth told him exactly what she thought of that.

Devlin gripped the back of the chair with both hands. 'Why are you here alone? Why did she not come with you?'

Morwenna's gaze skittered sideways and once more she smoothed her gloves over her fingers. 'I did not think it appropri-ate—'

'Does she know you're here?'

'That is none of your—'

'She doesn't, does she?'

Morwenna's head flew up. 'No, she doesn't. She had the effrontery to instruct me not to tell you. Not tell you! The very idea. But you have a duty—'

Hot anger welled up, tightening his muscles, demanding release. Devlin shoved the chair from him. It scraped loudly on the wood floor then collided with the table making Morwenna jump.

'You presume to lecture me, madam?' She flinched and took a step back. 'You who cannot control your own daughter?' He knew it was unfair. No one could control Tamara, least of all this foolish woman. But to listen while Morwenna Gillis made demands and issued instructions was beyond bearing.

Morwenna's eyes filled. 'Mr Varcoe, I beg you—' As she held out a beseeching hand Devlin turned away.

'Save your tears, madam. They don't impress me. Nor have I patience with such wiles.' Tamara hadn't wept. Despite her naked shock, the hurt she had been unable to hide, she had not wept. Her eyes had glistened, bright as moonlit water, but she had not allowed a single tear to fall.

Grinding his teeth he strode to the fire and crouched, seizing a log and stabbing the embers so that sparks flew. Then, remembering he must let the fire die for he would leave soon, he threw the log back on to the pile in the corner of the hearth.

He heard rustles and a sniff and a sigh as Morwenna wiped her nose. 'Mr Varcoe, I appeal to your better nature.'

'My—?' With a harsh laugh, Devlin spun round. 'But according to you I have none.' He watched hot colour climb Morwenna's throat and turn her face the colour of brick.

Holding herself rigidly erect, Morwenna clung to her dignity. 'It is true, this is not a match I would have chosen. But the choice has been taken out of my hands. To demonstrate the willingness of my husband and myself to make the best of the situation, you may consider your new boat a wedding gift. It will cost you nothing.'

Her condescending smile betrayed her. Thrown this bone, he was supposed to come to heel like a dog.

Hiding his fury, Devlin strode to the door and wrenched it open. 'You have said what you came to say.'

Startled, her smile dissolving, Morwenna stared at him. 'But—'

'No buts, madam. Out,' he jerked his head. 'You were not invited, nor are you welcome.'

Morwenna gasped, her gloved hand flying to her throat. 'You can't—'

'Oh, I can,' Devlin grated. 'Leave now or I'll put you out myself.' He held the door until she had reached the threshold. Knowing she would try to have the last word he didn't give her the chance. 'I doubt your husband has any notion of the offer you have just made.' The renewed surge of colour proved him right. 'But even if he did, I won't be bullied and I can't be bought.'

Stepping outside, she turned one last time, her mouth opening. He shut the door.

The wind was brisk and cutting as Jenefer walked up the main street. She had chosen her clothes carefully, wanting to create an impression of sobriety and willingness to work, while revealing nothing of the desperation that was her constant companion, or her anger at being in her current position.

As she opened the shop door a bell jangled. She inhaled the shop's particular aroma: cheese, from the big round missing a wedge on a slate at one side of the counter, the fishy reek of train oil from the barrel in the corner, and the earthy scent of potatoes and turnips in their sacks on the floor.

Hannah Tresidder came in from a room behind the wooden counter, wiping her hands on the apron that covered her brown serge petticoat. A cap covered her hair and a muslin kerchief was tucked into her calico bodice. The sleeves were pushed halfway up bony arms.

'Morning, miss. Sorry about your father an' all. Lizzie Clemmow was in earlier. She said you might come by.'

Jenefer detected a note of suspicion in Hannah's tone. There were dark circles of fatigue beneath her eyes and strain had etched creases across her forehead and between her brows.

'Mrs Clemmow has been a great help to me these past weeks.'

A glimmer of warmth softened Hannah's harassed frown. 'Kind soul she is.' Curiosity sharpened her gaze. 'I 'eard tell you was working down the pilchard cellars.'

Hating the fact that her circumstances were common knowledge and had probably been talked about and even laughed over, Jenefer stiffened. 'I did, for a few days.'

'Never fancied it meself.' Taking a cloth from beneath the counter, Hannah gave the wooden surface a brisk wipe.

Jenefer clenched her teeth to hold back the angry retorts that clamoured for release. 'It wasn't very pleasant.'

'Well, 'tidn what you're used to, is it? Any'ow, what can I do for 'ee?'

Jenefer gripped her purse a little more tightly. 'Actually, it's more what I might be able to do for you, Mrs Tresidder. Mrs Clemmow mentioned that your husband isn't well. I'm sorry to hear that. How is he?'

Hannah shook her head. 'Proper poorly, dear of 'n. He can't stop fretting about the shop, and that do make him all mithered so he can't sleep. Then I'm up and down half the night.'

No wonder she looked exhausted. 'I know nothing about running a shop, Mrs Tresidder, but I do know about keeping accounts. I managed my father's business accounts for several years. And after my mother died I took over the housekeeping budget as well. So, I was wondering, while your husband is ill, if you might find it useful to have help with the shop accounts?'

Hannah paused in mid-wipe, her frown returning. 'I don't know about that.'

Jenefer wished she could simply smile politely and leave. But she couldn't. She needed money and for that she needed work. 'You can rely on my discretion, Mrs Tresidder. I have never gossiped and I certainly don't intend to begin now.'

Hannah shook her head. ' 'Tidn that.' She darted Jenefer a look that combined wariness with hope. 'You'd want paying . . .' She let the sentence hang.

Jenefer held herself straight. 'Yes, I would. But if we can agree an overall amount, I would be happy to take half in cash and the rest in groceries.' She waited: hoping fervently that her offer would tip Hannah's decision in her favour.

Lizzie had warned her that Hannah didn't like parting with money. 'Tight as a gin, she is. Been like it all her life. But she knows she need help. And she knows she'll 'ave to pay for it. Take half and half would you? Half cash money and half in goods?'

Jenefer had nodded, agreeable to anything that would put food on her table and coins in her purse. Now she waited, willing Hannah to agree.

After wiping the counter once more, Hannah raised her head. 'All right. You give me a month and see how we get on.'

'Thank you, Mrs Tresidder. I'm sure we'll get on very well. It will be one less thing for your husband to worry about.'

Hannah clicked her tongue as she raised the counter flap, motioning Jenefer through and into the back room. 'I'd as soon not tell'n, but I suppose I'll have to. No offence, miss.'

'None taken.' Relief loosened Jenefer's tongue. 'If he's anything like my father, he'll fret because he can't do it, and fret just as much over allowing someone else to.'

Hannah rolled her eyes. 'You got that right.' She indicated an old and battered bureau behind the door. The top was rolled open but the writing surface was invisible under several ledgers. Above them pigeonholes were stuffed with papers. 'In some muddle it is. But I've had me hands full, what with looking after he and working in 'ere.' She hesitated as if weighing a decision then blurted, 'Look, when could 'ee start?'

Jenefer didn't hesitate. 'Now, if that would suit you?'

'Now? Proper job. See, 'tidn only the bills we got to pay, like what we owe for stuff we 'ave reg'lar from the farm: the milk, cheese, eggs and veg; Percy 'aven't been well enough to make up the monthly accounts for the customers.'

Having bottled up her worry for weeks, Hannah found relief in a torrent of words. 'Whole bleddy village do know Perce is bad, begging your pardon, miss. But Mrs Blamey said she wouldn't pay nothing till she'd checked the account. The rest is just the same. Send their maids in with a list, but don't offer a farthing.' Her tirade was cut short by the tinkle of the bell above the shop door.

'It sounds as if you have a customer,' Jenefer said quietly. 'Would you like me to wait until you come back before I touch anything?'

Hannah threw up her hands. 'No, if you're going to do it, you just as well start. I wouldn't know what I'm looking at anyhow.' She bustled out, leaving the door half-open.

Jenefer glanced round at boxes, crates and sacks stacked against the walls, at jars and packages piled on shelves, and wondered what she had let herself in for. The room was part store and part office. A small fire burned in the grate and a blackened kettle sat in the hearth. Crossing to the bureau, she sat down in the wooden armchair. As she turned the topmost ledger towards her she heard voices and realized more than one woman had entered the shop.

'Well, I got no patience with her,' snapped a sour voice Jenefer recognized. 'All they airs and graces she do put on. Give us six of they taties, Han, and a couple of turnips. That girl of 'ers is no better than a cheap whore.'

'Dear life, Mary-Anne, hush your mouth. You got no call saying such things.'

'Have too. She've only gone and got herself in trouble.'

'Who says?' Another voice was scornful, then softened. 'Two bars of yellow soap, please, Hannah.'

'Tess Mitchell. Her Ernie do work in Gillis's yard and he told Tess he could hear missus yelling at Tamara.'

Jenefer gave up trying to concentrate on the figures. *Tamara in trouble?* Jenefer knew there was only one kind of trouble the women could mean.

'Get on, Morwenna Gillis is always in uproar over something.'

'Not like this. Ernie said she was screaming fit to bust her stays.' Interspersed with the voices Jenefer heard the rustle of paper and purchases were wrapped, then the rattle of the till drawer and the clink of coins.

'Whose is it? Do Tess know?'

'Well, I heard she tried for Devlin Varcoe.'

'Never. I seen 'em both at the dance and they never went near each other. Give us a small slice of that there cheese, Han, and some boiling peas.'

'That don't mean nothing,' Mary-Anne objected. 'Mind you, does-n't have to be his. Who'd turn it down when 'tis offered on a plate like she do? Men! Led by their cocks, the lot of 'em.'

'Jealous, Mary-Anne?'

'She should be. Now 'er Charlie's gone, only hope she got is a blind man on a dark night.'

This earned a snort from Mary-Anne and a laugh from the rest.

'Tamara Gillis'll never hold him.'

'He'll get caught sometime.'

'Not till he want to be.'

'I wouldn't mind an hour with'n.'

'Sarah Collins, you hussy! What would your Jack say if he heard you?'

'She'd have to wake'n up first.'

The bell jangled and the door closed shutting off the women's voices.

Turning again to the bureau, Jenefer began sorting the papers into several piles as Hannah moved about the shop. The doorbell jangled again as another customer entered, made her purchases and left, exchanging greetings with someone else on the threshold. Soon these sounds faded from Jenefer's consciousness.

It was some time later when Hannah came back into the room, pausing with a gasp that made Jenefer look up.

'Dear life! I'd clean forgot you was here. Getting on all right are you?'

'Yes, but there's quite a lot to do. Would you like me to write out the customers' accounts as well as entering all the amounts in the ledger?'

'Be a lot of work, will it?' Hannah looked dubious.

'It's not difficult, it just takes time. If you've no objection to me taking the books home, I can work on into the evenings and get it finished more quickly.'

After a moment's frowning thought, Hannah gave a shrug and a nod. 'May as well.' As Jenefer stood and began gathering all the books and papers, she added, 'I got an old string bag here somewhere. Got paper and pen have you?' When Jenefer shook her head, Hannah pulled open the bureau drawer. 'Perce do keep it all in here. Take what you need.'

'Thank you.' Adding a metal-nibbed pen a bottle of ink and a dozen sheets of paper to the pile, Jenefer's glance slid to the six-inch thick wad of used newspapers at the far end of the table. She missed having something to read, and had no idea what was happening in the world outside the village.

She indicated the newspapers. 'Might I use one or two of those to wrap everything up? Then no one need be aware of our arrangement.'

Hannah glanced up, visibly pleased by Jenefer's suggestion. 'Yes, you take a couple. Old ones they are. I do have 'em back from Dr Avers for the privy or kindling and wrapping veg.'

Jenefer steeled herself. 'I need some vegetables myself, and eggs.'

Hannah brushed red work-worn hands over her apron. 'You going to be all day on they books are you?'

Jenefer nodded. 'I'll make a stew for tonight. Then I'll probably work on into the evening.' A thought struck her. 'Candles. Do you have any beeswax or spermaceti candles?'

Hannah's mouth pursed. 'Expensive they are.'

'I know. But they give such a lovely white light. It's impossible to read using tallow dips, and the smell is awful.'

'Right, well, would you say some tatties, turnips and onions, two eggs and three good candles would be fair pay for two days' work?'

Jenefer had no idea whether the offer was a generous one. Hannah Tresidder might well be taking advantage of her, having guessed she was not used to haggling and would find it difficult. But for the moment relief vanquished doubt. Even so, she was careful not to allow either to colour her tone. 'That sounds reasonable, Mrs Tresidder.'

The following morning Jenefer cleaned the ashes out of the range into an old bucket she would later take up the garden and tip down the privy. Picking up one of the creased, earth-smeared newspapers that had wrapped her vegetables, she glanced at the tiny print, resisting the urge to stop and read it more thoroughly. But just as she was about to crumple it and stuff it into the range a name leapt out at her.

Laying the paper on the floor she smoothed it as she read, her gaze flying over the words. The packet ship, *Lady Mary*, had been involved in a skirmish with a French privateer resulting in great damage to both vessels and considerable loss of life. *Lady Mary* was the packet ship on which Martin had sailed to America.

She checked the date at the top of the sheet. It was a month old. Clearly, after returning safely from America, the *Lady Mary* had made other voyages before the unfortunate events described in the newspaper.

Jenefer sat back on her heels. Why then, in all the time that Martin had been away, and despite all the letters she had written, had she heard nothing from him? Surely he could have sent letters back via the packet ships? Anyone would think he had forgotten her. That she could even consider such a thing was very lowering. Yet what else was she to think? It was as if he had vanished off the face of the earth.

She was tired of waiting for letters that never arrived, tired of being anxious and disappointed. As soon as she had finished the month's accounts for Mrs Tresidder she would make the journey to Martin's father's house in Falmouth. If her letters had been lost or misdirected, he might be unaware of all that had happened here. Surely someone at the house would be able to tell her more?

CHAPTER FOURTEEN

Despite the early hour the Roscoff quayside bustled with activity and the babble of different languages. The lugger had made a fast passage, aided by a steady north-westerly breeze that had dropped away just before dawn. But by then the danger of being sighted by a British Customs cutter was negligible.

As the sun lifted out of the sea, and soft pastels hardened into the clear sharp outlines of a winter morning, once again the wind began to freshen. It whipped the gunmetal water of the harbour into choppy waves tipped with foam as ebbing tide and on-shore breeze fought each other.

A fleet of fishing boats were tied by their bows and bumped against each other as their crews unloaded the night's catch. Moored alongside the north quay two large trading schooners already had their hatch covers off and winches squealed as cargoes were lifted out and swung across to the waiting wharfmen. Working in relays they heaved sacks on to wooden barrows and wheeled them across to stone sheds and warehouses.

His crew behind him, Devlin ducked his head as he entered his uncle's inn at the back of the quay. A narrow passage opened into two large rooms with low beamed ceilings and dark scarred tables flanked by high-backed settles or narrow benches. In the far wall of each room was a huge hearth, the ashes cold, fires laid but not yet lit. Further down the passage a staircase led up to private dining-rooms and bedrooms for well-to-do customers needing overnight accommodation. Devlin breathed in the smell of fresh bread, coffee and fried pork, and his mouth watered.

'Anybody home?' he called.

'Better be,' Danny Pawle murmured behind him. 'Bleddy starving, I am. Me stomach think me throat been cut.'

A bear of a man emerged from a doorway behind the wooden counter that separated the casks of ale and spirits from the rest of the room. His thick grey hair was tied back with a strip of leather. He wore a blue checked shirt: the rolled-up sleeves exposing brawny forearms, a knotted kerchief around his throat, and tobacco-coloured breeches. But despite his working clothes he was freshly shaved.

Seeing Devlin a grin lightened his face. Lifting the hinged flap he came out and clapped Devlin's shoulder as they shook hands. 'All right, boy? Good trip was it? 'Morning, lads.' He nodded to the crew. 'You'll be wanting your breakfast.' Without waiting for a response he turned and bellowed in French through the doorway, his grin widening as a woman's voice called back.

'Won't be long. How about a drop of something while you wait?'

'Proper job.'

'Wouldn't say no.'

Retreating behind the counter he soon had a row of tankards lined up on the bar. 'This one's on me, boys, and a drop of the finest to warm you up. You want more you pay for it.' He turned to Devlin. 'Jared not with you?'

'He's laid up: fever and a bad cough.'

'Not like him to be ill.'

'I miss him,' Devlin said, 'as we're two men short. But we had a fair wind coming over.'

'Good health to 'ee, Mr Varcoe.' Sam raised his tankard and the others followed suit, adding their thanks. They all drank deeply.

'Sit down, boys, sit down. Eve'll be out d'rectly.'

As his crew turned and settled themselves at one of the large tables, Devlin remained by the bar. Taking the purse from inside his jacket he dropped it on the counter.

Hedley glanced from it to Devlin, his brows climbing. 'Always welcome you are, boy. But I didn't think to see you back for a while.' He nodded at the purse. 'Where did he get it?'

Devlin propped one elbow on the counter and raised his tankard. 'He said he made a killing on our last cargo.'

Hedley frowned. 'Now how on God's green earth did he do that?' Opening the purse he poured the gold coins into his palm. After frowning at them he returned them to the leather purse, pulled the cords tight and tucked it inside his shirt.

'You heard about Harry Carlyon running aground during a chase?' Devlin knew that whatever happened around the Cornish coast, within the week his uncle would know about it. 'Half his cargo was lost and the rest impounded when his cutter went down. That doubled the value of mine.' Devlin shrugged.

Hedley nodded, but his expression remained sceptical. 'I know he's your brother, but I wouldn't trust him as far as I could spit. You watch your back.'

Eve appeared in the doorway carrying two heaped plates, with two more resting on her forearms. A buxom woman of middle age with rosy cheeks and fair hair escaping from her frilled cap, she smiled at Devlin as Hedley lifted the counter flap to let her through.

'*Bonjour, Capitaine.*' Her voice was soft and throaty, her eyes warm. *'Comment allez-vous?'*

'Bien, merci. Et vous, madame?'

'Bien aussi.' Her smile and nod made Devlin glad that he'd made the effort to learn a few words of French. He knew little of her background, only that she was not Breton, but from the Vendée and had ended up in Roscoff after her entire family was massacred during government reprisals after the failed Royalist uprising in 1793.

For eighteen hours a day her kitchen produced generous servings of tasty food, winning a well-deserved reputation among merchant seamen of half-a-dozen nations as well as those engaged running contraband to England. Thus the inn had become an important source of information about the war.

While the men huddled over their food at a table, Devlin pulled up a stool and ate his meal at the counter. 'Is there any more news about our agent?'

Hedley added a shot of brandy to his coffee. 'They've increased the reward for his capture.'

'They're worried then.'

'So they should be. The Royalists won't give up. The rising in October was a much bigger threat than the one back in April. People are sick of the republic and the war. They were promised freedom and equality, but what with the Terror and all the corruption, they're no better off than before the Revolution. There's no work, no money and little food. The government's shit-scared of a rebellion. That's why Barras had the rioters gunned down.' Hedley grimaced in disgust. 'A bloody massacre it was. I reckon he's made a big mistake giving so much power to that young general Bonaparte. You mark my words, he'll be trouble.'

Devlin forked up more food. 'They still don't know who the agent is?'

Hedley shrugged. 'Some say he's an army officer, others reckon he's a merchant or a diplomat. But 'tis all rumour. I pity the poor bugger, whoever he is.'

Setting down his fork, Devlin reached inside his shirt, withdrew Casvellan's letter, and passed it across to his uncle who palmed it and hid it so swiftly, Devlin could not have said where it had gone.

'I've got one for you to take back,' Hedley murmured. 'I was told it had come from Rennes. You'll have it before you leave. More coffee?'

'No, thanks.' Devlin cleaned his plate with a chunk of bread. 'These letters—'

'No use asking me,' Hedley interrupted. 'I run this place, do a bit of free trading, and mind my own business. I'll do my bit for England passing them on. As for what's in them' – he shook his head – 'I don't know and don't want to.'

Devlin couldn't blame him. Just handling the letters was a huge risk. If his uncle were caught the punishment would be severe. He stood up, patting his stomach. 'I feel better for that. Thank Eve for me.' He turned. 'Right, boys. Time to get the cargo loaded.'

It was mid afternoon when the mail coach pulled up outside the Royal Hotel in Falmouth's Market Street. A flunkey opened the door and Jenefer climbed out, aching and weary from the bone-rattling ride. 'Excuse me, in which direction is Wodehouse Place?'

'Down 'ere.' He pointed. 'Left up Well Lane, up the steps and turn left, then turn right at the end of the street.'

'Thank you,' Jenefer said, hoping she would remember. But he had already gone, clambering up on to the roof to unload chests and portmanteaux.

Jenefer eased her way through passengers waiting for their luggage and others waiting to board and set off along the busy street. Intimidated by the noise and crowds she walked quickly and tried to look as if she knew where she was going.

She passed a pair of well-dressed ladies who had paused to look at the hats displayed in a milliner's window. Noting their double-breasted coats with the new high waist Jenefer knew she would appear to them as dowdy and unfashionable. Immediately she felt ashamed for fretting over trivialities. Far more pressing matters demanded her attention.

Both sides of the street were lined with shops: a butcher's where braces of pheasants, partridges and pigeons hung above an open front displaying joints of beef, mutton and pork on a marble slab.

A greengrocer displayed cabbages, carrots, parsnips, potatoes, turnips and bunches of herbs. An apothecary's window advertised remedies for a vast range of ailments. A cobbler sat in his doorway whipping tacks from between his lips as he attached a new sole to a leather boot. The smell of fresh bread wafted from a bakery.

Every few yards, separating the shops on the lower side, alleyways led down to narrow quays. Beyond them she glimpsed the harbour and boats of every size and rig. The wind funnelling up these alleys carried the sounds of the waterfront and the acrid reek of hot pitch, stale fish, sewage and seaweed.

She hurried past groups of seamen lurching out of inns and alehouses. While some bellowed curses and threw wild punches, others whistled and shouted lewd remarks to painted women in gaudy gowns who loitered in shadowed doorways.

She had found Helston busy, but the main street there was three times the width of this one. Here fear that two carts would surely collide, or one of the ragged urchins darting between the wagons would fall to their deaths beneath the thundering hoofs and rumbling wheels made her heart beat uncomfortably fast. She felt battered by the noise, the raucous shouting, and the pungent smells of manure, decaying fruit, rancid oil, and beer-soaked sawdust.

But at least she was here. Had it not been for Devlin Varcoe's refusal to accept the money she had offered him for rent, she could not have afforded to make the journey.

Half an hour later she walked up the steps to the front door of Martin's house. A gleaming brass knocker on the black-painted door indicated that the house had not been closed up. So someone was at home.

The door opened. 'Yes?' The elderly woman wore a plain cap. Her simple dark gown, white 'kerchief, and chatelaine holding several keys proclaimed her the housekeeper.

'My name is Jenefer Trevanion. I'm the fiancée of Mr Martin Erisey.'

'He idn here.' The woman frowned.

'I know—'

'He's abroad. Which you would be aware of, if you was who you claim to be.'

'I am aware. But I—' Jenefer bit her tongue and started again. 'Is Mr Erisey Senior at home?'

The housekeeper shook her head. 'In London he is. There idn nobody here but me.' She started to close the door.

'Wait! Please! I understand that my coming here like this is … irregular. But my father died recently and I was expecting Mr Erisey's return several weeks ago.'

146

'Well, he idn back yet.' She stepped back once more.

'Letters,' Jenefer said in desperation. 'I wrote several letters. Were they delivered here?'

The housekeeper hesitated. 'Yes, they came. And I took them down to Mr Erisey's lawyer, like I was told.'

'His lawyer?'

'That's what I said.'

'Will you give me the address? Please? It is a matter of urgency. Otherwise I would not—'

'Hellings and Vincent in Market Street. Just this side of Bell's Court.'

'Thank you.' The door closed before Jenefer had finished speaking.

Her cheeks hot, her heart thumping against her ribs at the woman's rudeness, she turned away and retraced her steps. Daylight was beginning to fade and her anxiety was mounting when she arrived at the lawyer's offices.

Waiting outside a panelled mahogany door she listened to the low murmur of question and answer. She wondered what the clerk was saying and gripped her purse more tightly. Then the door opened and the clerk gestured for her to enter. As she went in, the door closed softly on his retreating back.

'Miss Trevanion? My name is Vincent. I am Mr Erisey's attorney.'

Dropping a curtsey, Jenefer sat down on a hard chair clearly designed to discourage visitors from lingering and watched the lawyer move round behind a large oak desk on which documents were neatly stacked in piles. He was a stocky man with a ruddy complexion and a paunch that strained against his waistcoat. Jenefer saw at a glance that his black frock coat and small clothes were of superior quality, his stockings spotless and his shoes highly polished. His grizzled wig indicated a man unmoved by the fashion for natural hair.

'How may I help you?'

His tone and expression were noncommittal. But as she met his gaze the kindness she saw there eased her tension and loosened her tongue. She told him of her changed circumstances, her attempts to contact Martin and her decision to come after reading of the packet ship's skirmish in the newspaper.

'Mr Erisey's housekeeper said she was told to bring my letters here to you.'

'As indeed she did.'

'Then you know where he is?' Hope leapt, only to be dashed as he shook his head.

'I'm sorry, I don't. My instructions were to forward any mail for Mr Erisey to an address in London.'

'Where?'

'I'm afraid I'm not at liberty to disclose that information. I sympathize with your predicament, Miss Trevanion. Unfortunately it is not within my power to alleviate it.' His expression softened slightly. 'You know there might be any number of reasons why you have not heard from him. His return might have been postponed due to the negotiations taking longer than expected. Or it may be that something as simple but infuriating as bad weather caused him to delay his sailing.' Placing his hands flat on the table he rose to his feet, a clear signal that the interview was at an end.

'I am sure you would have been informed had anything untoward occurred. I fear the only advice I can give you is to be patient.' His smile conveyed both sympathy and apology.

Jenefer rose. 'Thank you for seeing me.'

Out on the street once more, her head buzzing with unanswered questions, Jenefer stood for a moment. Why had her letters been sent to London? Why would Mr Vincent not give her the address? If Martin had received her letters, why had he not replied? *Where was he?* Far from satisfied despite the lawyer's assurances, Jenefer walked up the narrow slip and into the Packet Office.

Thinking quickly, she explained to the clerk that her fiancé had been a passenger on the *Lady Mary*, the packet mentioned in the newspaper as being involved in a skirmish with a French privateer. His voyage to America had been made many weeks earlier. But he should have returned to England by now and the lack of news was causing her grave concern. Would he be so kind as to check the passenger lists for the *Lady Mary*?

The clerk opened a huge ledger, ran his finger down the page and frowned. 'What date did he sail?'

Jenefer told him. The clerk turned the pages one at a time running his finger down the list of names.

'You sure you got the date right?'

'I'm positive,' Jenefer said.

With a deepening frown the clerk turned back several pages from his starting point and repeated his check. Then he looked up.

'I'm sorry, miss. He's not on the list.'

Jenefer stared at him. 'That can't be right. Please will you look again?'

The clerk tapped the ledger with an ink-stained finger. 'Don't matter how many times I look, if it isn't there, it isn't there.' He swivelled the ledger, pointing to each column. 'That's the ship's name, that's the date she sailed and that's her destination. And this here's the list of passengers. See his name, do you?'

Jenefer read then re-read the entries. Martin's name did not appear anywhere. She moistened dry lips. 'Perhaps – that's not the only packet sailing for America, is it?'

'No, there's—'

'Then maybe he mistook the name. Would you look to see if he is on the passenger list of any of the others? Please?'

The clerk sucked air through his teeth. 'Halifax for New York, you said? Only one sailing a month, the Sunday after the first Wednesday.' He turned pages as he spoke, ran his finger swiftly down the entries then shook his head again.

'Sorry, miss. His name isn't there. Wherever he's gone, it isn't America, not on a Falmouth packet.'

With contraband safely stowed aboard the lugger, the crew took turns to stand guard and snatch a few hours' sleep.

'Get some rest yourself,' Hedley advised as he unlocked a door and ushered Devlin into a private part of the house where a room was kept ready for him. 'You'll need all your wits about you on the homeward run.'

Removing his boots, Devlin stretched out on top of the counter-pane. The mattress was soft, the linen crisp and clean, and having been awake for almost thirty-six hours he was exhausted. Yet his mind would not stop.

It seemed he had only just closed his eyes when he heard his uncle's voice repeating his name, and a hand shaking his shoulder.

'Time to move if you're to catch the tide.'

Sitting up, Devlin swung his feet to the floor and rubbed his face, feeling beard stubble rasp against his palms. 'Coffee?' he croaked.

'On the chest. Here.'

Devlin looked up as his uncle thrust a slim package sealed with red wax at him. Stained and filthy, it had clearly passed through many hands on its way here.

'Hide it well, boy. If you're caught with it you're as good as dead.'

Devlin pushed the letter into the sole of his boot, pulled both boots on over his thick socks, stood up and reached for his coffee. 'They'll have to catch me first.'

An hour later, after a meal hearty enough to sustain them for a crossing that might take until dawn, the crew hoisted the big lugsail on the foremast. Then they set the main lug and staysail for raising once they had manoeuvred their way out of the harbour, and made ready to cast off.

Devlin bade his uncle goodbye.

'You watch yourself, boy,' Hedley muttered as they shook hands. 'I know family is family and all that. But I hear things. Word is that brother of yours have got grand ideas, but not the money to match. I wouldn't trust the bugger.'

Devlin's smile was grim. 'I haven't trusted him for twenty years.'

Darkness fell quickly. The wind had backed round to the southwest and was blowing strongly. Despite her load of casks, the lugger creamed through the water. Pale clouds chased each other across an inky sky and played hide-and-seek with the stars. Standing at the tiller, keen to get as many sea miles behind them as possible before the moon rose, he sniffed the air.

'Think it'll rain, skip?' Sam murmured beside him.

Devlin nodded. 'If we're lucky.' Cold wet clothes were a small price to pay for the protection afforded by poor visibility.

Hours passed. The wind remained steady, removing the need to change course or continually shift ballast. The crew split the watch, half making any necessary sail adjustments and keeping a lookout, while the others hunkered down out of the wind and dozed.

After midnight, knowing he needed a break, Devlin turned over the helm to Sam. Sitting on one of the casks his thoughts returned yet again of Tamara. To have a child out of wedlock would disgrace her and her family. Yet she had forbidden her mother to tell him.

He could not pretend he didn't know why. He had rejected her. And he had done so with deliberate cruelty. He had only to close his eyes to see her face: the naked hurt swiftly masked by pride, anger and contempt. Day and night that image haunted him. When he was busy he could banish her. But the moment his guard dropped . . .

He had neither time nor energy to spare for guilt. His way of life demanded quick decisions, forced hard choices. Most worked. Those that didn't he shrugged off. They could not be changed, only learned from. But when he thought of her he felt shame and that made him angry.

He had not forced or coerced her. She had led him on. He had expected her to pull away, but she hadn't and then it was too late and no power on earth could have prevented what happened. Hot, breathless, her mouth so soft on his, she had clung to him. He had never felt, never known – he slammed a door on thoughts he could not afford.

Half the village would say the scandal served her mother right for assuming such fancy airs and graces, and that Tamara deserved the trouble she was in. As if a child were a punishment.

He hadn't been wanted. He knew how that felt. Would he wish that on his own flesh and blood? His father had resented and blamed him for his mother's death. His brother loathed him. The feeling was mutual.

How could he be sure the child was his? What if she had been with someone else after him? Did he believe that? He could as soon believe the sun rose in the west. He raked both hands through his hair as his thoughts coiled and writhed like smoke. She had told him she loved him. He knew he inspired fear and respect, even admiration. But love? No one had ever loved him. So how could he believe her?

He thought of Inez and Arf. They had defied his father and taken him in, cared for him. Jared was more of a brother than Thomas had ever been. Yet, despite the warmth and kindness he had enjoyed in their home, he was an outsider. But he was used to that. He had never known any different. He had no fear of solitude. Alone was safer.

'Skip!' Ben's hoarse whisper roused him from his thoughts. 'A sail.'

On his feet in an instant, Devlin automatically glanced east. The horizon was growing lighter as daybreak approached. 'Where?'

Ben pointed south-east over the starboard quarter. 'Could be a free-trader coming from Guernsey.'

Devlin pulled the eye-glass from inside his jacket. 'Andy, shin up the foremast and take a look.'

Sam and Danny gave him a boost up. Joe and Billy, who had been sleeping, scrambled to their feet.

'What's on?' Billy whispered.

'Sails,' Ben told him.

Dropping the glass into Sam's waiting hands, Andy jumped down. 'Skip, I can't swear to it, but she look to me like the *Lark*.'

Standing on top of the casks, Devlin peered through the glass. 'It is the *Lark*.'

'Bleddy 'ell, not again,' Joe whispered. 'Talk about bad luck.'

'Bad luck be damned,' Devlin muttered. 'This is no coincidence.' Snapping the glass shut he returned it to his pocket. 'I'll take the helm. Sam, you and Billy run up the jib-topsail. Andy and Joe, set the square topsail. Danny, Ben, check the ropes and sinking stones.' He heard a sharp intake of breath. But no one spoke as each man hurried about his task.

Dropping the cargo so far from shore would mean it was lost for good, the water too deep to have any chance of finding it again.

'Right, boys,' Devlin growled. 'Let's shake her off.'

CHAPTER FIFTEEN

Wrapped in her counterpane, Tamara sat in her bedroom window with her back against the folded shutter. She hugged her knees as she gazed out over the harbour to the dark restless sea beyond. On the horizon the first glimmers of dawn paled the sky. Another day.

A shuffling in the passage made her turn her head. It was too early for Sally to be bringing her hot chocolate. The door opened and her mother crept in, closing it softly behind her.

'What is it, Mama? Are you—?'

Starting, Morwenna whirled round, pressing one hand to the ruffles over her bosom. 'Oh, what a shock you gave me!' she whispered. 'What are you doing? Why are you out of bed?'

'I couldn't sleep,' Tamara said.

'Hush! Keep your voice down.' Her mother's was a harsh whisper. 'Do you want to wake the entire household?'

Tamara sighed inwardly. It was more than likely that everyone in the house was already awake. Sally would be downstairs cleaning out the grates, lighting the fires and heating water. Her father had always been an early riser. No doubt he was drinking his morning tea downstairs in his study. As for herself, she often crept out at sunrise to saddle her mare and enjoy a gallop on the moor. Though she was careful to return home in time to wash and change before her mother emerged from her room where she would have lingered over her morning tea then spent an hour dressing.

'I'm not surprised you can't sleep,' Morwenna huffed, 'considering all you have on your conscience. If indeed you have given a thought to the grief you are causing your father and me.'

Knowing any response would add fuel to the flames of her mother's anger and anxiety, Tamara spoke the truth. 'I think of little else, Mama. But why have you come? Are you unwell? Do you want me to—?'

'What I *want* is to have a private conversation with you.' Gathering up her voluminous bedgown, Morwenna moved round the foot of the bed and sank on to the rumpled blankets. The grey light from the window fell across her face as she glared at her daughter.

'I fear for my health and it's all your fault. I can't sleep, I have such flutterings and palpitations.' Her voice broke on a sob and she pressed a square of lace-edged cambric to her nose.

Tamara swung her legs to the floor. 'I'm sorry you feel so poorly. Shall I fetch—?'

'You stay exactly where you are. I didn't come in here to talk about my suffering. Though this dreadful business has put years on me. Years!' She dabbed her eyes. 'I'm here because decisions have to be made.'

Watching her mother sit straighter and drop her hands to her lap where they fretted holes in the delicate handkerchief, Tamara felt her stomach tighten into a knot.

'I went to see *that man*.' Morwenna's eyes narrowed and her mouth pursed. 'Mr Devlin Varcoe.'

Tamara caught her breath. 'Mama, I asked you not to.'

'Someone has to sort out this mess if we're not to be the talk of the village. And I won't have it. Do you hear? Your father and I have a position to uphold. I will not have our name dragged through the mud and sniggered over. I won't!'

Anxious at the deepening colour suffusing her mother's face, Tamara started to rise.

'You stay where you are, miss,' Morwenna snapped. 'I haven't finished.' She wiped her nose. 'I had every right to speak to him. But I could have spared myself the trouble. He is the rudest, most disobliging man it has ever been my misfortune to meet. And if I never see him again it will be too soon. He had the effrontery to ask why *I* had come, not you. Do you know what he said?' Spittle flecked her lips and her chest heaved with indignation. 'He said he won't be bullied and cannot be bought. Can you believe that? How he had the nerve – never, *never* have I been so mortified.' She buried her face in her hands.

Tamara closed her eyes, her heart sinking like a stone as she pictured her mother haranguing Devlin. For the man who had so easily rejected her shy declaration of love, her mother's shrill demands would have posed no problem whatever. The chilling contempt of his response made her shiver and she drew the counterpane close around her shoulders. Aching to escape, she knew she must stay.

Her mother sat up. 'Though I did my best he will take no responsibility.' She inhaled deeply. 'Still, you must marry someone. And it will have to be soon, if you – and we – are not to be the talk of the village. I have lain awake half the night worrying. And I think I have it.'

Won't be bullied and cannot be bought. Had her mother tried to bribe him into marriage? Feeling a quaking in her chest Tamara clenched her teeth, teetering between wild laughter and shattering sobs. Her mother had done the one thing certain to make him refuse.

'Are you listening, Tamara?'

She swallowed hard. 'Yes, Mama. You said you have it.' Cold sweat beaded her hairline and upper lip. Beneath the counterpane her nightdress stuck to clammy skin while she trembled. Her head felt light and her stomach queasy. 'What do you have?'

'The answer, of course. You must have noticed that Thomas Varcoe has been very particular in his attentions to you these past months.'

She had noticed. Though she had neither sought nor welcomed his interest. 'I did nothing to encourage him.'

'No, you did not,' Morwenna scolded. 'And we must be thankful your coolness did not put him off. Indeed, I do believe it may have increased his regard. You must accept him.'

Stunned, Tamara raised her head. 'But he has made me no offer.'

Morwenna clicked her tongue. 'Don't be so difficult. That it a mere detail. A little encouragement is all that is needed to bring him to the point.'

'Are you—' Tamara was about to say *serious?* But her mother's determined frown and jutting chin were answer enough. She bit her lower lip hard as she fought the urge to scream. Her eyes stung and burned with tears she would not allow to fall. 'And what of my condition?'

Busily adjusting folds of material over her knees, Morwenna did not look up. 'If we are quick there will be no need for him to know.'

Appalled, Tamara stared at her mother. 'Mama, we cannot—'

Morwenna wasn't listening. 'He must be brought up to the mark as soon as possible. Indeed, it will answer very well. Then should the child bear any likeness to . . . that man,' she shuddered, 'it should not occasion comment.'

'Devlin has stronger features,' Tamara murmured. He was stronger in every respect, his build, his personality, and his character.

'For heaven's sake, Tamara! The similarities outweigh the differences, and that's all that matters.'

'But they loathe each other.'

'What had that to do with anything? And why should it concern us? As a matter of fact, it is all to the good.' Morwenna's mouth curled in a knowing smile. 'Devlin Varcoe will not tell his brother or anyone else the truth. His pride would not allow it. As for Thomas, what possible purpose would be served in telling him?'

'Mama, I can't—'

'You will do as you are told! It is your wilful, shameless behaviour that put us in this position. Now I have found a solution that will answer all the difficulties the least you can do is show some gratitude. I will hear no more argument, Tamara. You will marry Thomas Varcoe, and that's an end to it.'

'She's gaining, skip,' Sam said quietly.

Devlin glanced over his shoulder. Sam was right. Despite cramming every spare stitch of canvas on to masts now creaking in protest under the strain, the weight of the cargo held the lugger low in the water. This not only slowed her down, it meant her angle – despite shifting ballast to compensate – allowed the choppy water to slop in over the lee rail.

Despite desperate efforts on the pump, the water was coming in as fast as it was being forced out. Meanwhile the cutter was shortening the distance between them.

Though dawn had broken, a thick blanket of cloud hovered over the eastern horizon masking the rising sun. From behind it golden rays lit fast-moving, ragged-edged billows blowing up from the west, painting them orange and purple.

'What's the *Lark* doing out here anyhow?' Devlin heard Joe ask. 'Falmouth's her area. She got no business down this end.'

'The cutter knew we'd be here,' Devlin said grimly. 'Someone betrayed us.'

'Yes, but who, skip?' Billy panted, as he worked the pump. 'It wasn't none of us,' he added quickly.

'I know that.' Devlin was impatient. 'Right now I've no idea.' His first thought, God help him, had been his brother. Yet he could not imagine Thomas paying for then forfeiting a cargo, not to mention the profit he would lose. So if not Thomas, then who? 'But I'll find out. And when I do that person will wish he had never been born.' Glimpsing the looks his crew exchanged he knew they were remembering Charlie Grose.

'That's for later. Right now the cutter captain thinks he knows who we are. But unless he gets close enough to see our faces he can't be certain.' Devlin had always kept the lugger free of a name or any recognizable feature. Her black hull and dark brown sails made her indistinguishable from any of the hundreds of Mount's Bay boats.

'Shall us black up, skip?' Ben asked.

'You all know the law,' Devlin warned. 'Get caught with a blackened face while smuggling and you'll be hanged.'

'If they catch us we'll hang anyway,' Danny said.

'They got an eye glass aboard same as you, skip,' Andy said. 'But if we're blacked up they can't tell who we are.'

Devlin gave a brief nod. 'The soot bag is up fore'ard. Sam, take the helm. Andy, here's my glass. Let me know when they ready the guns. Billy, you stay on the pump. The rest of you get the casks over the side.' Though they groaned they didn't hesitate. By dumping the cargo they were throwing away much-needed money. But to be captured with contraband on board would mean at the very least transportation, at worst the noose.

In the small space by Sam's feet, Devlin removed his boot, retrieved the letter and stuffed it inside his shirt then pulled the boot on again. He could see the craggy cliffs of the Lizard ahead on the starboard beam.

'Skip!' Andy yelled. 'They're getting ready to—'

The gun's boom rolled across the water. Devlin saw the splash about fifty yards behind and to port.

'Bastard's trying to push us on to the Lizard,' Ben cried.

'Get those casks over,' Devlin snapped.

'They're reloading,' Andy called.

'Skip!' Joe shouted urgently. 'Squall coming!'

Following Joe's pointing finger Devlin saw a low-lying mass of purple-black cloud and beneath it a rippling curtain whose lower edge churned the sea into froth. It was heading for them at frightening speed.

'Get that topsail down! Drop the jib-topsail! Put a reef in both lugs,' Devlin roared and seized the tiller from Sam. 'I've got her. You help Danny.' As he spoke the wind suddenly dropped, and the sound of the men's grunts as they left the cargo to struggle with ropes and canvas seemed unnaturally loud. Watching them, seeing teeth bared with effort in soot-streaked faces, Devlin missed Jared keenly. They were a fine crew and they were doing their best. But there was too much to do and too few of them to do it.

Glancing back he saw the cutter enveloped by the squall as it hurtled towards them. The hissing of a million angry snakes grew louder. 'Brace yourselves,' he yelled. The wind returned with a mighty buffeting roar. Canvas snapped and the masts creaked loudly beneath the pressure of the straining sails as the lugger leapt forward.

Rain lashed down. It stung exposed flesh, rinsed off the soot and hit casks and deck like a cascade of lead shot. It pierced canvas smocks, thick oiled wool sweaters and shirts to soak and chill the skin. The noise was deafening, visibility non-existent.

Then, as swiftly as it had begun, the rain stopped as the squall heading towards the coast, masking the land behind its thick veil.

Wiping his wet face, and raking back his dripping hair, Devlin looked over his shoulder. Not only was the cutter still there, it was closer.

'Come on, move! Get rid of that brandy. Sam, take the helm.' Another boom echoed across the water. Crouching in the well, Devlin took the letter from inside his shirt. Casvellan had warned him and so had his uncle. Though he dared not keep it, it might yet save them.

Breaking the seal he unfolded the thick damp paper. It wasn't one letter, but two, one concealed inside the other. On the inside of the outer sheet were a few scrawled words. He tipped it sideways to catch the light and read, *Roscoff, end Feb, M.E.*

The letter inside was addressed to Lord Grenville. He hesitated, but it was too late now to turn back. Another boom echoed. This time he heard the ball howl past and Danny cursed as it splashed a fountain of water into the boat.

'Skip,' Sam's mutter was urgent. 'The next one will sink us.'

Icy rage surged through Devlin but he kept his voice low and level. 'Get the rest of those casks over the side. Sam, prepare to heave to. Danny, wave to let them know we're surrendering. Clean your faces all of you. Look sharp.' Turning away he broke the seal.

Ignoring the crew's mutters and the cutter captain's bellowed instructions, he skimmed the salutations.

. . . growing rumours of negotiations between Royalist factions and Louis XVI's brother, the Pretender to the throne. But while new landowners fear that a Royalist restoration would deprive them of their property, anger and dissatisfaction with the current regime indicates that a military coup appears not merely possible but increasingly likely. One name heard ever more frequently is that of General Napoleon Bonaparte. Despite his young age – he is but 29 – he is known to be an exceptional soldier and administrator. His defeat of the Royalist uprising in October of last year has fuelled his ambition and must consolidate his claim.

Sir, Having become a liability to my sources and with the risk of discovery or betrayal increasing daily, I shall head west. I hope to reach Roscoff by the end of February and pray for safe passage back to England. Your obedient servant, M.E

M.E? Devlin heard his uncle's voice. Some say he's an army officer, others reckon he's a merchant or diplomat. M.E. Martin? Martin Erisey? Jenefer Trevanion's fiancé? But wasn't he supposed to be in America on some diplomatic mission? Yet what better cover than for everyone to believe him on the other side of the Atlantic?

'Skip,' Sam muttered urgently. 'They're almost on us.'

Swiftly wrapping the letters around a lump of iron ballast Devlin dropped them overboard and watched them sink. Then rising to his feet he took the tiller. 'Drop the sails,' he ordered. As the lugger slowed, the cutter came up on the weather side. Several of her crew lined the side armed with pistols.

'We're done for,' Andy whispered.

'Stand fast, boys,' Devlin said quietly. 'No resistance, no heroics. Just do what they tell you. They have us now, but they won't hold us. You have my word on it.'

Back home from Falmouth, reeling from exhaustion and the shock of her discovery, Jenefer collapsed into bed and slept for six hours. Waking with a start just after dawn, her brain seething with questions to which she had no answers, she lit the range and made a pot of tea. Feeling stronger after two cups and some bread and butter, she washed and dressed, put on her hat and coat and hurried through the village, desperate to talk to Betsy.

Inez opened the door to her knock. 'Miss Jenefer! Dear life! You're out some early.'

'Good morning, Mrs Sweet. I'm sorry to call at such an hour, but I need to see my sister.'

Inez shook her head. 'Better not, miss. Proper poorly she is. Nothing to worry about,' she added quickly. 'Just this here chesty cold. 'Tis all round the village. Up half the night coughing she was, poor little maid. Wore her out it did. I mixed up some butter, sugar and vinegar to soothe her throat. She's sleeping now. Best leave her be. She'll get over it all the quicker.'

Bitterly disappointed, Jenefer did her best not to let it show. 'You're right. It would be wrong to disturb her. When she wakes up, please tell her I called, and that I hope she feels better very soon.'

'I'll tell her the minute she wake. Begging your pardon, miss, but you're looking a bit wisht yourself. All right are you?'

'Just a little tired.'

'Well, you look after yourself. Wouldn't do for you to catch it. Leave it a few days. Miss Betsy should be on the mend by then. You can have a nice chat, and I'd take it kindly if you'd stop for a bite of tea.'

'Thank you, Mrs Sweet. Betsy is very fortunate to have found such kindness.'

'No such thing,' Inez's cheeks pinked as she brushed the compliment aside. 'A dear little soul she is. Haven't complained once. Think the world of her we do. So don't you worry, miss. I'll take good care of her.'

Envy pierced sharply as Jenefer forced a smile. 'I never doubted it, Mrs Sweet. How is Jared? Is he recovering?'

'Better than he was, miss, thank you for asking. Weak as a kitten, mind. Took him quite bad it did. But he's on the mend now. He do visit with your sister while I'm busy. Does my heart good to hear 'em laughing.' Inez fiddled with her apron. 'I know he isn't what your father would have chose,' she blurted, 'but my Jared got a loving heart and he'll do his best by your sister.' She sighed and clicked her tongue. 'Fretting he is, about not being with the others. Can't wait to get back to sea.' She rolled her eyes. 'Men! Worse than children they are.'

Having no man and no child, Jenefer felt ill-equipped to comment. Instead she nodded, made herself smile once more, and turned to go. 'Good day to you, Mrs Sweet.'

' 'Bye, Miss Jenefer. You take care now.' She closed the door.

Walking back through the village, Jenefer barely noticed the nods and greetings of people passing on their way to work. Though they would always be sisters, Betsy was part of Jared's family now. They would have first claim on her loyalty. She didn't begrudge Betsy her happiness. But as life improved for Betsy, for her each day brought a new blow, and this latest was the most devastating.

Martin had not sailed to America. So where had he gone? And why? Why had he lied? Why had he not written a single letter? Why had he proposed marriage only to disappear? If he had lied about where he was going, what else had he lied about? Under these circumstances there could be no blame attached to her if she withdrew from her engagement. But that would remove the last semblance of protection she had. Where was he? Did he intend to return? *Was he still alive?*

*

Thomas studied his reflection in the mirror, made a minor adjustment to his neck cloth, then nodded in satisfaction. He turned aside, lifted his frock coat from the hanger, pushed his arms into the sleeves and settled the padded shoulders over his own narrow sloping ones.

Should he wait until the capture was confirmed? Surely there was no need. His arrangement with Mr Eddy, the newly appointed Supervisor of Customs responsible for this area of coast, was water-tight. Besides, with captured smugglers always landed either at Mousehole or Porthleven, it might be days before the news reached Porthinnis. Why should he wait? He had achieved the first of his objectives. He was finally rid of his hated brother.

Now for the second: Tamara Gillis. At the dance he had watched her, seen her gaze follow Devlin. He had glimpsed the flash of anger. There had been something else, something too swiftly gone for him to recognize it. He dismissed it for it didn't matter. He had an ally in her mother.

Morwenna Gillis was desperate for her daughter to marry well. But Tamara's wilfulness made families with eligible sons wary. They might like her charm, and even smile at her high spirits, but few would risk their family's future on a girl so determined to go her own way.

With no family – other than his soon-to-be-dead brother and his uncle permanently settled on the other side of the Channel in Roscoff – Thomas was free to please himself. He had wanted Tamara for years. Saying nothing, fearful of his father's ridicule or his brother's mockery, he had watched her grow from a coltish girl into a confident and striking young woman.

Taking over the business after his father's death should have brought him wealth and status. But things had gone wrong, people had let him down, and the resulting financial mess had left him terrified all his plans would come to nothing.

Now all that was firmly in the past. Within days the lugger's capture would be confirmed. Within a couple of weeks, a month at the most, his brother would be dangling from the hangman's rope with a broken neck, or locked in the hold of a convict ship on his way to some godforsaken country on the other side of the world.

Thomas smiled. Everything Devlin owned would be his. As was his right. Things would be very different then. Oh yes. Certain people would regret their lack of respect. He would enjoy taking his revenge. But that would wait, and be all the sweeter for it.

First he would marry.

For months he had played Morwenna Gillis like a fish, invariably polite even when her simpering curdled his stomach, paying her compliments, listening to her inane remarks, and only then making his bow to Tamara. And she, little hussy, murmured a greeting with barely a glance in his direction.

But that was about to change. Today she would notice him all right. Imagining the scene, the shock his news would provoke, himself solemn and restrained, dignified in the face of loss, he shuddered with pleasure.

CHAPTER SIXTEEN

Sitting at the table in the living-room, her sketchpad open in front of her, Tamara turned a pencil between her fingers and gazed out of the window. What was she to do? What could she do? Devlin had made his feelings abundantly clear. *Won't be bullied and can't be bought.*

Despite the shock and grievous pain of his rejection, she still loved him. She wasn't sure if she wanted to. But she couldn't simply turn it off, any more than she could turn off her hurt and anger. She admired his refusal of whatever bribe her mother had offered. What if he had accepted? She would have achieved her dearest wish – Devlin Varcoe as her husband. At what cost though?

Why waste time on such thoughts? He had turned her mother down, and she would have expected no less.

Regardless of how wrong she had been about his feelings for her, his integrity was one thing she could be certain of. In his own way he was the most honourable man she had ever met.

The laws he broke were bad laws made by men who had no idea of what life was like for ordinary people. The officers who enforced those laws took a share of the value of the cargo seized, contraband other men had risked their lives to bring over from France. Those same officers were rewarded with £20 for every man they gave up to the press gang. Where was the honesty or the justice in that? Perhaps she was a fool. She had been called worse. But though

Devlin had broken her heart, she could not hate him.

Nor did she want her parents to suffer because of her actions, which they would if she didn't marry quickly. But wed Thomas Varcoe? *Why not? Devlin did not want her.* But marry a man she didn't trust, who made her flesh creep? How could she? Yet what other course was open to her? If she ran, where could she go? How could she support herself? If she went to the parish her mother would die of shame. Besides, the overseers would demand to know the name of the baby's father. If she refused to tell them, they would either withhold relief or take the baby away.

Round and round her thoughts churned, all questions and no answers. Dropping her pencil she rested her elbows on the table and pressed fingertips to her aching temples.

The door opened. 'Beg pardon, ma'am, but Mr Varcoe's here.'

Tamara's heart lurched and she looked up, hope defying reason.

Sally shot her a glance of apology. 'Mr Thomas Varcoe.'

Morwenna sniffed. 'Wait one moment, Sally. Then show him in.'

Bobbing a curtsey, the maid left. As the door closed behind her, Morwenna adjusted her cap and her 'kerchief.

'We must be thankful that *one* Varcoe knows how to conduct himself.' She disposed herself more formally on the sofa. 'Sit up straight, Tamara. Pinch your cheeks, you're far too pale. It's not at all becoming. And for goodness' sake *smile*.'

The door opened. 'Ah, Mr Varcoe,' she simpered, as Sally stood back to allow Thomas to enter. 'What a delightful surprise.'

'You are kind to say so, ma'am.' Thomas bowed. 'It is always a pleasure to see you. And Miss Gillis, of course.' He inclined his head.

Though he did not attempt to hold her gaze there was a glitter in his eyes that made Tamara instantly uneasy.

He flicked up his coat tails and seated himself in an armchair, his high shirt points and carefully arranged neckcloth framing his face. 'I fear, ma'am, I am the bearer of bad news.' Adopting a sombre expression he gave his head a small shake. 'But perhaps I should come back when your husband is—'

'My husband is engaged in business at the boatyard and may be some hours,' Morwenna said quickly. 'As you are here, why don't you tell me and I will inform him when he returns.'

'Very well. It is no secret, ma'am, that my brother and I are not close. Yet I take no pleasure in the news that while he and his crew were bringing back a cargo from Roscoff, they were apprehended by one of the Revenue cutters.'

Tamara felt the blood drain from her face. She stared blindly at the table as a silent explosion of light filled her head and black spots danced across her vision. Bathed in icy perspiration, her shift clinging to damp skin, she willed herself not to faint. *Devlin captured? Had there been a fight? Was he injured? Where had he been taken?*

She clenched her teeth so hard that pain lanced through her jaw and temple. But it steadied her. To occupy her hands so their tremor would not betray her she took up her pencil again, turning it in her fingers. She could feel Thomas's gaze. He wanted her to ask. And she was desperate to know. But instinct kept her silent. Her mother felt no such reserve.

With a dramatic gesture Morwenna pressed a hand to her bosom. 'My dear, Mr Varcoe, what dreadful tidings. And your cargo? Was that seized as well?'

Tamara closed her eyes, biting the inside of her lip. Did her mother not realize how her question betrayed her? Her first concern was not for the men who had been taken, men from the village, men with parents, wives and families, but for the money the cargo represented.

'That is more than likely,' Thomas said. 'Even if the crew managed to drop the casks before they were captured, I doubt there is any possibility they can be recovered.' He spread his hands. 'I felt I should come and tell you at once. Clearly my brother will not now have need of the boat your husband is currently building. Indeed, if he is convicted – which I fear is certain – his lugger will be sawn into three parts so it can never again be used to run contraband.'

'What of your brother?' Morwenna asked belatedly. 'What will happen to him?'

Thomas's shoulders rose and fell. 'I fear the worst, ma'am. But even if he does not hang—'

'Oh!' Morwenna gasped.

'Pardon me, I did not intend to cause you distress.'

'Indeed, it is a shock. But pray continue. After all' – she darted a meaningful glance at Tamara – 'this must be far more painful for you than for us.'

As Thomas bowed his head in acknowledgement, Tamara felt a surge of loathing so powerful that the pencil she was holding snapped in two.

He looked up quickly. 'My dear Miss Gillis, I have upset you.'

Seeing through his expression of concern to the excitement beneath, Tamara looked directly into his eyes. 'No, Mr Varcoe. I am stronger than I look.'

Ignoring her mother's warning glare, Tamara held his gaze. He looked away first, but not quite quickly enough. What she saw tightened her skin in a shiver. He addressed her mother.

'As I was saying, ma'am, if he escapes the gallows he will face either transportation or many years in prison.' He shook his head.

'My dear Mr Varcoe,' her mother gushed, 'you have our deepest sympathy.'

Tamara tasted a warm saltiness and realized she had bitten through her flesh. She knew losing his boat would grieve Devlin. But to lose his freedom? He would sooner die.

Bruised and bloody from rough treatment by the cutter's crew who used their muskets to shove him down the companionway, Devlin ducked his head to avoid empty hammocks and slumped on to one of the mess table benches. Jeered and spat at as they followed, his crew ranged themselves alongside and opposite.

Designed for speed with low freeboard and her guns mounted on the deck, the cutter's accommodation was all below the waterline. The air was thick with the reek of stale food, wet clothes and unwashed bodies.

One of the cutter's men emerged from a cabin that another locked up behind him, carrying heavy iron shackles with chains attached.

'There's no need—' Devlin began, gasping as a musket stock cracked against his temple. His head jerked and he felt blood trickle down the side of his face.

'Shut your mouth! You speak when I say. Prisoners, you are. Smuggler scum. Any of you move while we put the chains on and you'll get a hammering.'

Another of the cutter's men laughed. 'Don't look so brave now, do 'e.'

Sam growled.

'Don't,' Devlin muttered. 'I'm all right.'

'Look at 'n!' A third man sneered over the clank of the chains as the heavy iron cuffs were locked around Devlin's wrists and those of his crew. 'Devil Varcoe. Don't look like no devil to me. Lost 'is cargo, lost 'is boat. Soon 'e'll dance at the end of a rope,' he mocked in a singsong voice.

As his mates laughed a voice called from above. 'Are those men secure?'

'Aye, sir,' the man nearest the companionway shouted.

'Then get back up here. I need a crew for the lugger.'

'You won't see that no more, *Mister* Varcoe,' one of the men sniggered as the rest clattered up the companionway. 'Cut 'n up for kindling they will.' The hatch slammed shut, leaving Devlin and his men in foetid darkness.

'What's on with these 'ere chains?' Andy whispered. 'And hitting skip like that?'

'Dunno, boy,' Danny murmured. 'But something 'bout all this do stink like a fitcher.'

'Last time the Rinsey boys was chased,' Ben said, his voice low, 'they cut the sinking stones off two strings of casks, heaved them overboard, and the cutter let 'em go.'

'Where d'you hear that?' Billy was sceptical.

'From my cousin down Mousehole. He heard it from one of the lads who was there.'

'Skip?' Andy hissed. 'You reck'n we should've gived 'em some casks?'

The chains jingled and clanked as Devlin raked his fingers across his aching skull. Danny was right. Something stank.

'Don't be bleddy daft, boy,' Sam growled. 'T'wadn luck they found us. They was waiting.'

'Yes, but how did they know? Who told?'

'What diff'rence do it make?' Ben cut in. 'We're dead men.'

'That's enough.' Devlin spoke quietly, but the men were immediately still. They shrugged off his flashes of temper. They were far more wary of his rage. Rare and tightly controlled, it meant trouble for whoever had crossed him.

'We're not dead yet. Nor will we be. Do what they tell you. Defiance will only get you a beating. They'll land us at Mousehole or Porthleven. If it's Porthleven we'll be in Justice Casvellan's parlour before nightfall.'

'You want that, skip?' Surprise made Billy's whisper a squeak.

'Better him than Sir Edward Pengarrick,' Danny murmured. 'That bastard wouldn't bother with a trial. He'd hang us just to warn off the others.'

'Danny!' Devlin warned. He understood their fear. The fact that he was gambling with their lives as well as his own was a heavy burden. Casvellan had warned him. Should he be caught there would be no assistance. But he had something Casvellan wanted: information.

Immediately Thomas left, Tamara went to her room and opened her closet. Ignoring her poppy-red coat, the colour wrong for her mood, she took out her dark-green one. Kicking off her slippers she pushed her feet into brown half-boots and quickly tied the laces, twisted her hair up beneath a dark green velvet hat with a stiff brim, and picked up her tan leather gloves.

'Where do you think you're going?' Morwenna demanded as she came downstairs.

'Just for a walk. I have a headache.'

'Very well, but don't go far. I would not be surprised if Mr Varcoe calls again later. He will think it only proper to speak to your father. And when he comes you must be here.'

'*If* he comes, Mama, surely it will be later this afternoon? I will be back long before then.' Tamara walked to the front door.

'So I should think! Well, go if you must. I shall begin making a list. There is so much to be done. Indeed I don't know how I shall cope with it all. Sally!'

Closing the front door, Tamara took a deep breath. The cold air stung her face and burned her lungs. But for now she was free. *Free to fret and worry as she sought a way out of the disaster she had brought upon herself.*

She walked up to the crossroads then turned on to the track that led across the moor. This was her favourite place. There were few trees, and those were stunted and leaned away from the prevailing wind. But up here amid the gorse, heather and bracken where there was so much more sky, she felt able to breathe.

She looked towards the sea, glittering like polished silver beneath a glassy sun. An armada of full-bodied clouds with gleaming white tops and blue-grey undersides sailed across a sky the clear blue of forget-me-nots. As her gaze turned west she saw one particularly dark cloud. It hung low, trailing a thick curtain of rain that hid the distant clusters of houses across the bay.

Where would Devlin be taken? What would happen to him? As she walked anxiety churned both her mind and her stomach. She swallowed hard to suppress the nausea. The sun shone brightly, but inside her warm coat she shivered. Then her gaze sharpened and her heart lifted. Instinct had brought her up here. Now, coming towards her along the track, was the one person to whom she could open her heart. Quickening her pace she waved. After a moment Roz waved back.

'I was so hoping I might see you.' Flinging her arms around Roz's slim shoulders Tamara kissed her cold cheek, and knew immediately all was not well with her friend. But she had learned not to ask.

Roz's drawn features softened in a brief smile. 'Now you have.'

Tamara linked their arms, so used to Roz's shabby serge petticoat, scuffed boots, and too-large coat that she no longer noticed them. Two years ago she had offered Roz some of her own clothes, things she could easily do without and would not miss.

Roz had been silent for a long moment. And Tamara realized what she had done, though with the best of intentions.

'I didn't mean – it's *not* charity.'

Roz didn't argue. Her silence said it all.

Tamara held out her hand, relieved as Roz took it. 'I'm sorry.'

Roz's smile was wistful as she nodded.

Nothing more was said. But later at home when she thought it through, Tamara understood, and could have kicked herself for her clumsiness. Of course she hadn't intended the offer as charity. But unable to reciprocate, Roz's acceptance of the cast-off clothes would have unbalanced their relationship.

Despite their different backgrounds, each had instantly recognized a kindred spirit. Both possessed talents they could not explain. Roz had an intuitive understanding of horses. Tamara's gift was more a sixth sense, a kind of precognition.

Tamara glanced at Roz's basket as they headed in the direction of the village, out of sight in the valley. 'Have you been collecting herbs?'

Roz gave a brief nod. 'Why did you want to see me?'

'Roz, I don't know what to do. I'm – I'm in trouble.'

Roz gave her a searching look. 'A child?'

Tamara nodded.

'Whose?'

'*Roz!* Devlin's, of course.' She glanced at her friend. But Roz remained silent, simply pressing the hand tucked through her arm, and Tamara felt gratitude welling up. People said Roz didn't talk. She did. What she didn't do was ask a lot of questions. She listened.

'Even now, after— You know I've loved him for years.' She glanced at Roz, who simply nodded. 'And I thought – I truly believed – but he— Oh Roz.' Her breath caught in her chest and her voice emerged small, broken and aching with hurt. 'He doesn't want me.' She fought her grief, grateful for Roz's silence and the comfort of their linked arms. Swallowing the choking lump in her throat she took a deep steadying breath.

'His brother came to the house this morning to tell us that Devlin's boat has been captured by a Customs cutter. My mother is frantic about the disgrace the family will suffer once my condition is known. She's insisting I marry Thomas.' She shuddered. The silence lengthened: growing tense and thick. 'Roz—'

'No.' Just the one word: quiet, shaded with pity, adamant.

Tamara heard the underlying sadness and knew she had caused it. But driven by compelling need she could not stop. 'If there was any other way, I wouldn't ask.'

'There is. You've just told me.'

'But if there's no baby there will be no humiliation for my family, and I won't have to marry a man I loathe. Please—'

'No.' Roz's tone was flat. 'I can't.' But she didn't withdraw her arm. 'You're not thinking.'

Tamara's strangled laugh verged on hysteria. 'I can't sleep for thinking. Every moment of the day it's—'

Roz stopped, pulling Tamara round to face her. 'If I did as you ask you could die. Your mother would seek someone to blame. She knows we're friends. I'd hang.'

Tamara stared into Roz's eyes, saw a truth that hadn't even crossed her mind. 'No! Oh God. I didn't—' Roz was right. She hadn't thought, except of herself, her own plight, her desperation to escape marriage to Thomas.

'Marry him. Have your baby. It's the only—' Suddenly Roz stopped. Her grip tightened on Tamara's arms. 'How did he know?'

'Who? Know what?'

'Thomas Varcoe. He came to your house this morning.'

'Yes.'

'We knew something must have happened.'

'We?'

'Me, the landsmen. Devlin was due back with a cargo. But we never received the signal. So how did Thomas know about his brother being taken? Who told him?'

It was late afternoon when Devlin, guarded by two dragoons, reached Branoc Casvellan's house. The dragoons were armed with swords, pistols and instructions to shoot him if he so much looked the wrong way. Though he knew some of the soldiers by sight, these two were strangers. And had, he guessed, been chosen for that reason.

But even had they been Porthinnis men, he would not have attempted escape. Not when his life and the lives of his crew depended on him reaching Trescowe and convincing the Justice to see him.

What if Casvellan refused? His warning had been clear: *no assistance.* But surely he would want the information contained in the letter? That was the hope Devlin clung to during the ride from Porthleven.

At first the supervisor had refused to let him go, agreeing only after Devlin shrugged and announced with a certainty he did not feel, that when the Justice heard of it, both the Customs Officer and the cutter's captain would lose their jobs.

Disclaiming all responsibility, the captain stormed out and returned to his ship. Careful to do everything by the book, the supervisor sent a message to the Riding Officer ordering *him* to call in six dragoons who had neither family nor friends in Porthinnis. When they arrived he appointed two to accompany Devlin.

Meanwhile, locked in a whitewashed room containing nothing but a wooden bench and a bucket while the remaining four dragoons stood guard outside the Custom House, the crew could only wait.

Stiff and sore, both from his beating and the long ride, Devlin obeyed the order to dismount. While one dragoon hammered on the front door, the other drew his pistol and aimed it at Devlin who stood perfectly still, hands raised, facing the soldier. The click of the hammer being cocked was loud in the silence.

In that instant Devlin realized that the dragoons had spent the entire journey expecting him to try and escape. That he hadn't increased rather than removed their anxiety. He sensed their unease. Any sudden movement would get him shot.

What if Casvellan was not at home? Sweat prickled his back.

The door swung open and the butler's gaze swung from the two dragoons to Devlin.

'You know this man?' the dragoon on the doorstep demanded.

Fearing the butler's denial, Devlin spoke up. 'Tell the Justice I have information for him.' Thirst and anxiety roughened his voice.

The butler's expression did not alter as his glance flicked from the caked blood on Devlin's temple to the dragoon's cocked pistol. 'One moment, Mr Varcoe.' He closed the door.

From the corner of his eye he saw the soldiers exchange a glance. Though they were still wary, he sensed an easing of their tension. But not his own. For his life and the lives of his crew depended on Casvellan reneging on his threat of no assistance. A tremor started in one leg and he shifted his weight. Instantly the pistol was raised. Aimed at his heart the barrel's dark eye was perfectly steady.

'Cramp,' he said, careful to remain absolutely still. Minutes passed. Anxiety and anger knotted his stomach. If Casvellan refused to see him. . . .

The front door opened once more.

Thomas left the Gillis household well pleased with his visit. He had hinted at his intention, and Morwenna Gillis was clearly anxious to secure him as a husband for her daughter. Tamara's reluctance did not deter him. Having wanted her for years, and forced to watch while she made sheep's eyes at his brother, he would relish her acceptance all the more. That she would accept was not in doubt. Her mother would see to it.

Should the wedding be a grand affair? It would not take many weeks for the lawyers to transfer all Devlin's assets to him. Once he was in funds it would be very tempting to host a lavish celebration. But did he really want to throw his money away on people who had openly questioned his business skills?

Anyway, the wedding breakfast was the Gillis's responsibility. Perhaps a small family occasion might be more suitable. Especially – Thomas found himself smiling – as he would still be in mourning for his poor dead brother.

Yes, that was a better idea. The money would be better spent on refurbishing the house. Tamara could begin work on it when they returned from their honeymoon. Where would he take her? Truro, perhaps? The season would be starting soon. Every night there would be balls, parties and dances where he could show her off. His new wealth would ensure invitations. Then they would return to their room at one of the best hotels.

He pictured himself in an armchair, holding a glass of fine cognac, watching Tamara, *his wife* who had promised to love, honour and obey him, as she slowly disrobed. He imagined the glow of firelight on her skin, her dark hair tumbling over her naked shoulders. . . .

The door opened, jerking him out of his fantasy. 'Willie Grose is 'ere,' his housekeeper announced. 'Want to see'n, do 'e?'

'No,' Thomas snapped. Then, 'Yes.'

'Which?' Maisy Roberts was impatient.

'Yes. Show him in.'

'He knows the way. I got work to do.'

He heard her footsteps down the hall. A few moments later the door creaked and Willie's head appeared round it.

'All right, Mister Varcoe? Cold again, innit?'

Thomas ignored the hint. 'Go down to the village and ask around. I need to know if the rumour is true.'

'What rumour?' Willie asked, exactly as Thomas intended.

'That my brother's boat has been captured by one of the Revenue cutters.'

'Bleddy 'ell! Where d' you hear that, then?'

'That's what I want you to find out,' Thomas said, hiding his enjoyment of Willie's confusion. Everything was working out exactly as he had planned. 'Is it just a rumour? I need to know, Willie.'

Willie's bafflement hardened into a scowl. 'Well, if 'tis true, 'tis no more'n he deserve after what he done to my brother.' He rubbed his hands together. 'Best place to ask will be in the Five Mackerel. But Jack don't let nobody sit in there without buying and I'll have to stay a while. So—'

'God alive,' Thomas muttered. Opening a drawer in the side table by his chair he took out some coins and dropped them on to Willie's grubby palm. 'Come back tonight, after dark.'

After drinking several glasses of brandy with his pasty, Thomas fell asleep. He woke with a start and checked the clock. It was almost four. Putting on his greatcoat, beaver hat and leather gloves, he left the house.

Reaching the harbour, he walked along the back of the quay past Devlin's workshop with its padlocked door. He turned up the cobbled alley and slipped in through the gate, closing it behind him. At the top of the stone steps that led up to his brother's loft he saw that door too was secured with a padlock.

He looked around to see if there was a stone, a pot, anything beneath which Devlin might have left a key. There wasn't. Descending to the yard he looked in the privy, feeling along the wooden lintel above the door, checking the walls and behind the door in case there might be a nail with a spare key on it. Surely there was more than one? What if he mislaid it? But if there was another, who would Devlin trust to hold it?

Jenefer was adding a column of figures when the brisk knock interrupted her. Setting down her pen and flexing cramped fingers she pushed back her chair. Who would come calling on her? It wasn't Lizzie or Ernestine whose knocks were familiar. *Betsy.* Her heart lurched and she snatched the door open. Then stared in astonishment at the man standing outside.

'Mr Varcoe.'

'Good afternoon, Miss Trevanion. I hope I haven't called at an inconvenient time?'

His smile was as insincere as his words. She had never liked him, and certainly didn't trust him, convinced that from the day they had begun doing business together Thomas Varcoe had cheated her father.

'As it happens I am rather busy.' No man of sense would expect to be invited in. Nor had she any intention of doing so. Yet she saw from his surprise and swiftly masked chagrin that he had presumed otherwise. Did he really believe the change in her circumstances somehow gave him right of entry? The sooner she disabused him of that notion the better. Though the cottage belonged to his brother it was, for the time being, her home.

'What do you want, Mr Varcoe?'

His smile stiffened then faded. She sensed his anger, saw the effort it cost him to remain polite.

'My apologies for disturbing you. I wondered if my brother had left a key with you? A key to his loft?'

Bemused, Jenefer shook her head. 'No. Why would he?'

'In case—' Thomas half-turned. 'It was just – I thought that as he had installed you in this cottage. . . .'

'You are offensive, sir!' She owed him no explanation. 'If there is nothing else?'

'Forgive me. I did not intend—' He bowed, abruptly formal. 'I beg your pardon, Miss Trevanion. I am in some distress. You see there is a rumour abroad in the village that the Revenue cutter – my brother's boat—' He broke off, shaking his head. 'So many people affected. . . .' With another brief bow he walked quickly away.

Jenefer closed the door. Thomas's words and the images they had conjured whirled in her head. Had Devlin been taken prisoner? Was he – God forbid – dead? She could not, would not, believe that. But fear slid down her spine like a drop of icy water.

With Devlin dead, Thomas would inherit all his possessions, including this cottage. Then he would take revenge on her by making demands she was unwilling or unable to meet. She would be homeless again.

But the rumour was still just that, a rumour. It had not been confirmed. Who had told him? Where had they heard it? Clearly he didn't yet have all the facts. But he would soon. What then? Crossing to the range she pulled the kettle over the flames and wrapped her arms across her body, cold and fearful.

CHAPTER SEVENTEEN

'The Justice is sitting. His rooms are in the building opposite the stables. He will see you there, Mr Varcoe, without your escort.' But as he took a step back, preparing to close the door, the dragoon raised his pistol. 'He don't go nowhere without us.'

Unmoved, the butler looked the soldier up and down. 'Mr Casvellan wishes to speak to your prisoner alone. I can assure you no harm will come to either of them while he does so. His clerk will be waiting to take Mr Varcoe to the Justice. Once relieved of your prisoner you may present yourselves at the back door where you will be given a mug of ale. You may also water your horses.'

Devlin watched his two escorts exchange a glance. One licked dry lips while the other gave a faint shrug.

Taking for granted the soldiers' agreement, the butler stepped back. 'I advise you not to keep him waiting.'

Pushing the pistol barrel gently aside with his index finger, careful not to betray even a glimmer of amusement as he wondered when and where the Justice had acquired his manservant, Devlin turned and started walking round the side of the house.

The swiftness and ferocity of the squall had allowed them no time to put on their oilskins. Stowed in the bow with spare sails these had been left aboard the lugger. When disembarking at Porthleven he had asked for them. This request had earned him further blows and the mocking response that they'd have no need of wet-weather gear where they were going.

So Devlin had ridden from Porthleven in clothes that were wet, cold, and very uncomfortable.

The clerk was a thin man of about forty with limp mousy hair drawn back in a queue. Dressed in black apart from his neckcloth and stockings, he peered over wire-rimmed spectacles perched on his prominent nose. His hooded gaze slid from Devlin to the dragoons and back.

'This way if you please, Mr Varcoe.'

Devlin followed the clerk up a wooden staircase to the second floor. A short passage led off the landing with a door on either side. One stood open. Devlin glanced in and saw a large table piled with ledgers of documents. Behind it, shelves from floor to ceiling were crammed with boxes, files and stacks of documents tied with different coloured ribbons. The second door was closed. The clerk knocked then, without waiting for an answer, opened it.

'Mr Varcoe, sir.' Standing back he gestured for Devlin to enter, then closed the door leaving him alone with the Justice.

Standing on the maroon-patterned carpet, Devlin was very conscious of his damp stained clothes and scuffed sea boots.

Seated in front of a window behind a kneehole desk the Justice stopped writing and laid down his pen. Leaning back in his chair he looked up, and his gaze narrowed.

'You have blood on your face.'

Devlin raised a hand to his temple, wincing as his fingers touched the swelling and crusted scab, then traced the dried runnels down to his jaw. 'No chance to clean up, sir.'

Rising, Casvellan moved across to the fireplace. Several logs burned brightly in the grate, their fragrance scenting the air. With his back to the flames he clasped his hands behind him and gazed levelly at Devlin.

'I thought I had made myself clear.'

'You did, sir.'

'Then you'd better have a very good reason for coming here.'

Devlin recognized the depth of Casvellan's anger. 'You will be the judge of that, sir.'

'Exactly so.' The quiet words carried a warning. 'I want everything, Mr Varcoe. Not what it suits you to tell me, or what you think I wish to hear.'

His life was in Casvellan's hands. If the Justice possessed other sources of information he might already be aware of what had happened. Total honesty, and trust in Casvellan's fairness were his only options.

Devlin began with the rumours circulating in Roscoff and his uncle's warning not to be caught with the letters. He continued by detailing the cargo, the arrival of the Revenue cutter and the attempted escape which included dumping the contraband.

'Did you fire on the cutter?' Casvellan asked.

Devlin shook his head. 'No. My boat isn't armed, neither is my crew, apart from the knives and axes that are part of our fishing gear. You don't carry guns unless you intend to use them. If you use them and you're caught, the law says you hang. I've always relied on skilled seamanship to get out of trouble.'

'Not this time.'

'It wasn't bad luck or carelessness that got us caught: the cutter was waiting for us. The captain knew where we'd be and when.'

Twin creases appeared between Casvellan's brows. 'Someone betrayed you?'

Devlin gave a terse nod. Anger burned in his gut each time he thought of it. Nearly everyone in the village was involved with the free-trade. Those who helped unload a cargo, the batmen who ran alongside the pack animals to deal with any would-be thieves, the farmer who had dug a storage pit beneath his barn and the priest who took care not to notice casks in his crypt. When the Riding

Officer came asking questions, the villagers shrugged and shook their heads. They hadn't heard or seen anything.

'Tell me about the letter,' Casvellan demanded.

Devlin repeated what he had read, closing his eyes to help him to visualize the writing and recall the exact phrasing, including the brief notation on the outer sheet. He concluded by describing briefly the treatment his crew had received at the hands of the cutter's men.

'Did you offer resistance?'

'Outnumbered four to one by men with pistols and muskets? No, we didn't.'

'So why. . . ?' he indicated the blood on Devlin's face.

'We were taken below. When two seamen brought out iron shackles and chains I said they weren't necessary. Damn it, we had no weapons. We weren't going anywhere. But they shackled us anyway.'

'Given your reputation, Mr Varcoe, are you really surprised?'

But Devlin had seen the flicker in Casvellan's eyes. The point made, he pressed on, 'Sir, I asked for this interview not only because of what was in the letter, information I believed you would want to know, but because I think I know who the agent is. If I'm right, the initials are those of Martin Erisey who is, or was, a diplomat. I know of him because he is betrothed to Miss Trevanion whose father financed our ventures. Colonel Trevanion died in the fire that destroyed their house.'

Casvellan nodded. 'I heard about that. Go on.'

'She – Miss Trevanion – believes Erisey to be in America. But he was expected back weeks ago.'

'I see.' Casvellan's frown grew more pronounced.

'Sir, it's clear from his letter he's in grave danger. He needs to get out of France. Let me go and bring him back.'

Casvellan didn't respond immediately. Knowing better than to press, Devlin waited.

'And in return? For we both know there is a price on your offer.'

Devlin met his gaze. 'My boat, and freedom for my crew and myself.'

Casvellan regarded him evenly, his expression revealing nothing. 'You want your boat and your freedom? After you were caught smuggling contraband?'

'They can't prove that, sir. We had nothing on board.'

'You ask a lot, Mr Varcoe.'

'I offer a fair trade, sir. And I know the man by sight.'

'Assuming you could make good on this claim, why should I agree such terms?'

'Sir, you trusted me to carry your letter to Roscoff. I've just given you important information. What can you lose? If I bring Erisey back he'll have more to tell than he could put in letters. That must be worth my freedom. If I'm killed while trying to bring him out' – Devlin shrugged – 'so be it. Better that than prison.'

Casvellan half-turned, staring into the flames for several moments. Then he raised his head. 'This agent is owed help to get home. However, if I agree your terms you cannot tell your crew where they are going or why.'

Devlin's mouth dried, but his response was immediate and firm. 'Can't do that, sir. It's no secret that free-traders sometimes bring back escaped prisoners of war from France. British Naval officers mostly, but packet men as well. I'm willing to use that as a cover story. But for this to succeed I need my mate, Jared Sweet. I won't lie to him, or to my crew. It's a matter of trust.'

In the silence Devlin heard his own heartbeat and the soft crackle of the fire, and willed the Justice to agree.

Eventually Casvellan gave an abrupt nod. 'All right. Is the Revenue cutter still at Porthleven?'

Devlin shook his head. 'Probably on its way back to Falmouth. The captain was furious about the Customs Officer allowing me to come and see you.'

Casvellan eyed him curiously. 'How exactly did you achieve that?'

'I gave him to understand his job could be at risk if he didn't, sir.'

'You *threatened* him?'

'Unarmed and surrounded by men with pistols and muskets? How could I—?'

'Enough, Mr Varcoe,' Casvellan gestured wearily. 'You will need your boat.'

'Don't you worry about that, sir. We'll—'

'But you will have to manage with only half your crew. Take it or leave it, Mr Varcoe,' he said, as Devlin opened his mouth. 'How many of your men are at Porthleven?'

'Six.' Devlin knew argument was pointless. But he didn't have to like it.

'You may choose three. The remaining three will be held at

Bodmin gaol both as hostages to your return, and,' Casvellan added coolly, 'to allay any suspicion among my colleagues that I might be entering into free-trading on my own account.' Returning to his desk, he took a fresh sheet of paper, picked up his pen and dipped it in the inkpot.

'I need the names of the men you wish to sail with you.'

Devlin raked both hands through damp tangled hair. His finger-tips skimmed lumps, scabbed cuts and tender bruises. Anger flared but he set it aside.

Who to take? Sailing short-handed on such a mission was riskier than anything he had previously attempted. It doubled the danger and there was a very real chance he would not succeed. Capture would mean death.

All his crew were skilled seamen. Yet those he would have chosen first he must leave behind. Sam had a wife and young son; Ben was the sole support of his father, Harry. Joe's mother was a widow whose two other sons had been snatched from their fishing boat by the press gang.

'Danny Pawle, Andy Voss and Billy May.' He waited while Casvellan wrote.

'And the names of those to remain behind?'

'Sam Clemmow, Ben Tozer and Joe Ince. Sir, can I tell them why—?'

'You will have no contact with them until you return with Erisey. Then I will arrange for their release, and their transport from Bodmin to Porthinnis. In the meantime they will be told nothing, for reasons that should be obvious.'

Devlin understood. What they didn't know they couldn't let slip. Secrecy was vital. If England had spies and agents in France then the reverse was almost certainly true. Though many French landed gentry had fled the Terror, some arriving in Cornwall, not all French spies and agents were of French nationality. The Irish hated the English and had allied themselves with the French Revolutionary ideals of liberty, equality and brotherhood.

Porthinnis was safe enough because outsiders would be recognized at once. But there was no knowing the origin or allegiance of prisoners held in Bodmin gaol – men and women sentenced to transportation or hanging as well as those awaiting trial.

Casvellan's voice broke into Devlin's thoughts. 'I've ordered that all six men be brought here under guard. On the ground floor of this building two rooms are used as holding cells. There is also a storeroom where you will wait. It is at least dry if not particularly comfortable.

'When your men arrive they will be divided, locked into the two rooms and their escort sent home. Once darkness falls, if you can remove Pawle, Voss and May without alerting the others, or anyone else, you will be allowed to continue. If not—'

'I'll get them out,' Devlin interrupted. The alternative didn't bear thinking about.

'Your remaining crew will be collected tomorrow morning by the prison wagon from Penzance. About your boat—'

'We should reach Helston around midnight and Porthleven soon after. We'll take her in the early hours, sir. I reckon it will be mid-morning before anyone notices she's gone.'

Scattering sand over the paper, Casvellan folded it. Rising, he crossed to the fireplace and tugged a bell-pull. Then he lit a taper and returned to the bureau where he held the flame beneath a stick of scarlet wax and dripped it on to the folded sheet. Lastly he impressed the molten wax with a seal.

The door opened admitting the clerk. 'Sir?'

'Give this to the dragoons. They are to carry it with all speed to the Customs Officer at Porthleven. You may inform them that their prisoner will remain in my custody.'

After the clerk had gone, Casvellan turned to Devlin. 'How long do you think?'

'Four days. Five at most.'

'James will bring down a basket of cold meat, bread, cheese, fruit, and ale, sufficient for four days.'

'Thank you, sir.'

'Good luck.'

Devlin knew he was going to need it.

Thomas smiled at his reflection in the tall cheval glass. Forty-eight hours had passed since his visit to the Gillis house. Having expected him to return that afternoon, or the one following, Morwenna Gillis would be in a state of anxiety, fearful in case he might have had second thoughts. That anxiety would give him considerable advantage when it came to negotiating Tamara's dowry.

An hour later he took his place on the sofa as he had done two days earlier. Morwenna's greeting had been so flatteringly effusive he had congratulated himself on his decision to delay his return. There was no doubting the relief in her welcome. As she continued to gush he was briefly surprised. Then he decided simply to enjoy the experience. It was all working out exactly as he planned.

He was about to cut short Morwenna's twittering with an enquiry about Tamara, when the door opened. Immediately her mother exhorted her in syrupy tones to come and greet their guest.

On his feet immediately, Thomas made his bow and Tamara curtseyed in reply. He waited until she sat, then resumed his place on the sofa from where he was able to take in every detail of her appearance. He was used to seeing her in one of the habits she wore for riding or walking in the village. But he guessed that today her mother had demanded she choose her dress in anticipation of his visit.

Her dark glossy hair was held off her face by a satin ribbon the same primrose shade as her long-sleeved gown of figured muslin. The low neckline would have revealed a considerable amount of *décolletage* but for the folds of fine white lawn that reached to her throat.

Though briefly disappointed he approved of her modesty. It seemed her mother's efforts to turn this wild minx into a lady were at last succeeding. Tamara's propriety of dress and demeanour in public would make the activity in their bedroom all the more exciting. At the stirring in his groin he crossed his legs and swiftly banished thoughts he would indulge later when he was alone.

'May I say how well you look, Miss Gillis? I am no expert on ladies' fashion, but that is a most becoming gown.'

'Thank you, sir.'

He felt a stab of irritation at her colourless tone. Looking more closely he saw that her cheeks, usually glowing with vitality, were today creamy pale. His irritation transferred itself to her mother. While he had no objection to Tamara being made aware of the honour of his proposal, this insipidity was not what he had expected, nor did he find it at all pleasing.

'Mrs Gillis—'

Morwenna shot to her feet. 'Please excuse me, Mr Varcoe. I will just see if my husband has returned. I have been expecting him this past half-hour.' She turned to her daughter. 'Tamara, perhaps our guest would care to take a turn in the garden?'

As the garden, a narrow stretch of grass with a small rose bed in the middle, lay between the house and the boatyard with all its attendant noise, Thomas desired no such thing. 'Another time perhaps,' he said firmly. 'The air is a touch chilly today, and I would not wish Miss Gillis to take cold.'

Reaching the door, Morwenna glanced back, her smile so wide it was almost a grimace. 'Then I will leave you to talk here by the fire.'

It was obvious to Thomas that she wished him to make an offer and had left Tamara alone with him for that purpose. In other circumstances such blatant manoeuvring would have annoyed him. Today, however, it made things easier. Even so he waited until he heard her footsteps fade. He wouldn't have put it past her to listen at the door. He cleared his throat.

'Miss Gillis – Tamara – I know this is perhaps not the best moment—'

Her head came up and she met his gaze for the first time since he had entered the room. 'You've had news? Of – of your brother, and the crew?'

Put off his stride by her interruption he frowned. 'No.' Then, remembering that appearances demanded some sign of grief and regret, he bent his head. 'No, alas. But I have to resign myself to the knowledge that even if my brother survived the attack and seizure of his boat, the court will demand the ultimate penalty.' He waited, allowing time for her to realize that Devlin wasn't coming back. When he looked up he was startled to see her watching him. She was even paler, but her eyes were dry, and he saw no hint of a quiver to her lips. He decided this was a positive sign, and uncrossing his legs, leaned forward.

'Miss Gillis, my dear Miss Gillis, I would not have wished it this way, but my brother's untimely passing means that as his next of kin, I will inherit all his estate. This responsibility would be so much easier to bear had I the support of a wife to whom I could turn for comfort. Your mother has led me to believe that an offer of marriage would be favourably received. So all that remains is for me to assure you of my deepest—' He stopped as Tamara rose quickly from her chair.

'Forgive me, Mr Varcoe.' Crossing to the window she stood for a moment then turned to face him. 'Before you say anything else, there is something I must tell you.'

Thomas sat back and fiddled with his cuffs as he tried to contain

his irritation. 'I must assume it is important. Otherwise such rudeness would be hard to tolerate.' He saw her throat work as she swallowed.

'I am with child.'

He stared at her. 'No.' Shock, disbelief and fury churned in his
chest. His heartbeat hammered in his ears and there was a metal-
lic taste in his mouth.

'I could not accept you without first—'

'Your mother knew?' Thomas's voice cracked. As Tamara nodded
he passed a hand across his face.

'She was trying to protect—'

Thomas clung to hope. 'You were attacked?' He could accept that.
God knew there were plenty of rough characters around the village.
And when they were in drink – though what she'd have been doing,
out alone at night – but it might not have been night. She rode alone
on the moor. What if some of the tinners. . . ?

'Tell me his name,' he demanded. 'I'll have him thrashed to within
an inch of his life. We can deal with this privately. There is no need
to involve—'

'Stop.' It was the weariness in her voice that silenced him. 'I was
not attacked.'

'Not? Then what? Who?'

She swallowed again, her calm fractured by fleeting anguish. In
that instant he knew. He wanted to block his ears, make it untrue.
It wasn't fair.

'Your brother's,' she said quietly. 'The child is Devlin's.'

All the bitterness, resentment and jealousy that had coloured his
every thought since the day his mother died giving birth to his
brother raged through him. His entire body shuddered and he
clamped lips and teeth tight so the howl of grief and fury that filled
his head would not escape. He wanted to smash, break, *kill.*

Yet despite *hating* that she had Devlin's brat in her belly, he still
wanted her. He wanted possession and control. He wanted to sate
himself on her body and tame her spirit. He wanted people knowing
she was *his.*

Devlin was dead – or as good as. Once the child was born it could
be got rid of. There were ways. In the meantime, proceeding with the
marriage would save her family from disgrace. They would owe him.
And by Christ he'd see that they paid. As for Tamara, as his wife she

was his property to do with as he chose. Thinking up new ways to punish her would give him almost as much pleasure as carrying them out. Another tremor shook him and he caught his breath just as Tamara spoke.

'You will not wish to—'

'On the contrary.' Rising from the sofa, Thomas crossed the room and took her cold hand in both of his. 'You need me.' As he brushed her knuckles with his lips the door opened. Morwenna stood on the threshold. Her smile was coy but her eyes were wary. He had been flattered by her effusive greeting. Only now did he understand the panic that underlay it. Oh yes, they would pay.

CHAPTER EIGHTEEN

Jenefer pulled the candle closer, resting her head on one hand as she added up the column of figures again, hoping this time the totals would match. Her eyes felt gritty and her head ached. But she was almost finished. If she could complete the work tonight she could take everything to Hannah in the morning.

To finish and be paid would mean one less worry. She was so tired, and it was weeks since she had slept right through the night. The moment she closed her eyes and tried to relax she was tormented by memories: arguments with her father, the fire, Martin's proposal, the pilchard cellar, Hannah Tresidder's back room, the packet clerk telling her that Martin hadn't gone to America.

Vivid random snatches, they flared like fireworks, denying her rest, waking her with fear and a racing heart.

Blinking then widening her tired eyes she focused on the figures. She heard a brief sound and assumed it was Ernestine next door. But it came again and she realized someone was knocking very quietly on the door.

Putting down her pen she rose from her chair then hesitated. Who would come calling at this time of night? Unless something was wrong. *Betsy?* Crossing to the door she lifted the bar and opened it. She gasped as Devlin caught her arm, whirled her inside and closed the door again.

Shock made Jenefer light-headed. Reaching blindly for the chair, she was pressed down into it and a cup pushed into her hands.

'Drink,' Devlin ordered.

She obeyed. Cold water soothed her parched throat and cleared her vision. She looked up at him. 'I'm sorry. I didn't expect to see— Your brother said there'd been a chase, the Revenue cutter – and you were probably dead, or if not—'

'Thomas told you?'

Jenefer nodded.

'When? Where?'

'Yesterday. He came here. He wanted a key to your loft.'

Devlin frowned. 'Why would he come to you?'

Heat climbing her throat to her cheeks, Jenefer glanced away, angry as well as embarrassed. 'He made assumptions about my living here.'

'He would.' Devlin's tone was scathing.

'If you remember, I did warn—'

'Yes, you did.' He frowned again. 'How did he hear about the chase?'

'I don't know. From one of the landing party maybe? When you didn't return—' She stopped as Devlin shook his head.

'They wouldn't have gone to the cove until the signal was given. Never mind that now, I need you to take a message to Jared Sweet.'

Jenefer gaped at him. 'It's far too late to go visiting. Everyone will be in bed. In any case Betsy is ill and Inez has forbidden callers.'

'For God's sake!' Devlin raked his hair in frustration. 'Stop being so difficult. I *know* it's late. That's the point. I'd go myself but I dare not risk being seen. I *must* get hold of Jared.'

'Why?' Jenefer demanded, anxious on Betsy's behalf. 'What do you want him for?'

As he paced two steps one way then two steps back, clearly battling with himself over whether to tell her, Jenefer's fear mounted.

He turned to her so abruptly that she jumped. 'All right. Perhaps you should know. But you cannot tell anyone. Not until we're back. Do you understand?'

'Tell anyone what? Back from where?'

'France. But I have only half my crew. The others are being held

185

in gaol to ensure my return. That's why I need Jared.'

'Why are you going to France? You've only just—'

'To rescue a British government agent.'

'Why you?'

'Because I know him by sight: it's Erisey.'

Jenefer heard the name but it took a moment for all the implications to register. '*Martin* Erisey?'

Devlin nodded. 'Bringing him back safely to England will buy our freedom. Now will you take the message?'

The blood pounding in her ears, Jenefer gulped water. Martin a government agent? A *spy*? That would explain his long absence, the lack of letters. But he'd said he was a diplomat. He had lied to her from the beginning. All right, so the danger of his job demanded it. But where did that leave her? If he had lied about his work, what else had he lied about?

Devlin was risking his life to rescue Martin because there was no other way to obtain his crew's release or his own liberty, but if they all got back safely, what then? Martin had made an offer for her, so he must have intended marriage. He had spent these past months risking his life for his country. All this raced through her mind in moments leaving just one thought: like Devlin she had no choice. She had to help. Decisions about her future must wait.

She set down the cup and rose to her feet. 'Yes, of course.' While she put on hat, coat and boots, Devlin gave her instructions.

'If your sister has taken Jared's room, he'll be on a truckle bed in the front room. You must wake him without disturbing anyone else.'

'I understand.' Jenefer's fingers trembled as she tied her laces, and nervousness made her voice strained. 'What do you want me to tell him?'

'He's to meet me as soon as possible.'

'Where?'

'He'll know, and it's safer if you don't. I'll leave now. After I've gone close the door *quietly* and count to twenty. Then you go.'

Obeying his instructions she waited in the shadows at the mouth of the alley for her eyes to adjust to the darkness. Then she hurried along the empty street. This end of the village was deserted. But she would cut through the narrow cobbled alleys to avoid the men coming out of the Five Mackerel.

She thought about the risk Devlin was taking sailing with only half his crew. But at least they were all alive.

Tamara wouldn't know that. Jenefer recalled the gossip she had overheard in the shop about Tamara and Devlin, the rumour that Tamara was in trouble. Betsy had always defended her friend, praising her kindness and her artistic ability. But she had been unable or – as she now recognized – unwilling to see past Tamara's apparently reckless behaviour, condemning her as wild and irresponsible.

But these past weeks her life had changed. She had changed. She had shot a tinner, worked – ineptly – in a stinking pilchard cellar, and bargained herself into a job. She had discovered more than was comfortable about her own limitations and gained insight into the lives of the village women.

Without Lizzie Clemmow, Ernestine Rowse and Hannah Tresidder she would be in desperate straits. She had no right to judge anyone. Nor could she allow Lizzie to continue worrying, fearing Sam was dead.

Waiting in the cave, Devlin tried to think ahead. An overcast sky veiled the quarter moon making the lugger difficult to spot. But the lack of wind worried him. They'd have to use the sweeps. Fortunately the pins were padded with oakum so the long oars wouldn't rattle. But with the crew already short of sleep, prolonged rowing would exhaust them before they got anywhere near the French coast. He could only hope that once away from land and into deep water they would pick up a breeze.

Alerted by the faint clink of a falling pebble he pressed back against the cave wall. A darker shadow moved across the entrance. Then he heard a whisper.

'Dev?'

'Here.' Pushing himself away from the rock, Devlin extended his arm and a moment later Jared's huge hand clasped his.

'What's on?'

Grateful for Jared's brevity, Devlin told him all that had happened.

'Sam, Ben and Joe will be held in Bodmin until we bring Erisey back.'

'You trust Casvellan?'

'What choice do I have? But yes, I do.'

187

'Where are the others?'

'Aboard the lugger, in the next cove. Jared, I need you with us.' Having explained the urgency of the situation, Devlin anticipated swift agreement. But as Jared remained silent, Devlin's surprise turned to angry disappointment.

'Lost your nerve? If that's what love does—' He bit the words off, instantly ashamed, not understanding what had prompted them.

Hearing Jared's intake of breath he waited for the tongue-lashing he knew he deserved.

'What would you know about love?'

Jared's scorn made him even angrier. Clamping down on his temper and other emotions he dared not acknowledge, he forced himself to be calm.

'It's small compensation for the risk, but I'm paying triple the rate for a smuggling run. Surely a man planning to marry by special licence needs all the money he can get?' He was putting Jared in an intolerable position. But he had no choice. Jared was worth two men. Without him they had little hope of success. Even with him the entire venture was a desperate gamble.

'When are you going?'

'Now.'

'Jesus, Devlin!'

Devlin knew what was on Jared's mind. Betsy had lost her father and her home; Jared was her security, her future. But when she woke in the morning he would have disappeared and she'd have no idea where he'd gone or if he would return. He thrust the thought aside.

'We *have* to go now.' He couldn't hide his urgency. 'Someone is bound to notice the lugger is missing and we need to be halfway across the Channel by then.' Damn it, in all the years they had been running contraband he had always brought them back. Why should this trip be any different? They could do it. Then, once they were home – he tried to imagine then but couldn't. The pictures wouldn't come. Refusing to worry and unable to stand the thickening silence he pressed on.

'Casvellan has provided food, ale and blankets. The only thing we're short of is wet-weather gear. The cutter's crew kept ours.' He took a breath. 'So, are you in or out?'

'In. But this is the last—'

'Don't,' Devlin interrupted, strain roughening his voice. 'Please.' He had damaged their friendship, perhaps irreparably. Yet what could he have done different? 'Let's get this over first. Then we can talk.'

'Nothing more to say.' Jared's murmur was lost in the darkness.

Spooning up stew, Thomas chased each mouthful with a gulp of brandy, and brooded. He wouldn't have thought it possible to hate his brother any more than he already did. But Tamara telling him she was with child by Devlin had added a new and bitter dimension to his loathing. Had she been raped he wouldn't have minded so much. Knowing she had resisted and been overpowered would have been some small comfort. *Damn him. Damn them both. Why couldn't she have lied?*

Raised voices and a clatter of booted feet in the passage brought his head up as Willie Grose burst in through the door.

'What the hell?' Thomas roared.

'Hark a minute,' Willie panted. 'Wait till you hear what I got to say. Be glad I come over, you will.'

'Get on with it then,' Thomas snarled.

'I just come from the Five Mackerel. One of Casvellan's stable lads was in supping ale while he waited for a carthorse to be shod. We got talking and he said he'd seen the prison cart arrive this morning and three of your brother's crew was put aboard in chains.'

'What d'you mean, three? He usually sails with—'

'That's all there was, just the three. Sam Clemmow, Ben Tozer and Joe Ince.'

'What about my brother? Wasn't he—?'

'See, that's what's strange. The boy said he seen your brother yesterday. Afternoon it was, and him guarded by two dragoons. One had a pistol pointed at 'n. But he never got in the wagon. The boy haven't seen hide nor hair of 'n since.'

Not dead, and not on his way to gaol. So where was Devlin? Fear made Thomas queasy. The food and brandy curdling in his stomach, Thomas pushed his plate away, threw down his napkin and rose from the table.

'That bit o' news have got to be worth the price of a drink or two,' Willie said hopefully. 'Go back again, shall I? See if there's any word about where the others is to?'

Taking coins from the cache in the side-table, Thomas dropped them into Willie's dirt-ingrained palm. 'Find out what you can, but keep your mouth shut.'

Within the hour Thomas was astride his horse and riding hard for Porthleven. Despite the air's chilly bite he arrived at the harbour sweating profusely. Not from the activity, but dread of what Devlin would do if he learned who had betrayed him. Pausing outside the Customs House he removed his beaver hat and wiped his forehead and upper lip with a handkerchief. After taking a few moments to compose himself he entered the building.

As an anxious clerk opened the door to Eddy's office, Thomas saw the supervisor sitting behind his desk, his face dark red with anger, anger that would be turned on him unless he was quick to deflect it.

'Well, Mr Eddy.' Tucking his hat under his arm he tugged off his York tan gloves and slapped them against his thigh. 'I have been hearing the wildest stories.'

'I daresay you have, sir. And they are no stranger than the truth. All that money!' He slammed his hand on to the desk, making Thomas flinch. 'And nothing to show for it. Not a single cask. They dumped the lot over the side. But at least I had prisoners. Where are they now? Tell me that! Gone, that's where!' he snarled before Thomas had a chance to say a word.

'Casvellan sent a letter.' Eddy rummaged among the mess of papers on his desk. 'Ordered me to have them brought to Trescowe under guard. He's the Justice so I couldn't argue. I couldn't have kept them here anyway. Where am I supposed to hold six prisoners? And now the boat's gone as well. It was here last night. Now it's gone. I've had men out asking. Waste of time. Nobody saw anything. They never do. That boat would have fetched a tidy sum at auction. Even sharing it with the cutter's captain and crew, I would have recouped something. Where did it go? Who's had it?'

Thomas's mind raced, fuelled first by terror then by fury. 'I think I know,' he spoke through gritted teeth. 'Casvellan ordered the crew taken to him? He's sending them to Roscoff for contraband.'

'Casvellan?' Eddy frowned as he considered. 'I'd be very surprised. I've never met the man, but from what I've heard he's straight as a die. Nothing's been said to me about him being involved with the trade.'

'Exactly,' Thomas retorted, convinced now. What other explanation could there be? 'No one would ever suspect him. Why else would he have kept Devlin Varcoe out of gaol?'

Eddy's head came up, his eyes sharp with curiosity. 'How do you know that?'

'I have my sources,' Thomas sat back. 'For instance, I know that of the six men taken under guard to Casvellan's house, only three were put aboard the prison wagon this morning. Where are the other three? And where is Devlin Varcoe? They were all at Trescowe yesterday. Now they've vanished. I'm telling you, Casvellan has them making a run.'

'Just say you're right—'

'I am, and I'll prove it. Varcoe will be returning with a cargo of contraband either tomorrow or the night after. Write me an order for Lieutenant Crocker to call out the dragoons. I'll have it delivered as soon as I get back to Porthinnis. You'll get your contraband, and I'll see Varcoe on the end of a rope. He won't cheat me again.'

Riding away with the signed order in his pocket, Thomas's mood swung wildly between elation and panic. Devlin must die. His own future depended on it.

After delivering Devlin's message to Jared, Jenefer had hurried back to the cottage and crawled into bed, shivering as much from nerves as from cold. But sleep had been impossible. She knew now where Martin was and what he'd been doing. But that knowledge only made her feelings about him even more confused.

For months he had braved discovery and death on a daily basis. She could not begin to imagine what life must have been like for him, living a lie, having to keep moving, always at risk of betrayal. How had he managed to survive? Of course she wanted him to come back safely. But if he did, what then? She was betrothed to a man she didn't know.

It was a little after three o'clock when she walked up the path to the thatched house next to the boatyard. A thick veil of cloud hid the sun and the milky sky was luminescent. With no wind to carry it away the sound of hammering and the rhythmic scrape of a saw seemed very loud.

Devlin had warned her to tell no one. But he should have reached Roscoff by now. She knew what it meant to be denied the truth: to live with fear and anxiety. Why should Tamara suffer that? Yet Jenefer still wasn't sure she was doing the right thing.

The young maid who answered her knock looked tired and

191

harassed. Jenefer's twinge of sympathy made her realize how much more aware of others she had become.

'Good afternoon.' She met the girl's gaze with a smile. 'Is Miss Gillis at home?'

Before the maid could reply, Tamara's mother appeared in the hall behind her. 'Miss Trevanion. This is a pleasant surprise. My goodness, you poor girl, what a time you've had. Is it true you've been working in Mr Casvellan's pilchard cellars?'

Detecting relish beneath the spurious sympathy Jenefer's smile faded but she kept her voice level. 'Briefly. I wasn't very adept. Is Tamara at home, Mrs Gillis?'

Morwenna waved the maid away. 'Go back up, Sally. I'll be with you shortly.' She turned again to Jenefer. 'I'm afraid not. And you find me in the middle of preparations for her wedding.'

Stunned, Jenefer could only stare at her. 'Wedding?' she managed finally.

'Indeed.' Morwenna beamed as she clasped her hands over her lace-frilled bosom. 'Mr Thomas Varcoe offered for Tamara and she has accepted him. Naturally, due to the difficult circumstances, it will be a quieter wedding than her father and I would have wished.'

'Difficult—?' Jenefer repeated faintly, thinking of the rumours and astounded that Tamara's mother would mention such matters at all, let alone to a relative stranger. For though they lived in the same village social meetings between the Gillis and Trevanion families had been rare.

'Yes.' Morwenna nodded with great solemnity. 'It is quite a tragedy. His brother is missing and we must prepare ourselves for the worst.' She sighed, shaking her head. 'But life must go on.' Her brave smile implied valiant effort for her daughter's sake. 'It is, I'm sure, what Devlin would have wanted.'

For a moment Jenefer was speechless. Then courtesy and her mother's training came to her rescue. 'My apologies. I have come at a bad time. I – I wish them very happy.' She turned away.

'Will you not leave a message?' Morwenna could not contain her curiosity. 'Tell me and I will tell my daughter the moment she returns. I am very busy but—'

'Thank you, no.' Jenefer edged away.

'It's not your sister, is it? I hear she's been poorly. Betsy is such a dear girl. Tamara is very fond of her.'

Beginning to wish she hadn't come, Jenefer continued backing down the path. 'She's much better, thank you.'

'Tamara will be glad to hear it. Good day to you, Miss Trevanion.' The door closed with a snap.

Perhaps it was as well that Tamara was out. If Devlin were killed bringing Martin home, Tamara would be no worse off than she was now. Why tell her he was alive when by tomorrow or the night after he might not be? She had accepted *Thomas* Varcoe? Why would she have done that? It didn't make sense.

CHAPTER NINETEEN

Earlier that afternoon, her nerves shredded by her mother's cease-less instructions, these interspersed with reminders of her good fortune, Tamara had begged to be excused.

'I'm sorry, Mama, but I have a dreadful headache.'

'My dear girl, why didn't you say so? Here, come and lie down. I will ring for Sally to fetch—'

'No, Mama, thank you. I will be better much sooner if I walk in the fresh air.'

'You do look pale. Very well then, go out if you must. But make sure you wrap up warm. I cannot be doing with you catching a chill. And while you walk, try to recover your spirits. You should remember your good fortune. When I think—' She shuddered. 'I shall expect you back in an hour. No later, mind. I need you here. There is so much to do.'

'I only distract you, Mama. You will get on far better without me.'

As she fastened her green jacket, Tamara tried to feel grateful that her family would be spared disgrace. Thomas had held her hand and promised to take care of her. But while his mouth smiled his eyes had raged. Recalling the touch of his soft damp fingers made her flesh creep.

Once out of the house she walked quickly up on to the moor, her favourite refuge since her early teens. She loved the space and soli-tude. Usually, being up here able to look down on to the village, the harbour and beyond to the sea, allowed her to distance herself from whatever troubled her. It put problems into perspective. But today there was no escape from what she had done.

Though there had been no alternative to accepting Thomas, every fibre of her being rebelled. But Devlin hadn't wanted her. Even if he still lived he was bound for prison, and then – there was no *if*. He was alive. He was. Had he been killed, she would have sensed it. She would know.

What could she do but marry Thomas? But how would she bear to? She hugged herself, the ache almost unbearable. She yearned for Devlin, grieved for Devlin. But she also felt something deeper than loss, darker than grief. It was fear: a premonition of something terrible.

She tried to persuade herself such imaginings were due to shock, or her condition, the pressures of a marriage she dreaded yet could not avoid. But in her heart she knew it was none of those things.

She tilted her head back. The air was totally still. She could hear the harsh cawing of rooks. Yet the nearest trees were at Trescowe, a quarter of a mile away. Her eyes flew open and every muscle in her body tightened. She looked around, desperately seeking an explanation for her unease.

Her gaze swept over the village, from the cottages on the seawall, tiers of houses separated by alleys, the church, the chapel, Thomas Varcoe's house, then down again to the harbour and quay. Seeing Devlin's workshop with the net store and his loft above, memories flooded back. And with the images came sensation as she relived all that she had felt. Her heart swelled as if it would burst and a low cry escaped before she could stop it. Biting hard on her lower lip she choked down sobs, her chest heaving with the effort. Blinking away tears she dared not allow to fall – for her mother might notice and that would provoke a tirade – she focused on the barking shed, the pilchard cellars then her father's boatyard.

She started to turn away but her attention was caught by a figure skulking by the bushes near the gate of Lieutenant Crocker's house. She watched the figure hurry up the path and push something beneath the door.

Raising her hands to shade her eyes as the man scurried down the road, she recognized the way he moved. According to Roz, Willie Grose liked to tell anyone who would listen that he was Mr Varcoe's right-hand man. Yet she had just seen him at the Riding Officer's door.

Had he and Thomas fallen out? Was this an act of revenge? She ought to warn Thomas. But he would want to know how she knew. Where had she been that allowed her to see this occurrence? He had already annoyed her by telling her mother he didn't approve of young women risking their safety and their reputation by going out without a chaperon.

She started walking, the path so familiar she was barely aware of it.

Marriage to Thomas would be a cage to which he held the only key. Watching his face when she told him of her condition, she had seen his fury. No matter what he told her mother, or his promises to protect and care for her, she was under no illusions. Her whole family was in his debt. But it was she who would pay. She would be his property to use as he chose. How would she bear it? At least she would have her baby. *Would she?*

'Miss Gillis?'

Startled, Tamara glanced up. It took her a moment to realize she had reached the crossroads, then another to recognize Betsy's sister. But what was she doing here? As Tamara's gaze sharpened, so did her instincts. But Jenefer spoke first.

'I called at your house. But your mother said—'

'Is Betsy—?'

Jenefer shook her head. 'No, she's much better. I came – I hoped to see you.'

'Me? Why?'

After a quick glance round Jenefer blurted, 'He's alive.'

A rushing sound like a great waterfall filled Tamara's head. She heard a gasping cry, and realized with faint surprise that it had come from her throat. The ground tilted under her feet and an arm gripped her around the waist.

'I'm sorry – I shouldn't have – are you ill?'

Swallowing her nausea, her skin prickling, Tamara sucked in a deep breath. 'No, I'm all right. It was just— Please, could we go to your house? I need to know – and it won't be possible – my mother.'

'Of course. Here, take my arm.'

Tamara's legs felt boneless. Her shift clung to her clammy skin, and her throat was parched. But none of it mattered. She had believed. And she was right. *Devlin was alive.*

They cut across the quay. The water in the harbour was eerily smooth. It reminded her of pitch then of black satin.

A few minutes later they turned into the opeway that led to Devlin's cottage. Once inside, Tamara sank on to a chair and watched Jenefer shovel coal on to the embers, open the damper and pull the kettle over the flames.

'You are sure?' Tamara asked, desperate for reassurance as Jenefer took off her coat and flung it over the banister rail. 'It isn't just a rumour?'

'No, I'm sure. I've seen him.'

'Where?'

'Here. He came here. He wanted me to take a message to Jared Sweet.'

Tamara stood up, but swayed as her head spun and quickly sat down again, supporting her head on her hands. Anxiety coursed through her.

'Don't try to move until you've had some tea,' Jenefer warned.

'But he's all right? He's not injured?'

'There were bruises on his face and temple.' Jenefer set the kettle down and put the lid on the small teapot. 'Forgive me, but is it true what your mother told me? That you are to be married to *Thomas* Varcoe?'

Her mother. Tamara pushed her fingers through her hair. Reluctant to get involved in explanations she raised her eyes. She cared little for what people thought of her, but hoped she might still protect her parents. 'It's difficult – complicated.'

Jenefer tipped milk into each cup then poured the tea. As she pushed the cup across, Tamara saw her hand was shaking.

'I know. It's hard to keep secrets in this village. You mentioned rumours. I heard one. I was not gossiping,' she added quickly, 'I was in the shop and couldn't help overhearing. It – they were saying—'

'About me?' Lifting her cup with both hands Tamara sipped. With each mouthful of hot tea she felt her strength returning.

Sitting opposite, Jenefer nodded. 'You and Devlin.'

'Ah.' Tamara met her gaze directly. 'I love him. But he—' To her horror her voice cracked. She put her trembling lips to the cup, swallowed more tea, and with it the lump in her throat.

'I'm sorry,' Jenefer said.

'Why did he want Jared?' Tamara lowered the cup, clattering it on to the saucer. 'Oh God, surely he can't be making another run? But if he isn't, then where *is* he going?' Her head hurt and she rested on her hands as she tried to work it out.

'When Thomas came to our house he told my mother that Devlin was either dead or a prisoner. If he believes that, then he can't have put up the money. So who has?' She looked up. 'What if Thomas lied? What if he does know Devlin's alive? What if he's found out Devlin is making a run for someone else? Thomas hates his brother. While I was up on the moor I saw Willie Grose push something under Lt Crocker's door.' Tamara gazed at Jenefer. 'Willie wouldn't do that on his own account; Thomas must have sent him.'

'Devlin is making another run,' Jenefer said. 'But it's not for contraband. He's trying to rescue a government agent.'

'How do you know?'

'I didn't want to take the message so he was forced to tell me. But he swore me to secrecy.'

'What was the message?'

'Just that Jared should meet him.'

'Did he say where?'

Jenefer shook her head. 'He said Jared would know, but it was safer for me not to.'

'If Thomas has alerted Lt Crocker to call out the dragoons, Devlin will be sailing into a trap.' Cold rage at Thomas's duplicity had banished all trace of her faintness and the tea had given her energy. She felt strong, determined, and impatient. 'Thomas said Devlin was either a prisoner or dead. If he was a prisoner, how did he get free? Someone in authority must be involved in this. Devlin must have made some kind of bargain and his side of it is to rescue this agent.'

'But what if—?'

'He'll do it,' Tamara insisted. 'He's the bravest, most skilled seaman on this coast.' Then she noticed Jenefer was shaking.

'What is it? What's wrong?'

Jenefer looked up. She was laughing, but her face was creased with anguish and tears streaked her cheeks. 'Do you know who this agent is?'

'Of course not.' Tamara was bewildered. 'How could I?'

'I do. His name is Martin Erisey.'

Startled because she recognized the name, Tamara tried to recall where and when she had heard it. As realization dawned, she gazed at Jenefer, tightness gathering at the base of her skull. 'But isn't he—?'

'The man to whom I am betrothed? The man with a life I knew nothing about? A man who has lied to me since the day we met?' As Jenefer's voice climbed, Tamara reached across the table to touch her arm. 'Yes, that's Martin Erisey. I wish him no harm. Indeed, I hope he escapes, and survives the voyage home. But as for our engagement – I don't know. I just don't know.'

'This is not the time for such decisions,' Tamara said gently. 'I must go. I need to warn Devlin.'

'You can't. It's too late. He came last night. If Jared went to meet him, surely they will have sailed at once?'

Tamara sank back. 'Of course they would. He wouldn't dare wait. The risk of being seen, or someone talking.'

'I should go and see Betsy. She will be so worried. I'm ashamed I haven't told her.'

'Devlin swore you to secrecy for good reason.' Tamara raised her hand to forestall Jenefer before she could speak. 'I know why you told me, and I'll never be able to thank you enough. But God willing they should be back before dawn tomorrow. It might be better if you wait until then. You're under great strain.'

Jenefer's mouth twisted. 'After all that's happened these past months I should be used to that.'

Tamara buttoned her coat. 'I must go home. I was only going out for an hour and my mother will be fretting.'

Jenefer followed her to the door. 'What will you do about Thomas?'

Tamara shook her head. 'I don't know. I can't think about that now.'

As she closed the front door Tamara saw Sally emerge from the kitchen clutching some burning feathers and a small dark bottle.

'Oh, miss, thank God you're home,' the maid whispered. 'In some state she is. She's shouting for her drops. But I didn't like to—'

'That's all right, Sally. I'll see to it. Just give me a moment.'

'Tamara? Is that you?'

Crossing to the bottom of the stairs and gesturing for Sally to go on up, Tamara called, 'Yes, Mama. I'm just coming.'

'How could you!' Morwenna cried as Tamara entered. Lying on

her bed with several pillows at her back, she inhaled the smoke as Sally passed the feathers under her nose, grimacing and pushing the maid's hand away. 'Where are my drops? I need my drops.'

Tamara took the bottle from the maid. 'Go on downstairs,' she said softly.

'Want me to leave the feathers, miss?'

'No, take them with you.'

As Sally scuttled out and Tamara closed the door behind her, Morwenna pressed a tear-soaked ball of cambric to her nose. 'Be back in an hour I said. But you've been gone over two. I've been almost out of my mind with worry.'

Measuring five drops of laudanum into a small glass of water, Tamara carried it across to where her mother lay. Morwenna snatched it and drained the contents, then sank back against the mound of pillows. Retrieving the glass, Tamara sat on the side of the bed. Her mother's eyes were red-rimmed and swollen almost shut. Concern replaced her initial impatience.

'Why, Mama?' she asked gently. 'I told you I was going for a walk. You know how I lose track of time.'

Morwenna's face crumpled. 'I thought you'd run away,' she sobbed. 'I was afraid you weren't coming back. People would ask where you were and there'd be a scandal and I couldn't face it, Tamara. It would be the death of me.'

Because the thought of flight had crossed her mind only to be dismissed, Tamara was able to meet her mother's fearful gaze. Leaning down she pressed her lips to the puckered forehead. The skin was damp and hot. She took her mother's hand, hoping the tincture of opium would work quickly.

'Well, here I am,' she soothed. 'I'm truly sorry you were so worried.'

'Yes, but where were you?'

The familiar undertone of complaint was preferable to the abject terror she'd heard in her mother's voice a moment earlier.

'I met Jenefer Trevanion and she invited me back with her for a cup of tea.'

'She called here while you were out. What did she want?'

'Nothing very much.' The lie slipped easily from Tamara's tongue. To protect Devlin she would lie to God Himself. 'Just to let me know that Betsy is making a good recovery and hopes I may be free to call on her next week.' She hesitated. 'Mama, why did you tell Miss Trevanion?'

'Why shouldn't I?' her mother demanded. Bright patches of colour bloomed in her cheeks. 'It's no more than the truth. And the sooner people know the better.' Her gaze dropped to Tamara's waist then slid away. 'I had every right to tell her.' She wiped her nose. 'I hear she's living in the cottage *that man* bought when it was a ruin.'

Tired, wondering whether Devlin had yet reached France, whether he had managed to find Erisey, whether they had got away safely, Tamara held on to her temper.

'Yes, that's right.'

'Well?' Morwenna prompted, settling herself more comfortably, her eyelids perceptibly heavier. 'What is it like?'

Tamara had not intended to frighten her mother. But having done so the least she could do now was indulge her curiosity.

The clock had just struck nine when Tamara said goodnight to her parents and went up to bed. The laudanum's calming effect had enabled her mother to get up and eat her evening meal, which in turn would help her to sleep.

A fire in the small grate had taken the chill from her bedroom and flames from the glowing coals added their own light to that of her candle. She was grateful for the warmth. The stresses of the day had left her physically and emotionally exhausted. And when she was tired she always felt cold.

Carrying a copper warming pan, Sally slid it between the sheets, moved it back and forward then left it as she crossed to take Tamara's gown.

Undressed to her shift, Tamara sat in front of her toilet table, opened the drawer and took out her hairbrush.

Sally closed the wardrobe door.

'Like me to do that would you, miss?'

'Not tonight, I can manage.' She just wanted to be left alone.

'All right if I go then?' Sally crossed to the bed and removed the copper warming pan. 'I just heard mistress come up.'

'Yes, of course.'

Still the maid hesitated. 'You sure I can't fetch you something, miss? Hope you don't mind me saying, but you do look awful tired.'

'It's not been an easy day.' Swivelling round Tamara forced a smile. 'I'll be fine tomorrow. I just need a good night's sleep.'

' 'Night then, miss.'

'Goodnight, Sally.'

After brushing her hair and exchanging her shift for a night-dress, Tamara blew out the candle and climbed into bed. Lying on her back she rested her right hand on her belly and thought of the child growing inside her and, as she did every night, of Devlin.

She pictured his face: dark brows raised as he mocked, the hunger in his eyes as he drew her close, the gentle warmth of his lips the first time he had kissed her; the weight and strength and heat of his body. She had felt so *safe*. Yet the price of those wonderful moments was rejection and bitter anger. It hurt. How it hurt. Hot tears leaked beneath her closed eyelids and slipped down her temples into her hair.

He did not want her, and she must marry his brother. But right now all that mattered was that he returned safely.

Told by his uncle where Martin was waiting, Devlin had not recognized the dishevelled unshaven man clad in peasant clothes. Though the local fishermen shook their heads, warning of the coming storm, Devlin knew he dared not wait. The moment Martin was aboard they left.

Thin, haggard and clearly exhausted, Martin asked for food, ate what he was given, then wrapped himself in a blanket and crawled into the sail locker out of the way.

Forced south by the north-easterly wind, Devlin had to keep tacking. This meant shifting ballast, making the tired men even wearier. As the night wore on and the wind rose to a near gale he ordered both lug sails dropped leaving just the staysail to maintain their heading. The wind pressure on the masts alone was driving the lugger forward through heaped up seas half the height of the fore mast. Waves breaking all around gleamed white in the darkness and the shrieking wind blew foam in long streaks from the crests.

The muscle-straining pitch and roll added to the crew's difficulties, forcing them to hold on with one hand and bale with the other. Devlin needed every ounce of his strength to hold the tiller steady while Jared did the work of two men.

Each time the boat plunged into a trough the wind noise eased before rising again to a thrumming scream as they reached the crest and were hurled down the slope into the next trough. Soaked and chilled, deafened by the gale, Devlin yelled at the men to swap sides and change jobs. He had to keep them moving. He knew how tired they were, and that the urge to sleep was becoming harder to fight.

By morning the wind had veered towards the south. But instead of blowing itself out it seemed to be strengthening. Running before it they were in constant danger of a following wave breaking on top of them. The air was thick with spray and hard to breathe. Salt had made Devlin's eyes sore and they burned with tiredness.

If he died who would miss him? His brother certainly wouldn't. The crew would find work on other boats. Jared would marry Betsy.

He had worked hard and been successful. Money and reputation had bought him everything he wanted: property, his lugger, and women. He had earned his crew's respect and loyalty. Jared had been more of a brother to him than Thomas, though he might have damaged their friendship beyond repair.

Would Tamara miss him? Why should she? She had loved him, and he had thrown her gift back in her face. He wished now – too late – that he'd had her courage. But conditioned from childhood to expect rejection he had kept even those kindest to him at a distance.

The lugger teetered on a foaming wave-crest. Caught by the wind it began to twist. Jared lurched to help him and Devlin hauled on the tiller with all his strength as the boat plunged.

CHAPTER TWENTY

Gradually Tamara became aware of a loud roaring. She opened her eyes. It was still dark, and the noise was the wind. Suddenly rain splattered like gravel against the window making her jump. Outside she could hear the boom, crash and hiss of breaking waves.

Her mother's shriek catapulted her out of bed and she fumbled for the tinderbox on her nightstand. She had just lit her candle when the door opened and she saw her father. Hastily dressed in breeches, shirt and waistcoat he raised the lantern.

'Good, you're awake. Come and see to your mother. I have to go down to the yard. I've got two boats up on props. If this wind gets any stronger—' He shook his head, superstition stopping him in case voicing his worst fears made them happen.

'Is she ill?'

'She's afraid the wind will take the roof.' Anxiety made him terse.

'What time is it, Papa?' Seizing her robe from the foot of the bed she pulled it on and hastily knotted the sash. Grabbing her candleholder and shielding the flame with one palm she padded barefoot after him.

'About five I think.'

That meant another hour until sunrise. Where was Devlin? Was he still off the French coast? Had he reached Cornish waters? Was he caught up in the storm?

She entered her parents' room and her mother looked round from the open drawers of a chest. She was clutching an armful of shifts and nightgowns. Her eyes were wide, her frilled bedcap awry. 'Quick! Empty the closet. We must take everything downstairs before the roof goes. Listen! Can't you hear it? I need my clothes. I cannot be seen like this. I have a position – my dignity. Come *on*, Tamara!'

Terror had put her beyond reason, so Tamara didn't waste time trying. Crossing to her mother's side she set down her candle then took the clothes and dropped them on top of the disordered bedcovers.

'I'll bring them. But first let's go downstairs to the living-room. I'll make up the fire so you'll be warm and safe.' Their arms linked, she drew her mother firmly towards the landing and stairs.

'But the roof?' In the flickering candlelight her mother's face was haggard with fear.

'Mama,' Tamara reassured, 'this house is over fifty years old and has withstood countless storms.'

Her mother stared at her, plagued by doubt but wanting to believe. 'But all that groaning and creaking—'

'Is just the wind under the eaves.'

Tamara opened the living-room door and guided her mother to an armchair, then set the candle on a side table. 'There. It's much quieter in here. I'll fetch a blanket so you'll be comfortable while we wait for it to pass.'

But it didn't pass. It grew worse. The wind howled like a ravening animal looking for a way in. As her mother's fear became frenzy, Tamara resorted to another larger dose of laudanum. She sat holding the trembling hand as her mother slid into somnolence then eventually slept.

Back upstairs, Tamara gathered armfuls of clothes and brought them down, laying them in an armchair where her mother would see them as soon as she opened her eyes. Outside the wind screamed. At the front of the house it roared in the chimneys, rattled doors and windows, and hurled torrents of rain at the glass until Tamara began to fear the panes would shatter. Knowing there was nothing more she could do until daylight, she rejoined her mother, lay down on the sofa and closed her eyes.

She was floating, weightless, the sun warm on her eyelids. Then suddenly the water roughened, tossing her about. Breaking waves slapped her face, filling her nose and mouth. Out of her depth, choking, unable to breathe, she floundered, struggling desperately, and felt one foot touch the bottom. She opened her eyes and the water was red. Her lungs strained. She had to breathe. She opened her mouth – and jerked upright, gasping, her heart pounding, the rapid pulse loud in her ears. She felt the same terrible apprehension she had experienced up on the moor, and knew it meant death. *But whose?*

The candle had gone out. In the grey light of morning she could see her mother still sleeping in the other chair. Sweating and shivering from her nightmare, she stood up, stretched to ease the tension from her neck and shoulders, and went to open the curtains.

The garden was strewn with debris. But her gaze skimmed over it, drawn to tangled wreckage strewn about the harbour, all that remained of the fishing boats moored to the quay. Smashed by the waves, they had been abandoned by the ebbing tide.

At the mouth of the harbour huge waves pounded the wall with a sound like distant thunder. Breakers reared, curled and crashed on to the beach, leaving a red line as they receded. *Her dream – blood – death.*

With a strangled gasp she ran to the door and raced up to her room. Wrenching open her curtains she could see the listing hulk of a ship driven on to the rocks during the night. Rags of canvas flapped on broken masts. Already a few villagers were struggling down the beach to salvage what they could.

Weak with relief – *it was too big, not a lugger. Not Devlin.* She sagged on to the window seat swallowing repeatedly as she fought dizziness and nausea.

As soon as she could stand, she threw off her robe and nightgown, pulled on her shift, her green habit, stockings and boots. Tying her hair at the nape of her neck so it wouldn't blow across her face and get in her way, she ran downstairs again and almost collided with Sally who was carrying the ash pail and small shovel she used to clean out the fireplace.

'Has Mrs Voss arrived?'

'Not yet, miss. I nearly didn't get back myself. There's chimneys down and slates flying. 'Tis some bad all the way up to the farm. Still, I got the milk all right. Mr Reece's thatched roof was tore off. Straw everywhere there is. The Mitchells and the Tallacks been flooded out. Their windows is all smashed and front doors stove in. The sea went in the front door and out the back. Poor souls, some terrible mess it is. I've never known nothing like it. The rain's stopped for a minute but that won't last.'

'Leave the fire for now, Sally. Make some tea and toast for my mother. She had a bad night so I brought her downstairs. She's in the small living-room. I hope she's still asleep.'

'What about you, miss? Bring some for you, shall I?'

'I'll have something when I get back.'

'You're never going out? 'Tidn safe.'

'I won't be long.'

Not daring to open the front door in case the wind took it off its hinges or she couldn't shut it again, Tamara went out the back way. As she picked her way through the off-cuts of wood, pitch pots, frayed rope and scraps of canvas blown from the boatyard to litter the grass and path, the gale tore at her clothes and made her eyes water. Once through the gate she crossed the open ground between the yard and the broad foreshore, her boots slipping on the thick layer of seaweed tossed up by the tide. *No spring tide had ever reached this high.*

She stumbled across the beach trying to avoid more debris, and saw the crimson tide-line of her dream. It wasn't blood: it was red coats. The stricken ship had been carrying marines, drowned as they tried to reach the shore.

Some villagers were dragging their finds up the beach. Others pulled corpses out of the water only to rifle their pockets. Moses Carthew, the Methodist preacher, ran from one group to another, waving his arms as he threatened hellfire and damnation. They ignored him. What need had the dead of possessions?

The rain began again, hard, heavy and almost horizontal.

Realizing there was nothing she could do she retraced her steps. The wind shoved and pushed, making her run while the rain hammered her scalp and soaked through her jacket.

Sally met her in the passage. 'I done me best, miss, but she won't eat nothing. Working herself into some state she is.'

Struggling against anger and impatience, Tamara nodded. 'I'll see to her. Make a pot of coffee and cut three thick slices of heavy cake, will you?' She went in to her mother. Knowing reassurance would be a waste of time she measured out a dose of laudanum and poured it into her mother's open mouth.

'Mama, I'll be back again in just a moment.'

'Where are you going? Don't leave me!'

'I'm taking coffee and something to eat to Papa and the men in the yard.'

'Sally can do that,' her mother cried pitifully. 'I need you.'

Shutting the door, Tamara hurried to the kitchen. She wrapped the cake in a clean napkin, put it in a basket beside the coffee pot and three cups, and went out once more into the driving rain.

The devastation shocked her. Toppled from its props, Devlin's new lugger lay on its side amid the wreckage of the smaller boat on to which it had fallen. Her father crouched beneath the only boat still standing, hammering wedges to hold additional props in place while two of his shipwrights anchored the hull with ropes and iron spikes.

Seeing her he straightened and waved her away. 'Go back in the house. It isn't safe.' He had pulled an old black oilskin over his clothes, but his head was bare, his hair plastered to his scalp.

She held up the basket and waded through the debris towards him. He looked exhausted and beaten.

'Papa, I'm so sorry.'

'Go on, lass. Nothing you can do here.'

The wind pushing her along, Jenefer tried to avoid broken roof tiles and scattered bricks from fallen chimneys. She had stayed at the Sweets' just long enough to tell Betsy, Inez and Arf where Jared had gone and why.

But now as she passed alleys leading down to the harbour and caught glimpses of the raging, white-capped water, she wondered whether knowing that Jared was somewhere out in that maelstrom had added to their worry rather than relieving it. Yet recalling

Betsy's pallor, the dark circles under her eyes, and the anxiety emanating from both Inez and Arf at their son's sudden and unprecedented disappearance, their dread that he had been snatched by a press gang, how could she not have told them?

She had seen Dr Trennack down on the beach supervising the loading of corpses on to a wagon.

Ahead of her, carrying whatever they had been able to rescue from their flooded homes, Denzil Laity, Arthur Tallack and Jacca Benney ushered their wives and children up the through the alleys to higher ground. The tide was rising again, and with the wind behind it, would flood the properties on the quay.

This was her chance to repay all the kindness she had received. As chapel steward, George Ince would hold a key.

When he opened his door to her urgent knock she didn't waste time. 'Mr Ince, please will you open the chapel? I've just seen three families who've been forced out of their homes. There will be many more before this is over. They need somewhere safe, warm and dry to wait out the storm. I'm going to fetch Lizzie Clemmow and Ernestine Rowse. I'll ask them to contact everyone they think will be willing to bring any food and blankets they can spare and meet me there.'

As she was speaking his expression altered from surprise to relief that someone had taken charge and something was being done. Nodding, he reached behind the door to grab his coat from the hook.

'I'm on me way. Put up a notice shall I? There's a blackboard and chalk in the back room.'

'Thank you, Mr Ince. That's an excellent idea.'

Hurrying home she saw Moses Carthew.

'Kneel in fear of the Lord all you sinners!' he bellowed as he marched towards her, wild-eyed and gesticulating. 'He has sent a tempest to punish those who traffic in the demon drink!'

Jenefer knew that both the Laitys and the Benneys were staunch Methodists and teetotal. Furious with the minister, she resisted the temptation to suggest that he come to the chapel and do something to help. Those people had suffered enough. The last thing they needed was this deranged man shouting at them.

Back at the cottage she put all her vegetables, cheese and butter into a basket, rolled up a blanket and grabbed her purse. Running next door to Lizzie she outlined her plan.

'If you take my veg, I'll bring my big pan,' Lizzie said, opening the table drawer and taking out one large and one small knife.

'We're going to need plates, bowls and spoons,' Jenefer said.

'Mrs Avers.' They spoke simultaneously. Every summer the doctor's wife hosted the village fête in her large garden.

'Do you think Harry might come and help?' Jenefer asked, referring to Ben Tozer's father, Lizzie's other neighbour.

'He'll be mad as fire if we don't ask'n,' Lizzie said. 'I'll go and fetch him while you get Ernestine. She got a lovely great pan she use for making jam.'

Jenefer nodded. 'Now all we need is a stove.' She turned to Lizzie's ten-year-old son and gave him her purse. 'William, take this to the bakehouse. Ask Mr Rowe for as many loaves as the money will buy. Tell him I'll be in shortly.' As William scampered off she turned to Lizzie. 'I'd use my range, but Mr Rowe's is bigger and much nearer the chapel.'

Lizzie snorted. 'That man wouldn't give you a cold if he could charge for it.'

Jenefer's brows rose. 'Do you really think he'll refuse me, when it's for such a good cause?'

Pausing for a moment, Lizzie eyed her. 'No. He won't bleddy dare.'

Standing at the living-room window, Thomas peered through the eye-glass that had been his father's. Despite the fire burning in the grate and his warm clothes, a shiver tightened his skin as he peered through the eyepiece at the turbulent sea. Low grey cloud raced above mountainous spume-streaked waves.

No one could survive in that. Not even his hated brother who had the luck of the devil and more lives than a cat. The dragoons would find nothing but wreckage and bodies.

He turned to look towards the harbour. Even inside the seawalls the broken, foam-capped waves were several feet high. Sturdy fishing boats that last night had been moored alongside were now splintered planks tossed on the water. On the quay huge stones lay amid shingle hurled up by the waves.

Bearing the brunt of wind and sea, parts of the eastern sea wall had disintegrated. If the gale continued the rising tide would demolish the rest of it leaving the inner harbour and quay without protection.

But of more immediate concern to him was the visible damage to workshops, cellars, barking sheds and net stores. Not only had

windows been smashed and their frames broken, on several buildings, including Devlin's, the heavy double-doors had been stove in
and now lay flat on the ground or hung askew on their hinges.

People milled about, battling against the wind. But there was
little left to save. Already the waves were exploding against the
quay, hurling spray roof high.

He had been up for hours, waiting impatiently for the gale to
ease. But this was no ordinary storm. Instead of blowing itself out it
was growing stronger. The wind had veered round to the south-east,
directly behind the rising tide.

Thomas knew he dared not wait any longer. If he didn't go now,
the building and everything in it might fall to the storm.

With a small axe concealed up the sleeve of his caped greatcoat
and his beaver hat pulled low over his eyes, he hurried down
through the village. Though he kept to the narrow streets behind
the quay, the thunder of the waves was deafening. Feeling the shock
through the soles of his boots, his heart tripped on an extra beat.
Moistening his lips he tasted salt. The air was dense with spray that
made his eyes sting.

As he opened the gate in the alley it crashed back against the
wall. He struggled to shut it again. He didn't want anyone to see
him, or coming in offering help he didn't need. Keeping close to the
wall he climbed the stone stairs and used the axe to smash the
padlock. It clattered on to the stone by his feet, the sound drowned
by the screaming wind and pounding waves.

Inside the loft he paused for a moment. Two windows overlooked
the harbour. But salt and spume had frosted the small panes block-
ing much of the grey morning light. Crossing to one of the windows
Thomas peered out, and stumbled backwards as a huge wave
smashed on to the quay with a deep boom that shook the building.
It exploded into a blizzard of froth and spray, flinging broken
planks, stones, mangled crab pots, and other debris against the
front wall and in through the broken doors.

Dropping the axe he turned to flee. But after two steps dizziness
made him stagger. He grabbed the back of a chair and held on with
both hands, head bent, eyes closed. His heart pounded so fast his
gorge rose and he feared he might vomit. He plunged trembling
fingers between his throat and collar, wrecking the careful arrangement of his cravat in his haste to loosen the starched cloth.

As he sucked in shaking breaths his pulse began to slow. He straightened, flexing his shoulders and jutting his chin. He wasn't leaving until he found what he had come for.

Picking up the axe he crossed to the oak chest. He smashed the padlock and threw back the lid. Tossing shirts and stockings on to the floor, he found a small brandy keg and a stone jar. Setting both aside to take with him he continued emptying the chest. With the last of the clothes thrown aside revealing nothing, he stood up, flinching as another wave battered the building.

Crossing to the shelf he swept everything to the floor, watching for a leather purse. The sound of smashing crockery and clatter of pewter and enamel was lost in the deafening noise outside. He upended the ewer and the buckets, flung them aside and peered into the two lanterns. He wrenched open the wooden cupboard and went through the pockets of Devlin's waistcoats and the jackets he sometimes wore instead of his oiled wool guernsey.

Another wave hit making the floor shake. He heard a loud crack then a deep grinding rumble and quickened his search, reaching under folded shirts and trousers. He felt inside shoes then threw them behind him and turned spare sea boots upside down. *Nothing.*

He slammed the cupboard door in temper but it fell open again as he staggered towards the bed, disoriented and off-balance. The rumbling stopped. The cupboard toppled forward and crashed to the floor making him start. He should leave. He would go in just a minute.

Breathless from the unaccustomed exertion, he lurched toward the bed with the strangest sensation of walking uphill. Seizing the bedclothes he flung them into the mess on the floor. *Where was Devlin's money?* He staggered to the table, wrenched open the drawer and fumbled for a sharp knife. Slashing first the pillow and then the mattress he pulled the stuffing out, shouting his frustration when once more he found nothing.

He glared around him, panting and sweating, and his gaze fell on the keg. *Too light to be full. Yet there had been no sound when he shook it.*

As he lunged forward to grab it the windows shattered. Glass flew inwards, slicing his face and hands. The wooden frames buckled and snapped. Weakened by the barrage of waves, the lower walls crumbled. In a salvo of loud cracks the floor collapsed. Thomas knew brief outrage then bowel-loosening terror. He was falling . . .

CHAPTER TWENTY-ONE

Returning to the house Tamara found her mother gazing sleepily into the fire. Backing out and quietly closing the door, she went upstairs to change. The gale shook the window and blew a chilly draught under the door. Shivering, she stripped off her wet clothes and pulled on a clean shift, a simple white petticoat and a high-necked long-sleeved gown of pale green figured muslin. After towelling her hair almost dry she combed out the tangles then twisted it into a chignon.

Pausing by the window she peered out at wild sea and low cloud blurred by spray into a grey murk. *Where was he?* Wrenching her gaze away, she gathered up her linen and her sodden habit and took them downstairs. In the kitchen Sally had set her boots on the brass fender to dry.

'Take this through to the dining-room shall I, miss?' Sally poured steaming brown liquid into a china cup. 'I made chocolate. I know you can't stomach coffee just now.'

Remembering Devlin's pewter mug and the brandy he had given her to stop her shivering, Tamara dragged her mind back to the present.

'Thank you. I'll stay here. It's warmer.' She sat down at the kitchen table. Sally put a plate in front of her. On it was a slice of heavy cake studded with currants and lemon peel. 'I'm not—'

'C'mon now, miss.' Sally didn't let her finish. 'You need your strength. Got to think of the little one,' she added softly. 'Eating for two now you are.'

Tamara's eyes filled and she compressed her lips to still their quivering. Not trusting her voice she gave a brief nod and raised the cup.

Swallowing the cake she drained the last of the chocolate. Already she felt stronger. She hadn't realized how hungry she was. As she stood up, someone knocked loudly on the back door. Sally opened it and William Clemmow looked past her to Tamara.

'Please, miss, I got a message from Miss Trevanion. She's in the chapel looking after people who been flooded out. She says if you aren't busy please could you go and help.'

'I'll come at once. Wait,' she called as he turned away. 'Did Miss Trevanion want me to bring anything?'

William shrugged uncertainly. 'She and Miz Rouse and my ma was all carrying veg and blankets and pans. I had to go to Rowe's and buy all his bread.'

'Thank you, William.' She gave him a penny out of the tin on the shelf. 'You go on back. Tell her I'm right behind you.'

Sally closed the door behind him. 'Miss, are you sure?'

Tamara paused briefly in the doorway. 'He's out there, Sally. In this. If I don't keep busy I shall go mad.'

Rolling up four old blankets taken from the chest on the landing, she laced up her second-best boots, buttoned her poppy-red great-coat, tied a shawl over her head and left the house once more.

Waves crashed over the quay and exploded against the buildings at the back. Shock took her breath as she saw the heap of rubble and wood, all that remained of Devlin's workshop, and the loft where he had lived, where she had lain with him, loved him.

Refusing even to consider it an omen she told herself it meant nothing. His property, like a dozen others that had been damaged, was simply a casualty of the storm. When he came home he would rebuild.

She closed her eyes and conjured memories. Devlin busy on his boat, a blue checked shirt tight across his broad shoulders, dark curly hair ruffled by the breeze; black brows lifted in mockery, the corners of his mouth tilting as he teased her. He was so strong, so vital. *He could not die.*

Gasping, she forced herself onward. Jenefer needed her. The rain had stopped again, but the air was heavy with moisture and salt. As she cut through the back streets Tamara caught up with a family she recognized. Husband and wife were hollow-eyed. Each carried a big bundle: all they had had time to grab. Two older children led the younger ones, all of them shaken by the violence that had destroyed their home.

'Mr Jory, take your family to the chapel,' Tamara urged, briefly slowing her pace to theirs and shouting above the noise of the wind. 'Miss Trevanion has arranged food and shelter for those who need somewhere safe. I'm going to help her. I'll see you there.'

In defiance of the intermittent rain, one of the chapel's double doors had been fastened back. A black-painted board with *All Welcome* chalked on it was propped just inside visible to anyone approaching.

In the vestibule, relieved to be out of the buffeting gale, Tamara loosened the shawl and pulled it off as she walked into the chapel.

The building was already half full. Wet and shivering, their faces pinched with shock and pale as wood ash, families sat among their pitifully few possessions. Above the smell of wet clothes and unwashed bodies she scented something savoury and appetizing, and saw Lizzie Clemmow with a tray crammed with steaming cups, mugs and bowls moving from group to group. Ernestine Rouse followed with two large platters piled with hunks of bread smeared with butter and topped with a sliver of cheese.

Craning her neck Tamara saw Jenefer at the far end standing beside a table on the small platform from which Moses Carthew preached his notoriously threatening sermons. Starting forward she passed sullen-faced Mary-Anne Grose who jerked her chin towards Jenefer.

'Who do she think she is? Telling everybody what to do.'

Hands on her hips, Hannah Tresidder rounded on Mary-Anne. 'Don't you ever stop bleddy moaning? Doing a 'andsome job she is. Just like that there story in the Bible about the loaves and fishes. Look aound, maid.' Hannah's gesture encompassed everyone in the chapel. 'Where'd they be now if 't wasn' for Miss Trevanion? Out on the street, wet and cold.'

'Mr Carthew—' Mary-Anne began.

'Him?' Hannah snorted. 'Bleddy useless he is. Preach hell and damnation from sunrise to Thursday he would. But where's he to? Eh? Not in here helping, that's for sure. Miss Trevanion never belonged in no pilchard cellar, dear of her. But she wasn't above trying. So stop your craking. I got no patience with it. Worth two of you she is. If you can't be useful, get on home out of it.'

'No need to be like that,' Mary-Anne began, but Hannah was already hurrying away.

Tamara reached the table at which Jenefer, a stained apron covering her gown, was ladling steaming broth from a huge pan into another trayload of cups and bowls. She glanced up, her face shiny with perspiration. Her smile was warm and conveyed relief.

'Thank you so much for coming.'

'I was glad to. I need to be busy. It's the only way I—' Tamara cut herself off and took a breath. 'What would you like me to do?'

'Quite a few people have minor injuries. Almost everyone has cuts and bruises either from things falling on them, or because they tripped on debris in the streets on their way here. Doctor Avers was in earlier and treated some. But he's been called away. I don't like asking you to go out again, but you know Roz Trevaskis and I don't. Her salves and ointments would really help.'

'I'll go and ask her to come down,' Tamara said, and turned to retrace her steps. As she eased her way through towards the door, more people were arriving, hesitating at the entrance. She saw the relief on their faces as Lizzie Clemmow called them by name and urged them to come inside.

'Find yourselves a seat,' Lizzie called. 'I'll be there d'rectly. Soon as I got some more broth, all right?'

Covering her head with the shawl and tying the ends at the back, Tamara made her way toward the seaward end of the village where Roz lived with her mother and younger brother. Their home was a cramped and dark cob-walled cottage behind the Five Mackerel inn.

As she reached the corner, her streaming eyes narrowed against the raging wind, she saw that the outermost in a row of three small dwellings on the seawall had disappeared. The second had lost its roof and with each mountainous wave more masonry was torn from the walls and swept away by the seething water.

An old man stood in the doorway of the innermost cottage. Spray cascaded over the roof drenching the man and woman pleading with him. Two fishermen joined them, pointing to the foaming turbulence in the harbour, but still the old man shook his head.

A gigantic wave reared over the cottage. Grabbing the couple the fishermen ran, dragging them up toward the road. The breaker smashed on to the cottage, flinging sheets of spray high into the salt-laden air. Some spilled into the harbour the rest retreated taking the roof with it. There was no sign of the old man.

Horrified, powerless to help, Tamara forced her shaking legs to move. She could do nothing here, and Jenefer needed Roz. She dropped her gaze as she passed the couple, not wanting to intrude on the woman's grief as the man tried to comfort her. It had happened so fast. The little house had been there one minute, yet between one breath and the next, half of it had been washed away.

Storms were a regular occurrence every winter and the village was grateful for the bounty they brought. But she had never seen seas like this. *Devlin was out there.* What chance did he have in the lugger when a much bigger troopship had foundered? Panic beat like dark wings in her head. Her breath sobbed as she fought over-whelming dread.

If she gave in to fear, acknowledged the possibility – *the likeli-hood* – that he might not get back . . . *no!* She had to trust, to believe he would survive. She couldn't pray. Her own mother had called her wicked and thoughtless and selfish. Why would God listen to such as she? All she could do was have faith in Devlin, in his skill and his strength. Out there with only half a crew, the other half depending for their freedom on his return, he needed all of it, and more.

Trembling, she pounded on Roz's door. Roz opened it. Behind her Tamara glimpsed Mary Trevaskis, open-mouthed and snoring in a chair by the fire.

'Jenefer Trevanion needs your help.' Steadying her voice, Tamara quickly explained.

Roz studied her, then gave a brief nod.

'My boots are muddy so I'll wait out here,' Tamara said to spare her friend. She had never been invited inside. Understanding why, she felt no resentment.

A few moments later Roz emerged carrying a basket containing jars and bottles. She wore her overlarge coat and a faded poke bonnet tied under her chin. Without a word she slipped her arm through Tamara's. Huddled close, they hurried back towards the chapel.

Midday came and went. As word spread through the village more people arrived at the chapel. Though the number of homes completely devastated was relatively few, many more had lost chim-neys or tiles, or had their windows smashed. The thatched roofs of two houses had been ripped off and straw lay scattered in drifts and clumps along the full length of the street.

Some people came seeking the comfort of company while they waited for the gale to ease. Few arrived empty-handed. Several brought food; others clothes outgrown or saved to be cut down.

Roz moved quietly and efficiently from one group to the next. She bathed cuts and grazes with a lotion of marigold and goldenseal, then applied a soothing salve and bandages where needed.

Tamara deliberately kept herself occupied. Two o'clock came, then three. To her intense relief there was plenty to do. Barely aware of her surroundings, or of the other women's chatter, she chopped vegetables, sliced bread, folded squares of torn sheet into pads, and wound strips of linen into bandages. Then she began drying the cups and bowls Sarah had just washed.

She glanced up startled, as the cloth was taken out of her hands. 'It's time you had a rest,' Jenefer said gently.

'I'm all right,' Tamara protested. She had to keep busy. *Devlin.*

Pushing her down on to a chair, Jenefer thrust a cup of savoury vegetable broth into her hand. 'No, you aren't. You're as white as that sheet,' she said softly. Straightening up she glanced round. 'Is there any more bread?'

Lizzie hurried towards the table carrying a large cloth-wrapped parcel. 'Tide's turned and the wind's dropping,' she announced. 'Here's three barley and one wheat. Ernie says that's the last he can do today. Still we shouldn't need—' As Jenefer moved aside and Lizzie saw Tamara, she frowned. 'Dear life, miss, you do look—'

'Tired, I know.' Tamara pulled a wry face raised the cup. 'Miss Trevanion is feeding me.'

'The broth'll do for a start, but you need more than that,' Lizzie said. Swiftly slicing the fresh wheat loaf she spread one piece with butter then thrust it at Tamara forcing her to take it.

'I really don't—'

'Yes, you do.' Lizzie was firm. 'Come on now. You got to think of—' She stopped, a blush colouring her cheeks, and turned to Jenefer. 'Tell her, miss.'

'Lizzie's right,' Jenefer said. 'You've worked as hard as anyone here. And I doubt you had very much sleep.' As Tamara moved one shoulder, she added softly, 'I imagine the noise of the storm was very upsetting for your mother.'

Glancing up, Tamara saw understanding and sympathy in both women's faces. Her eyes prickled and she looked quickly away, not wanting to appear weak. She had never wept easily. And though these past weeks her emotions had risen much closer to the surface and were far harder to control, she would not start now, especially in public.

'You got to look after yourself,' Lizzie whispered. ' 'Specially now.'

Jenefer nodded. 'The day's not over yet.'

Tamara cleared her throat to try and dislodge the choking lump.

'Thank you.' The broth was hot and tasty. She swallowed and felt its heat soothe and settle her stomach. Putting the cup on the table she took a bite of the buttered bread.

Ernestine bustled up, her round face flushed. 'Miz Trevanion, George said he just seen Mr Casvellan coming up the street. On one of his hunters he is, leading a pack mule with two great baskets—' She broke off as the Justice entered. The chatter died away leaving the chapel silent but for the rushing of the wind outside and the wail of a hungry baby.

Tamara didn't move. Her chair on the platform at one side of the table allowed her to watch the Justice's approach. People edged away, the women bobbing, the men knuckling their foreheads. She saw Roz glance up, then quickly bend her head as she continued applying salve to the back of Minnie Kessell's arthritic hand. But in that instant Roz's expression, normally guarded, betrayed her and Tamara's heart went out to her friend.

As Casvellan reached her Jenefer straightened up and wiped both hands on her apron. One hand rose as if to check her hair, but she quickly dropped it again and made a curtsey.

'Good afternoon, sir.'

'Miss Trevanion, I must congratulate you. All this.' His gesture encompassed blanket-wrapped families and the women moving among them with trays of mugs and bowls, and platters of bread and butter. 'It's quite remarkable.'

'You are kind to say so, sir. But I cannot take all the credit. Almost everyone in the village has contributed in one way or another.'

'Following your example, Miss Trevanion,' he smiled. 'I am reliably informed.'

As Jenefer acknowledged the compliment, Tamara studied the Justice's face. Had he seen Roz? Did he know? His expression gave nothing away, but he would be aware that everyone was watching him. He was the law and, as virtually the whole community had some connection with free-trading, few villagers felt easy in his presence.

'I understand a troopship ran aground during the night?'

'So I believe, sir,' Jenefer replied.

'Survivors?'

Tamara shook her head as Jenefer caught her eye.

'Sadly no.'

'What of the dead?'

Jenefer clasped her hands in front of her. 'Miss Gillis, do you know?'

Tamara straightened in her chair as Casvellan looked at her. 'On my way here I saw Dr Trennack on the beach with several men. They were loading the bodies on to one of the farm wagons.'

'I see.' Casvellan nodded at her. 'Thank you.' He hesitated. Tamara waited, sensing he had another question. But he switched his gaze to Jenefer. 'There is food, clothing and blankets on a mule outside. I'm sure you will find a use for them. I had thought that – no matter.'

As he inclined his head and started down the aisle, Tamara realized that the loss of the troopship might have been one reason for his arrival. But he had another. *He had come to see if Devlin was back.* That was the question he had not asked.

He was the only man with the power to order custody of Devlin and his men transferred from the Supervisor of Customs to himself. It had to be the Justice who had freed Devlin and half his crew in order for them to rescue Martin Erisey. And Casvellan was the only man with the power to send the remaining crewmen to gaol as hostages.

He had come to the village because the lugger was overdue. Were it not for the storm Devlin would have been back hours ago. And the dragoons would have been waiting. But sea conditions must have persuaded the lieutenant that a landing was impossible, for she had seen no sign of him or his soldiers.

Now no one knew where Devlin was, or even if – he *was* alive. He was. If anything had happened to him she would know.

The Justice had almost reached the door when Arf Sweet burst in. 'Boat in the bay!' he panted.

Tamara bolted from her chair, clutching the table as her head spun. Jenefer caught her.

'It may not be—'

'Of course it is,' Tamara cried. 'No one else would be out there in this. I have to go.' Grabbing her coat she started down the aisle, pushing her arms into the sleeves as she squeezed past knots of people arguing about whether to stay in the chapel.

'What's the bleddy point going down the beach?' one woman demanded. 'Want to see 'em drown, do 'ee? Cos that's what'll 'appen.'

No, no, it won't. Tamara told herself as she took the quickest route. *They haven't come all this way and survived those appalling conditions to fail now.* Instinct told her Devlin wouldn't attempt to come into the harbour. Even though the wind was easing it was still far too dangerous. It was all too likely that the boat would be driven against the quay wall and smashed.

She walked then ran along the narrow streets. Arf had left the chapel immediately after announcing the news. Seeing his stocky figure ahead she could imagine his anxiety for it mirrored her own. Willing them to make a safe landfall, terrified they might not. Fearing to watch, yet unable not to. Jared was his only son. Devlin her only love.

She followed him on to the beach. Blowing in from the sea, the wind caught her coat and gown so their skirts flapped behind her. It tugged curls loose from her chignon and she tasted salt on her lips.

The onshore wind meeting the ebbing tide piled the waves high. From beach to horizon the sea was wild and white with foam. As more people arrived gathering behind her, Tamara caught snatches of their conversations between gusts. She scanned the sea, her gaze sharpening as she glimpsed the lugger. But no sooner had she spotted it, than it vanished, diving into a trough before appearing again on the next crest.

'Bleddy suicide it is, trying to land in this lot.'

'Well, they can't stay out there, can 'em.'

'Varcoe's the only man could do it.'

'He's the only man would try. Mad he is.'

'No such thing. But he might 'ave bit off too much this time.'

'Where're they to? I can't see 'em.'

Impatient with the comments and not wanting to be distracted as she willed Devlin to safety, Tamara moved down the beach, never taking her eyes from the small triangle of brown canvas that kept disappearing behind the curling wave-crests.

While she watched, her mouth and throat grew dry as she realized that the huge waves were followed at intervals by an even fiercer roller. When it reared, curled and crashed an evil cross-sea raced along the trough.

Devlin was beyond exhaustion. A voyage that usually took then between six and seven hours had already lasted sixteen. He ached in every muscle from the effort of trying to hold a course while Danny, Andy and Billy baled, fighting to keep the sea out of the boat. Erisey was doing his best to help, but weakness made him slow.

Standing shoulder to shoulder with Jared, both of them soaking wet and chilled to the bone, Devlin pushed the tiller over to keep the lugger stern-on to the waves.

It was now, when they were at the end of their strength and within a cable's-length of safety, that they faced the greatest danger. It needed only one false move for the boat to be smashed to splinters and them to pulp. The only way to survive the breakers was to try and ride them, guiding the boat through the thundering surf and as close in-shore as possible.

People crowded the top of the beach. At least there were no dragoons. Then he saw a red coat, billowing in the wind. His heart clenched like a fist. Since early that morning and all the time the storm had raged he had felt her presence. Ashamed of his behaviour – not of what had happened between them, but of his brutal actions afterward – he had tried to put her out of his mind, telling himself he could not afford distraction. But as the hours passed and reaching home began to look ever more unlikely, he had allowed her back in.

As he and Jared fought the boat and the storm-lashed sea, he relived his memories of her: spirited, infuriating, generous, passionate. If this was to be his last day, he knew now that someone had thought him worth loving. She was different, rare. And she had loved him. *Tamara.* He held the thought, drew strength from it.

It made no sense but he had felt her there with him, an impression so strong he had almost looked over his shoulder, certain he would see her close behind him. He had resisted, knowing it impossible, mocking himself for a fool. And yet . . .

Now she was on the beach. Had she come down for him? Despite the wound he had dealt her? Her red coat was vivid against the grey shingle and darker rock. Had she worn it so he would see her? Know she was there? His narrowed eyes were sore from the salt spray and burned with exhaustion. He peered shoreward, focused on that poppy-red beacon of hope.

The boat reared on a gigantic wave that lifted her quarters and swung her bow round broadside on. Devlin fought grimly. They *could* still make it. Then a cross-sea he hadn't seen snatched the boat and tipped it on its beam-end.

He heard Jared's harsh cry of fear, and saw Martin Erisey, the man who held the key to his freedom and his future, hurtle past, mouth wide, arms and legs whirling. He had an instant in which to choose.

As the icy water took his breath, Devlin dived after Jared, who had not wanted to make this trip, and who could not swim.

Vaguely aware of the others and of Erisey, all shouting, choking, floundering, he focused on Jared. Kicking off his boots before they could drag him down, he lunged for his oldest friend. Hooking him under the chin, Devlin struck out desperately for the shore, kicking frantically for the surface as the breaking waves pounded them under.

He broke surface again, gasping. His burst of strength was ebbing, but above the deafening roar of the surf he could hear people shouting encouragement, urging him on. Jared's huge hands gripped his forearm like twin clamps. The drag and weight was almost too much for his screaming muscles. Spitting water, gulping air, he saw terror on his friend's face, the fear that he might let go.

Dredging up a final despairing effort as a wave lifted them high them smashed down and raced past, Devlin touched solid ground. He staggered forward and felt Jared pulled from his grasp. Coughing up water from his burning lungs, he saw Arf, wet to the waist, tears streaming down his face, lift his son's arm over his shoulder and drag him out of the boiling surf.

Tamara was running towards him. The joy on her face cracked his heart. Then he saw terror. She was shouting but he couldn't hear. He raised his hand. *No closer – the waves – not safe.* As he heaved in a breath to shout, the cross-sea struck, hurling him off his feet.

CHAPTER TWENTY-TWO

The scream hurt Tamara's throat. She hurled herself forward. If the next wave broke on him, the undertow would suck him back and he would drown. Plunging into the wild foaming water she grabbed his flailing arm, felt his fingers grip hers and hauled with all her strength. Her coat billowed around her, red as blood, as she fought the sea for the man she loved.

She felt her skirts seized and then hands caught her and they were both pulled to safety as the curling breaker crashed, swirled furiously around their knees then retreated with an angry hiss.

She managed a few staggering steps then her legs gave way and she sank on to the shingle, sobbing for breath. Devlin collapsed to his knees beside her, hands on his thighs as he heaved in great gulps of the sweetest air he had ever tasted. Seawater had scoured his throat, but it was the fist-sized lump that made swallowing impossible. He looked at her, humbled.

'You could have drowned.' The hoarse whisper was all he had strength for.

'You would have,' she said chattering teeth, shaking with reaction and relief. 'I could not have borne it.'

Struggling to his feet he grasped her hand, helped her up then pulled her against him, terrified at how close he came to losing her. He sought words that would tell her of the shame that had haunted him, his fear of trusting, of loving, of betrayal. The task was too great.

'I'm sorry,' he rasped. 'So sorry.'

She lay her face on his shoulder, listened to the thud of his heartbeat. He was alive, safe. 'You're home. The rest doesn't matter.'

His arms tightened and he rested his dripping head against hers, his voice cracking as he whispered, 'Don't let go.'

She turned her face up, met his gaze. Scalding tears spilled down her cold cheeks. But she made no attempt to stop them, for they were tears of joy. 'Never.'

'Tamara! For heavens' sake! Have you no shame? What will people think?' her mother squawked, crimson and breathless as she hurried across the beach leaning heavily on her husband's arm.

'She wanted me to marry Thomas,' Tamara whispered to Devlin.

'You won't,' Devlin growled.

'No,' she agreed calmly, then turned to her mother. 'Mama, people will think what they want to think.'

Ignoring Morwenna, Devlin addressed her husband. 'Mr Gillis, I'm going to marry your daughter. I would like—'

'You can't!' Morwenna cried, then rounded on Tamara. 'I forbid it. I will not have that man in our family. In any case, you cannot marry him,' she announced, tossing her head, 'you have already accepted his brother.'

'Only to spare you disgrace, Mama. Devlin is the father of my child. I will marry him or no one. I should like your blessing. But—'

'You have it.' John offered Devlin his hand. 'She's yours, Varcoe. Always was, had I the wit to see it. Take care of her.'

'John! How could you?' Morwenna cried. Realizing they had an avid audience, her hand flew to lace-edged ruffles frothing from the open bosom of her coat. 'Oh! I want to go home. Now, Mr Gillis!'

'In just a moment, my dear.' He turned again to Devlin. 'I'm sorry, Varcoe. The gale hit us badly. Your new boat. . . .' He shook his head. 'I'm sorry.'

Devlin glanced towards the water's edge where the lugger lay on its side. *One never launched and beyond salvaging, the other badly damaged.* His arm tightened around Tamara's shoulders. Soon he would have a wife and child to support. He looked at his future father-in-law.

'Later,' he said.

With a nod, John turned away. Clinging to his arm, Morwenna stalked up the beach, her chin high, ignoring the watching crowd.

Devlin tensed. 'Where are the others? Did they get ashore? Erisey?'

'They're all safe. Mr Erisey is over there,' Tamara pointed. Devlin's crew, each surrounded by family, were being helped up the beach. One man sat alone, his head hanging in exhaustion, arms resting on his bent knees. Devlin saw Jenefer Trevanion bend and place a blanket around his shoulders.

Martin Erisey glanced up. 'Jenefer? I must explain—'

'No, Martin.' She shook her head. 'It's too late for that. Perhaps if you had told me at the beginning—'

'I couldn't.' His voice was raw and harsh. 'I was sworn to secrecy. But it need not affect—'

'Don't.'

Watching Jenefer silence the man she was to have married, Devlin drew Tamara closer and she looked up at him.

'What is it?'

'Erisey and Miss Trevanion,' he murmured, and Tamara followed his gaze.

'. . . no future together,' Jenefer was saying. 'In your heart you know that. Come, you need dry clothes and a hot meal.' She offered him her hand.

He grasped it. 'I'm sorry.'

Silent, she helped him to his feet.

'Mr Varcoe.' Devlin looked round as Casvellan bowed briefly to Tamara.

'A brave move, Miss Gillis. Risky, but courageous.' He turned to Devlin. 'Well done, Varcoe. Few men could have done what you did.'

He offered his hand and Devlin shook it. 'I will send word to Bodmin. Your men will be home by the end of the week.'

'Thank you, sir.'

'However,' Casvellan added with a hint of steel, 'after such a fortunate escape you would be most unwise to tempt fate again. Whatever you may have been in the past, Varcoe, you were never a fool.'

Devlin glanced at Tamara, saw the love in her eyes, and knew he must not cause her any more grief. 'Sir, I would leave the sea tomorrow, but I know nothing else.'

Glancing toward the crowd, who quickly decided they had business elsewhere and began moving away, Casvellan nodded. 'A man unafraid of hard work, willing to adapt and learn, could be of great use to me.' He turned back to Devlin. 'You will want a few days to sort out your affairs. Come and see me after the weekend.'

Stunned by the offer, Devlin swallowed. He had always been his own man, giving orders not taking them. 'Sir, I'm not sure—'

'Of course not. Wait until we've talked. Miss Gillis.' Bowing once more to Tamara, who bobbed a curtsey, the Justice left them and started toward Erisey.

'Come,' Tamara said softly. 'You need food and sleep.'

Devlin raked a hand through his hair. 'Where?'

'Tonight? Home with me.'

He looked down at her, one dark brow lifting. 'Your mother—'

'Will have seen Mr Casvellan talking to you. When she hears you have been invited to Trescowe to discuss a proposition' – Tamara smiled wryly – 'by tomorrow our marriage will have been her idea all along.' As Devlin raised her hand and kissed it, the touch of his lips made her shiver with anticipation.

Devlin's face darkened. 'Have you seen my brother?'

Tamara shook her head. 'Not for days.' She sighed. 'He'll need to be told.'

'He can wait. You are all that matters now. You and our child.' He drew her close.

Tamara looked into his eyes. No longer cool and guarded, they revealed the depth of his love, his need of her. 'There was only you, Devlin,' she said softly. 'Then, now, always.'